MONSTER JUICE

Stomach-Turning
Tales of Terror

D0062552

GROSSET & DUNLAP
Penguin Young Readers Group
An Imprint of Penguin Random House LLC

Text copyright © 2014 by M. D. Payne. Illustrations copyright © 2014 by Amanda Dockery and Keith Zoo.
All rights reserved. *Boogers from Beyond* and *Burpstronauts* first published in 2014. This bind-up edition
published in 2015 by Grosset & Dunlap, an imprint of Penguin Random House LLC, 345 Hudson Street,
New York, New York 10014. GROSSET & DUNLAP is a trademark of Penguin Random House LLC.
Printed in the USA.

Cover illustrations by Amanda Dockery and Keith Zoo

The Library of Congress has cataloged the individual books under the following Control Numbers:
2013957922, 2014947289

ISBN 978-0-448-48912-4   10 9 8 7 6 5 4 3 2 1

The Guts:

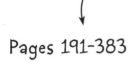

Boogers from Beyond

by M. D. Payne

Grosset & Dunlap
An Imprint of Penguin Random House

To Ben, whose support
is strong as llama spit

Prologue

The old monster quivered with fear.

"Thank . . . uh, thank . . . you for seeing me," it stammered while bowing low.

A dark, hooded figure slowly approached the old monster. His long, shimmering cape extended past his feet, and he appeared to be floating a few feet off of the ground. In his long arms he held a purring cat. The figure stroked the cat with gloved hands.

A hiss-like voice came from within the dark hood. "You've come a long way. I hope for your sake that the journey was worth it. Speak. But prove to me why I should listen."

From somewhere deep underground, a massive

roar shook the ancient throne room. White dust from the high ceiling slowly rained down on them, causing the cat to hiss.

"There, there," said the figure soothingly to the cat. "You'll feast soon."

The old monster brushed the dust off of his shoulders, trying to fight through his fear. "I can get you into their new facility," he said. "I can give you all of them."

"You offer me nothing. I've already weakened their defenses," said the floating figure. His eyes glowed from somewhere deep in the hood. The cat hissed in agreement as its eyes, too, began to glow. "Their old facility has been destroyed. Their spirits have been crushed—they will be easy to pick off. I have already won. Those old monsters just haven't realized it yet. As for you, I will have you drained of every last drop of lebensplasm for wasting our time."

The cat hissed at the monster as the hooded figure motioned to two guards who had appeared at the door. The figure floated up toward a massive hole in the stone ceiling. The cat growled ominously as they rose.

The guards, cloaked in red, moved toward the old monster.

"No, wait!" screeched the old monster as he fell to his knees. "They're stronger than you think. They're the strongest ones left, thanks to Paradise Island. The

Director has chosen a new, secure facility. You'll never be able to defeat him without my help."

The hooded figure ignored the monster's pleas.

"And you'll never find his *pendants* without me," added the monster.

The hooded figure paused his rise and extended his hand. The cloaked guards immediately halted their advance.

"Did you say 'pendants'? That fool has more than one?!" howled the hooded figure.

The old monster rose to his feet as the guards backed away.

"You have my attention," the hooded figure said as he hovered just above the ground. "Now tell me *everything* you know about the location of these pendants."

"He has one piece that he wears around his neck," the old monster replied confidently. "And the other he keeps hidden. I can find it and bring them both to you."

"And what do you ask for in return?" asked the hooded figure.

"I'm sick of being eternally old," said the old monster. "I'm sick of being weak. And I know how this all is going to end. If I don't do something now, you'll just drain me like all the rest. I need you to promise you won't harm me."

"Very well," said the hooded figure, "you have my word. You shall be considered one of us. Now, I have—"

"Wait," the old monster cut him off. "It's not just about me. There's something more I need you to do."

"SOMETHING MORE?" the voice hissed from deep within the hood. "You dare to ask me for more than your pitiful soul? What more could you want?"

"My sister," choked the old monster, holding back tears. "I need you to bring my sister back. You can do that, can't you?"

"Yes, but why should I?" hissed the hooded figure. "This talk of family disgusts me."

"I would rather die right now, at this very spot, than keep on without her," said the old monster. "But I'm much more useful to you alive, am I not?"

"For the time being," said the hooded figure. "But don't dare to disappoint me. There are fates worse than being drained of your energies until you gasp your last breath, I can assure you.

"I don't trust you to do this alone," the figure added as he dropped the cat onto the floor.

He clapped his hands, and the two guards once again stood at attention. "Bring me Test Subject Q," demanded the hooded figure.

"Q?" asked one guard. "But, Master, I thought you had deemed Q unworthy."

"Did I ask you to think?" threatened the hooded figure. "If I wanted you to think, I'd have you working in the lab—now bring me Test Subject Q!"

The guard left and returned a short time later with a huge woolly monster with terrible fangs—like a mutated buffalo mixed with an abominable snowman. He held it with a glowing leash that crackled as the monster rose and swiped its huge paws in the air.

"Let it loose," said the hooded figure.

"Master?!" the guards yelled.

"DO IT!"

The old monster watched, horrified, as they let the beast loose, and it immediately turned on them. It grabbed the closest guard. There was a screech as it shoved its furry face into the guard's hood.

CRUNCH.

"Oh, wonderful." The black hooded figure chuckled and clapped his gloved hands.

"Is this the creature you want me to use?" the old monster asked. "I'll never be able to control it!"

The woolly monster, finished with the guard, turned to the old monster and the hooded figure. It galloped at them.

"No," said the hooded figure over the roar of the terrible woolly creature. "This is."

He pointed at the cat, which took off for the advancing monster.

The monster stopped in its tracks, shrieked in terror, and turned around.

The cat chased it out of the huge doorway, and the

old monster could hear a terrible struggle, the sound of splashing and hissing, tearing flesh, screaming, and then utter silence.

The cat quietly padded its way into the room and licked a bit of blood off of its muzzle.

"I give you . . . the SANGALA!" said the hooded figure. "THIS is the tool that you shall unleash upon the unsuspecting. THIS is the tool that shall tear you to shreds if you dare disappoint me."

Once again, the eyes of the cat glowed ominously like the eyes of the hooded figure. The old monster was very afraid.

"Now, bow down!" The hooded figure's voice boomed throughout the room.

The old monster bowed down and slowly backed out of the massive chamber.

In the Beginning . . .

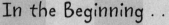

"All right, smell test," said Shane. He had created a three-point test for Lunch Lady's cafeteria food.

We all leaned in and began to sniff.

"I think I'm good," said Ben. "It doesn't make me feel sick or anything."

He sneezed.

"But you *are* sick," said Gordon. "Can you smell anything but your own boogers?" He leaned in and took another mega-whiff of his food.

"Poor *habibi* has a cold," said Nabila, Ben's not-girlfriend from Egypt. Her nerdy brown eyes looked sadly at Ben through her thick glasses.

Nabila put her tray and Ben's tray in front of Gordon.

"Would you mind smelling ours?" she asked. "As you know, I have—"

"Yeah, yeah," said Gordon as he snatched the trays. "You have no sense of smell. I remember. How convenient."

After two more mega-whiffs, Gordon gave a thumbs-up.

"Okay, visual check," Shane continued.

We all grabbed our forks and began moving our food around to make sure nothing was hiding in the folds. I slowly lifted off the top of my Blandburger and peered inside.

As I replaced the bun, I saw some kid headed our way. He had a full tray of food and it looked like he was planning on sitting at our table. I hated to be cruel, but we couldn't have outsiders listening in on our conversations. It was for their own good.

"Ben," I said while elbowing him. "Someone's coming."

"Not again," said Ben, and he started to make himself gag.

The kid looked at him strangely, but still tried to put his tray down.

Ben's whole body began to spasm as he returned the boy's look. Then it happened.

BLAARRP!

Ben spewed a small splatter of barf onto the table.

The kid slowly backed away and then ran off.

"Okay, *now* are we free to discuss saving the old monsters from monster juice drainage?" yelled Ben as he wiped a few leftover chunks from his mouth.

"You don't have to yell it," said Nabila as she cleaned up his mess. "There are still kids at other tables."

"Sorry," Ben said. "My ears are all clogged."

"Good barfin', buddy," said Gordon, patting Ben on the back. "Perfect targeting. Always the right amount."

"Half the time, I really do need to barf, you know," Ben said, snotting.

"Speaking of barf," Shane added as he poked at his food, "the thought of what's in here makes me want to hurl."

"Are you sure we have to search our food every day?" asked Gordon as he shook at his Pepperphony Pizz-ugh. "So what if Lunch Lady feeds us something again? We'll probably need it to battle a new breed of monster."

"I guess Gordon is right," said Shane. "Chris ate roaches, we beat roaches. We ate zombie piranha, and were better against the underwater skin monsters. But I just wish Lunch Lady would warn us, you know?"

"I still can't believe she fed you sussuroblats," Nabila said to me. "Was it the whole roach? That must have been a big burger. Did she include any lips? I think that's probably where all the magic is . . ."

I gagged at the thought of eating sussuroblat lips. A

bit of barf rose into my mouth and I quickly swallowed it. Another kid who was trying to sit down eyed me with disgust and then changed her mind and headed for another table.

"Aw, thanks," said Ben.

"How was the meeting between your mother and Director Z?" Nabila asked me.

"The good news is that Director Z convinced her nothing strange was going on at the old retirement home before it burned to the ground," I replied. "The bad news is that he did *such* a good job, she asked to hold her next PTA meeting at the new place! She's meeting with him today for a tour, and then Sunday they'll have the meeting."

"I think she's still investigating," said Shane. "Their friendly meeting over tea wasn't enough."

"I agree," I said. "Which is why we all have to make sure nothing goes wrong during the tour. I'm terrified she'll see something that will make her freak. So we *all* need to be there to make sure everything looks perfectly normal—*great*, even."

"Aw, come on!" said Gordon. "I have wrestling practice after school. Didn't Director Z say all the old monsters would be on their best behavior?"

"We've all seen those guys on their 'best behavior,'" said Shane, "and it's the worst."

"It's pretty bad," said Nabila.

"Yep," snorted Ben.

"Arrrgh, I guess you're right," Gordon said, rushing out of his seat. "I'm gonna see if anyone's practicing at the gym right now. See ya later, losers."

Ben blew a huge snot rocket into a tissue, crumpled it up, and tossed it onto Gordon's tray.

"I'm not sure he's finished," said Nabila.

"Well, he's finished now," I said with a chuckle.

"Wow," my mother said as she parked the car. "It's . . . well, it's HUGE! So much bigger than Raven Hill. It's beautiful."

She stared in awe at Gallow Manor Retirement Home as Ben, Shane, Gordon, and I stumbled out of the cramped backseat. The huge stone manor looked like a small castle.

"Just wait until you see what it looks like inside," Nabila said as she got out of the passenger seat. "It's amazing!"

"Be cool, or she'll suspect something is up," I whispered to Nabila. "It's not *that* great."

We walked to the huge, wooden, iron-studded front

door and rang the bell. Beautifully sculpted bushes sat on either side of the door with huge, colorful stained-glass windows above them. I glanced at one of the snow-covered bushes and could have sworn I saw two eyes looking at me through the cold. I did a double take, and by the time I looked back, the eyes were gone.

My mom's visit has me so nervous that I must be seeing things, I thought. *Everyone was warned to be on their best behavior.*

Before I could ask anyone else if they had seen the mysterious eyes, Director Z himself opened the door.

"Mrs. Taylor," said Director Z, pale and skinny, but always well dressed. "It's delightful to see you. Please, come inside from the cold."

My mother eyed every square inch of the foyer as we entered. The marble floors were scuffed, the tapestries on the wall were worn, the fireplace was slightly charred, but at least it didn't look like it could fall down at any time like Raven Hill had. *The best thing that ever happened to that dump was the fire that turned it to ashes*, I thought.

"I specifically said that your services weren't needed tonight," said Director Z, eyeing me.

"Oh, we had a lot of . . . um . . . stuff left over from yesterday," I said.

A few of the residents rolled past in wheelchairs.

Shane waved at Clarice, the banshee, who gave us

a dirty look from behind her walker. The old monsters had gotten stronger since they'd returned from Paradise Island. So we had begged them to act as old as possible for my mother.

"Thanks so much for putting my mind at ease when we spoke before," my mother said as Director Z took her coat. "I just keep thinking of how sad it was that you lost everything because of one faulty light switch."

"We're all dealing with the tragedy as best we can," said Director Z. "I'm lucky to have an amazing nursing staff, and your son and his friends were a huge help during our transition into the new facilities. We're so grateful to have them."

"I'm just so glad that Chris was at Kennedy Space Center when it all happened," said my mother.

She gave me a look that said, *I'm still not sure you were actually there . . .*

A Nurse walked over to grab our coats. Nabila and I gasped when we saw him. Ben sneezed in surprise, and a booger landed with a plop at Gordon's feet.

"What is it?" asked my mother.

He put on a uniform that actually fits, for my mother, I thought. I was used to seeing the Nurses—the massive, doofy men with huge heads who helped keep the old monsters in line—in one-size-too-small nurses' uniforms.

"Oh, nothing," I said as calmly as I could.

"What a beautiful coat, Madam," said the Nurse. "It really brings out the color of your eyes."

This time Shane gasped while my mother blushed at the compliment.

Director Z leaned in and whispered to us, "It took me an entire week to teach him that. So proud! As you can see, I've got everything under control. Your presence really isn't necessary."

The Nurse took the coats and headed to a nearby closet. My mother turned to us just as Director Z leaned back into place.

"What courteous staff you have, Director," said my mother.

"Please," said Director Z, "call me Zachary."

As Director Z and my mother turned and walked ahead of us, I looked behind to see a skeletal hand reach out of the closet and grab our coats from the Nurse.

Here we go, I thought.

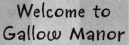

Welcome to
Gallow Manor

Director Z led my mother out of the beautiful marbled foyer toward the West Wing. Not knowing what to do, we followed them. After only a few steps, we could hear a pounding behind us.

"It's Roy, the Old Bigfoot," whispered Shane.

"Get outta sight!" Gordon hissed at the monster.

We waved him away frantically, but the shaggy gray bigfoot kept pounding his way toward us. The sour scent of his stinky old feet (which were, in fact, HUGE) increased with each step.

"Director Z?" Old Bigfoot asked. "I've been looking for you all day."

Director Z and my mother stopped.

Before they could turn around, Ben ran up to them and barfed on Director Z's shoes.

"Whhhhhharrrf," said Ben. "I'm so sorry."

"Oh dear," said my mother, too busy with barfy Ben to notice the stinky sasquatch. "Are you okay?"

She leaned down to help Ben.

"Director Z?" Old Bigfoot asked again.

Now Director Z was trying to wave him off, but he kept coming.

Shane ripped down one of the old tapestries, jumped up, and covered Old Bigfoot from head to hairy toes just as my mother turned around.

"My, aren't you just so cold," I said, wrapping the tapestry tightly around him. "Let's get you to your room."

Shane hurriedly shuffled Old Bigfoot off down the West Wing before my mother could see him—or smell him.

The rest of us stood there, staring at my mother and Director Z.

"Soooooo . . . ?" I asked Director Z.

"Yes, it does look like you might have a lot of 'stuff' to deal with." Director Z sighed, shaking Ben's barf off of his shoes. "Why don't you run off and make sure nobody else needs to be taken care of."

I gave Director Z a dirty look and headed down the hallway with my friends.

As soon as Shane had safely plopped Old Bigfoot

back in his room and closed the door, we heard growling from the room in front of us.

"Uh-oh . . . ," said Shane, rushing ahead. "Sounds like someone else is on their 'best behavior.'"

Three mangy old werewolves dragged their butts around a carpeted drawing room with a beautiful fireplace and very expensive antique furniture.

Lamps shook on rickety old tables. Fur was flying everywhere, and the smell was outrageous. The werewolves didn't even look like old dogs anymore— their coats were still somewhat gray, but they had all of their fur back. Not one of them had peed on a rug in weeks.

"Waaaaah-choo!" sneezed Ben, splattering a fine leather chair with snot.

"Guys!" I yelled. "That's disgusting! Stop it! Right now!"

"Arooo—" one started to howl with relief at having his itch scratched, but Shane was able to grab him and clamp his half-toothed mouth shut.

Another one hit one of the tables, and sent a beautiful stained-glass lamp over the edge.

"Eeek," I squealed, rushing forward and catching it just in time.

"Hey!" Ben yelled from the entrance. "They're coming down the hall!"

"Close the door," said Shane.

"There *is* no door," cried Ben.

"Shoot!" I yelled. "Think fast."

"Can you change back into human form?" Shane asked the flea-ridden werewolves.

"Nooooo, wait!" I said, still holding on to the lamp. "They might just keep doing it when they are in human form. Do you want to see that?"

"Ew!" said Gordon.

"Hurry!" said Ben.

Nabila ran over to a creaky old window, unlatched it, and threw it open. There was a terrible screech—paint flakes sprayed everywhere—and the room was filled with a fresh, cold breeze.

"Out!" She pointed to the open window.

The werewolves cocked their heads and stared at her with funny expressions.

We could hear the click of Director Z's perfectly polished dress shoes coming up to the entrance.

"This is gonna be bad," said Ben, scurrying deeper into the room to hide behind a bookcase.

"FETCH!" yelled Gordon, throwing a small stick of wood from the fireplace out of the window.

The werewolves jumped up from the slightly brown carpet, sprinted to the window in a flash, and jumped out one by one. As the last tail cleared the window, my mother and Director Z entered the room.

"We have several sitting rooms with period furniture

and art from the time when this home was constructed. Apparently, it was built by a shipbuilding family from Britain," said Director Z. "Oh, Chris! Do be careful while cleaning that lamp. You would pay dearly if ever you were to break it."

"Of course," I said, finally placing the lamp back on the table. "Just getting the dust off so nobody's sneezing around here."

Ben sneezed from behind the bookcase.

"Oh, Chrissy," said my mother, "you do such wonderful work for these old folks."

"Would you mind closing the window, Nabila?" asked Director Z.

"Of course, Director," said Nabila.

Director Z took a big whiff and stared at the carpet.

I gave him a look that said, *Get her out of here before she notices!*

"Now," said Director Z, quickly leading my mother out of the room. "Shall I show you the music room? Chris tells me you can play piano. Have you ever played a harpsichord?"

They walked across the hallway and opened the door to the music room. As soon as it had shut, we rushed into the hallway.

"We've got to stay ahead of them," I said, panicked, "or my mother might see something!"

We rushed past a number of closed doors. Luckily,

most of the residents had listened to us, and were keeping quiet in their rooms.

We peeked into a sitting room to see a few old folks playing cards, staring at chessboards, quietly talking, or warming themselves in front of the marble fireplace.

"Lookin' good! Lookin' normal!" yelled Shane, giving all the old monsters a big thumbs-up. "All that's left is the dining room, the kitchen, and—"

"The bathroom!" screeched Nabila, pointing farther down the hallway. "Look!"

Up ahead, a steamy green fog poured out of the bathroom. There was no mistaking that smell.

"Swamp gas!" yelled Gordon.

Through the open door, Gil, the swamp creature, happily sang and farted in the shower.

Behind us, my mother and Director Z emerged from the music room. I could feel the hair stand up on the back of my neck. We lined up from wall to wall to keep her from seeing the green cloud down the hallway.

"Let's just take a quick look at this room," said Director Z, leading my mother into the second sitting room. "The fireplace is exquisite."

"We've got to close the bathroom door," I said, and we turned around to see a zombie stumble out of the bathroom.

"Arrgh! Can't *breathe!*" he moaned and passed out on the hallway floor.

"Wow, farts strong enough to knock out a zombie," said Shane. "I'm constantly impressed by Gil."

"No time to be impressed," I yelled. "We've got to move this zombie before my mother walks down the hallway."

"What about the gas?" yelled Nabila.

Gordon rushed up to the zombie, who was still moaning, and quickly dragged him back into the bathroom.

"No!" the zombie wailed. "Barely survived."

"Barely survived?" Gordon said. "Did you forget you're already dead? Just stay low, under the cloud."

Gordon slammed the door shut, cutting off the green cloud, just as my mother and Director Z came out of the second sitting room.

"Now on to the kitchen," said Director Z as they breezed past us.

My mother wrinkled her nose slightly, but didn't say anything.

After a pause, we rushed after them, through the dining room and into the kitchen.

"This is perhaps the most stunning marblework in the entire manor," said Director Z. "Italian marble, very sterile, perfect for preparing meals for those with special needs—and for your PTA members on Sunday."

"Looks clear in here," whispered Shane, patting me on the back.

Before I could finish saying, "WHEW," there was a great SQUUUUEEEAAAK.

The huge wooden door to the walk-in refrigerator slowly swung open in front of my mother. A gnarled hand gripped the dark wood ominously.

My friends and I stood in shock. There was nothing we could do.

Grigore, the vampire, stumbled out clutching a large plastic bag of blood. He was slurping happily on a plastic tube.

"Ahhh!" my mother screamed, jumping back, surprised.

"WHA!" Grigore screeched, just as surprised, and tossed the blood bag up into the air.

"Oh no," said Ben.

"Oh my!" said my mother as the bag fell back down onto the ground with a SPLAT, and sprayed blood all over Grigore's shoes and pants.

"Nooooo!" he yelled. "My blood!!!"

"Blood?" My mother suddenly looked horrified.

Director Z was, for once, stunned.

"Oh . . . ," Grigore said, looking at my mother. "You can't know. You shouldn't know."

He held his right hand in front of him, made his hand into a claw, and squinted into her eyes.

"You are getting very sleepy," he said.

"No," she said. "I'm not."

"Do. Not. See. Meeee . . . ," purred Grigore.

"But you're right in front of me," my mother said, annoyed. "Covered in—"

"Tomato soup!" I interrupted. "Grigore, how many times have I told you—you can only eat at scheduled mealtimes. What a silly old dude, right?"

My friends and I laughed nervously.

I looked at my mother, hoping she'd believe me.

"But he screeched the word *blood* after he dropped what is clearly an IV bag of blood." My mother furrowed her brow in my direction.

"I am deeply sorry that my resident has scared you," said Director Z, "but Grigore really is one of the more—how do I put this without sounding rude—demented patients here. I assure you, this is not normally what happens at my facility."

"I'm not demented," said Grigore, offended. "I—"

Gordon hissed, raised his fist, and gave Grigore a dirty look. My mother was staring too hard at the blood to notice.

"Right . . . right!" screeched Grigore. "I'm the King of Transylvania! That's vhy I thought this delicious tomato soup vas bllllooooooood!"

"Yes," Director Z quickly added with a smile, "and it's a funny coincidence that the bags we serve all our soup in would look like IV bags to you—we find that serving soups directly from a plastic pouch, using a plastic tube

23

to suck, gives our residents a sense of comfort. Spoons are simply too harsh."

We all stared at my mother, wondering if she would believe our terrible story. She stood there with her mouth open, shocked.

She finally turned to me with a look of anger and said, "Chris, what is going on here?"

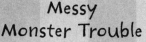

Messy
Monster Trouble

"How could you kids act like this?" my mother scolded. "Are you just going to stand there? Clean the poor old man up!"

"Of course," I said, relieved. "Director Z, where's the cleaning supply closet again?"

"In the back of the dining room," replied Director Z. "Mrs. Taylor, while the children assist Grigore, please allow me to show you the view from the West Tower above the dining room. It's spectacular."

"Yeah, and at night, the stars are amazing out here," I said nervously, trying to get my mother to think about anything but the blood-splattered old vampire in front of her. "I've got my telescope set up in the tower."

"We'll be right back," Shane said to Grigore.

"One of you should stay and keep an eye on him," my mother said.

"Of course," said Nabila. "Ben and I will stay behind."

The rest of us walked out into the dining room.

"Is it this door?" I asked Director Z, who continued walking toward the hallway with my mother.

I grasped the doorknob of the already slightly open door and peeked inside to see bizarre-looking instruments and a huge, grainy photograph of the moon on the wall. The moon had—

"Not that door," said Director Z, who pulled me out of the room before I could explore further. My mother stood in the hallway, looking around at the decorations.

"But the moon," I whispered so my mother didn't hear. "It had a face! Like a real face, not just the craters and hills that make up what we *think* is the face."

"Do you see the moon everywhere, *Moon Boy*?" Gordon said, chuckling.

"It would be best if you forgot about this room for now," Director Z hissed as he closed the door.

Shane opened the next door, revealing a gaggle of mops and every kind of cleaning solution you could imagine.

"This is Ben's dream," said Shane.

"I'm sure it shouldn't take you too long," said Director Z. "Please meet us at the bottom of the stairs and we'll all continue to the East Wing."

He led my mother up the spiral staircase with a warm chuckle.

We grabbed as many supplies as we could and went back into the kitchen to find everything perfectly clean. Nabila and Ben stared wide-eyed at Grigore.

"What happened?" I asked.

Nabila and Ben kept on staring.

"I realized after you left that I could just slurp up all of the blood myself," said Grigore. He stared off into the distance and added, "Like a cat licks up blood."

"Huh?" I said. "You mean like a cat licks up milk?"

"Yes," he said. "Of course that's vhat I meant . . . maybe I am a little demented like the Director says."

Nabila and Ben were finally coming back to the real world.

"You guys okay?" asked Gordon.

"He was so fast," said Nabila. "So creepy."

"And hungry," added Ben, shivering. "I don't think I'm going to be able to sleep tonight."

We left Grigore, and I walked over to the door of the mysterious moon room. It was locked.

"Dang," I said.

"What did you see?" asked Shane.

Before I could answer Shane, Director Z and my mother appeared at the bottom of the stairs.

"Let's head to the other side of the manor, where

there's one room in particular that I think you'd like to see, Mrs. Taylor," said Director Z.

The East Wing was filled with empty rooms. Gallow Manor had a lot of space.

As Director Z led us down the long hallway, organ music blared. It was a louder and darker song than Horace usually played.

We passed by beautiful, dark oil paintings in dusty frames. We passed a suit of armor that stood guard with an ax.

"We have quite a collection of Victorian art. As you can see—"

"WHAT?!" my mother screeched. "I CAN'T HEAR YOU OVER THE MUSIC."

The organ music got crazier and spookier.

"MY APOLOGIES!" Director Z yelled over the music. "I HAD TOLD HORACE NOT TO PRACTICE WHILE YOU WERE HERE, BUT AS YOU KNOW, MANY OF OUR RESIDENTS ARE HARD OF HEARING."

"THAT WOULD EXPLAIN THE VOLUME," my mother yelled back.

But Director Z and I both knew that Horace had amazing hearing. Something else was going on here.

"RUN UP AHEAD AND TELL HIM TO SHUT UP," I yelled to Gordon with a panicked look that said, *Be careful.*

The closer we got to the banquet hall, the louder it got. My mother and I covered our ears. Director Z pretended not to notice. My teeth rattled in my mouth.

Gordon opened the door . . .

. . . and the last note from the organ echoed through a massive banquet hall.

"Well," said my mother, gasping at the beautiful banquet hall as the rest of us came through the door. "This is quite nice."

"Horace?" My squeak echoed off the high arched ceiling.

Huge iron chandeliers hung above a beautiful wood floor, and all around the room was a balcony. In the back, above a stage, was a massive set of pipes, with a small keyboard below.

But the organ player was nowhere to be seen. And the only way out was through the door behind us.

My look of concern made Director Z speak before I could.

"So, Mrs. Taylor," he said, perfectly calm. "We can arrange seating for a number of different occasions. I assume our collection of one hundred folding chairs will work for your PTA meeting?"

"Wow," she gasped, clearly forgetting the fact that an organist had just pulled a disappearing act. "Yes."

"Wonderful," Director Z said, clapping his hands together. "Then we'll make all the preparations

29

necessary for your big day on Sunday. Chris, you and your friends should come extra early tomorrow."

As we were leaving Gallow Manor, I noticed Horace walking down the hallway to the West Wing. I rushed over to speak with him.

"Was there a secret door?" I asked. "Is that how you got out so quick?"

"Pardon?" he asked, looking confused.

"In the banquet hall just now you were playing a crazy, loud song that ended right when we opened the door."

"I don't know what you're talking about," said Horace. "I just woke up from a nap. The Director gave me strict instructions to lay off the playing while your mother was here."

"Really?" I asked. "That's so strange . . ."

"Chrissy," shrieked my mother from outside, "let's get going!"

The mystery would have to wait.

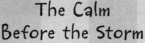

The Calm
Before the Storm

Early the next morning, Ben, Nabila, Shane, Gordon, and I arrived back at Gallow Manor to help set up the banquet hall for the PTA meeting.

"I'm so excited to spend the day with the monsters," said Nabila as she pulled a handkerchief from her fluorescent pink fanny pack. She handed it to Ben, who couldn't stop sneezing. "I really like the idea of working *with* them, rather than *for* them."

"It depends on the monster," said Gordon. "Murray is always so cranky, Griselda is bossy, and Grigore is plain batty. Not to mention the zombies are ... well ... *zombies*."

"I'm just happy that the monsters are finally doing something other than drooling," Shane said. "You saw

31

how helpful they were during the move. All the monsters are getting stronger."

"Yeah, but they're still old," said Ben. "They just went from insanely ancient to just plain old."

"But if we do have another attack," Shane said, "they should be strong enough to fight. I've been teaching them some moves."

"I don't even want to think about another attack," I said. "I just want to survive this PTA meeting without my mother attacking."

"I don't know about surviving your mother," said Director Z, who had walked up to the entrance of the banquet hall to meet us, "but it would be hard for someone to attack the manor. We have extra protection in the main facility with a deep dungeon to fall back into if we need it. But we won't need it with the charms and seals that have been put on the facility. And Shane and Gordon's emergency action plans have all been memorized by the residents, who, I assure you, are ready for a fight if it happens."

Someone on the other side of the hall huffed. We turned to see Murray standing at a podium. He waved his wrapped hand dismissively at Director Z.

"It doesn't matter what you do, Zachary," said Murray. "We're all done for. The great lebensplasm drinker in the sky will take every last one of us before all is said and done."

"What's got into Hotep?" Shane said while pointing his thumb toward the podium.

"I don't know how many times I have to tell you," grumbled Murray. "My name is Murray. Not Hotep."

"You've got to be kidding. Murray's not a mummy name," said Shane. "It just doesn't feel right. You're totally Hotep."

Gordon snickered. "Told you Murrayhotep was a grump! He barely helped the other monsters move into this place—half the time he had disappeared to who-knows-where."

"Well, I'll have you know—" Murray started to say.

"Let it be, Murray," Director Z said. "We have a lot to accomplish before the parents and teachers arrive."

"You always side with the humans, Zachary," Murray said as he stormed out of the hall. "This is why you will always fail."

My first job was to clear out the massive sections of giant spiderwebs that covered most of the hall. I stood with a broom and a pair of hedge clippers as I stared down at least a half dozen fist-size spiders.

33

"I told you guys that the East Wing is off limits today!" I said to the agitated spiders.

In unison they shook their hairy spider legs at me and then reared up, exposing insanely long and pointy fangs.

"I have to take down your webs," I continued. "There's no way around this."

Griselda, the head witch, approached with a small black bag.

"All right," she cackled, "I need a refill of leg-of-spider. Any volunteers?"

The spiders quickly formed a line and scurried out of the door.

"Ve need three more chairs over here," called Grigore, who was helping set up the seating.

Shane rushed over to him with three more chairs.

"It's great to see us all working as a team," sniffled Ben as he helped set up the catering table. Nabila smiled at him as she came over to help with the chairs.

A few zombies ambled aimlessly past her, shuffling chairs from place to place. Nabila huffed and said, "That's good, Jane and John. Just open up the rest of the chairs—I'll straighten things up."

I dodged the zombies and made my way over to Director Z, who was adjusting the podium. Across the hall Gordon waved his arms, trying to get my attention. He was fiddling with the speakers.

I grabbed the microphone. "Testing, testing, one, two, three . . ."

Gordon gave me a thumbs-up from the back row.

"Awesome," he said as he jogged over. "Now that we're finished setting up, I can play fetch with the werewolves in the North Wing. That hallway is HUGE!"

"Not so quick," said Director Z. "We have a few errands to run."

"What!?" the five of us said at the same time.

"Speaking of werewolves," continued Director Z, "we need to go to the pet store in town to pick up chew toys, and Medusa's snakes are almost down to their last mouse. We should probably head to the butcher's and the blood bank as well. That's a lot to carry, and I'll need all of you to help."

"How are we getting there?" asked Nabila.

"We'll take the company car," Director Z replied.

We all looked at the Director in shock.

"You have a car?" asked Nabila. "Why didn't you tell us? This whole time, you could have picked us up and saved our parents the trouble."

"Did you think I just walked around to get from place to place?" Director Z asked. "Of course we have a car. I just don't like to take it out that often, and I don't think your parents would appreciate it if I started picking you up in it."

"Why?" asked Nabila.

"You'll see," he replied, and motioned us out the door.

We walked to a beautiful carriage house off the east side of the manor. It had three huge wooden doors. The one in the center was open, and inside was a brand-new, sparkly and clean . . .

"Hearse?" Shane chuckled. "Okay, I can see why you don't take this out too often."

Ben gulped. "I don't think I can ride in this."

Director Z opened the back door to reveal an old coffin.

"Like I said," Ben mumbled as he choked something back down, "I don't think I can ride in this."

"You can ride in the front with me," said Director Z.

"Is anybody . . . ," Nabila said and pointed at the coffin.

"No," Director Z replied, but then a funny look came over his face. "Well, maybe. You might want to knock."

We all piled into the hearse, and Director Z reversed it out of the carriage house. Before he was able to turn down the road, a Nurse jumped in front of the car.

Director Z slammed on the brakes. All of us, and the coffin, slid up toward the front seats.

"Boss," the Nurse said, knocking on the window, "we've lost Murray and Grigore. Again. They should be helping us with the food, but we can't find them anywhere!"

"I'm sure they'll wander back," said Director Z. "Until the residents get used to this place, they're going to keep getting lost. Have three Nurses check each wing."

A creaking sound came from the back of the hearse. A gnarled hand made its way out from below the cover of the coffin.

"Wha!? Guys!!" Nabila squealed, backing away from the coffin.

Whatever Ben had choked down earlier erupted down the front of his shirt.

"I'm here," croaked Grigore. "I'm just a little down. It's just I . . . I vas thinking about somevone I'd lost . . . and vas trying to hide avay."

"See," said Director Z as he slowly pulled the car away from the Nurse, "we've found one already. Go back to bed, Grigore. Everything is fine."

Two hours later the hearse pulled back into the carriage house. Gordon was slumped in his seat. He had been terrified that someone from the team would see him riding around in the big, black death boat. Once Director Z turned off the ignition, Gordon practically jumped out of the car, yelling, "Pietro! Howie! Calling all mangy mutts for a game in the North Wing hallway."

"Gordon," I yelled. "Aren't you going to help carry anything?"

"No time," he called back.

"Just be careful in the manor," Director Z added. "If you break anything, you'll pay for it."

That's strange, I thought, *we've broken plenty of things in the past and he never made us pay for anything. Now he's mentioned it twice.*

Shane struggled to get out of the hearse, holding on to a huge bag that squirmed and squeaked.

"Hey," he said, and I gave him a little push through the door. "Do you remember when we had to hand-feed the mice to poor Medusa's snakes? Now they're chomping at us before we can even get the package open."

"Things have certainly changed," I said. "I think—"

Spray from a wet sneeze blew across my face. Nabila whipped out her handkerchief and offered it to me.

"Sorry," Ben snorted. "We should probably go soon. I've run out of allergy medication."

"I'll call my mother after we catch up with Gordon. I might want to toss a few balls myself," I said.

The werewolves were going crazy in the North Wing.

"FETCH!" yelled Gordon. He tossed a large red rubber ball, and the three werewolves went tearing down the huge hallway, which was as wide as a small soccer field.

They nipped at each other, and then one of them ran back to Gordon with the ball.

"Can I try?" I asked.

"Sure," said Gordon.

"I'm next," said Shane.

"Make sure to throw it really far, or they'll just stand there and wait for you to try again," said Gordon.

"Oooof," I yelped as I tossed the ball as far as I could.

The three werewolves went scurrying off with a howl.

One grabbed the ball and came running back at me . . . FAST!

"Wait," I said. "Slow down!"

Faster and faster he ran, until he knocked my feet out from under me. I fell into Ben, sending him headfirst into a pedestal that held a large vase.

"Are you okay?" asked Shane as he picked me up.

Ben was holding on to the pedestal for dear life. But the vase jiggled as Ben swayed, trying to steady himself— it had edged right to the side.

"Don't move!" said Shane as he headed for Ben.

Ben's eyes widened, and I noticed his nose begin to twitch. "Ahh . . . ," he said. "AAAAAAH . . ."

"Whatever you do," I said, moving in behind Shane, "don't finish that sneeze."

"CHOOOOOOO!"

He shook the pedestal violently, knocking the vase over in a shower of snot. Shane dove to catch it, but the snot-covered vase slipped through his fingers and smashed into a million pieces.

"Sorry," coughed Ben. "I told you we should have gone home."

Shane sat up and wiped his boogery fingers on Ben's shirt. "Do you have any superglue in that fanny pack of yours?" he asked Nabila.

"Something tells me this is beyond superglue," I said.

Before we could figure out what to do, the whole hallway began to shake. The candelabras on the wall vibrated and jerked in and out. The windows rattled. Instinctively, the werewolves tucked their tails and ran.

Then a scream came from somewhere within the walls and echoed through the hallway.

"AAAAAARRRGGGGGHHHHH!"

A gate slammed down behind us, sealing us in from the rest of the manor.

We were trapped!

The Storm Before the Calm

"Weeeee. Wiiiiiilllll. DESTROY. Youuuuuuu."

After sitting trapped in the hallway for what seemed like an eternity, we were starting to make out what the voices in the hallway were saying.

"We?" asked Shane. "Who are you?"

"It's not the 'we' part that's bothering me," Ben added. "It's the whole 'destroy you' bit that is freaking me out."

"We won't be able to stop them if we don't know who they are," Shane replied.

"Yeah, why won't you show yourselves?" I screamed.

"I wouldn't question them," Nabila said. "It might anger them further."

Just then a wind picked up, and the tiny pieces of the broken vase swirled like a small tornado.

"Cover your eyes," I called out.

"The dust!" Ben squealed. "I can barely breathe!"

Nabila ran to Ben while Gordon ran to the gate that blocked the hallway and shook the iron railings like a crazed prisoner, trying to escape.

The tornado headed for us, and we all backed up against the gate.

"There has to be a switch!" I yelled over the howling wind. "A lever! Something!"

Shane, Gordon, and I frantically searched for a way out while Nabila dealt with Ben, who was having a full-on allergy attack. She handed him an inhaler from her fanny pack as he collapsed at the bottom of the gate.

"Guys, we have to get him out of here!" yelled Nabila. Her hair whipped in the wind.

"Over here," yelled Gordon. "I think I've found it!"

The tornado had almost reached us. Shane and I had to struggle against the wind to get to Gordon, who was struggling with a small iron door. Shards of the vase whizzed past us, one or two cutting small slits into my pant leg.

"That tornado is going to tear us to shreds if we don't hurry," I said.

As the three of us struggled to open the door, the wind howled, "NOOOOOOOOOOO!"

The small iron door sprung open so fast we were thrown onto the floor. Shane jumped back up and pulled down the lever that was inside.

With a great creak and a rattle, the iron gate began to rise.

As it rose, the tornado shot back down the hallway and blew a window open. The pieces of vase blew out and into the sky and met with dark clouds.

Lightning struck the window, which closed with a BAM.

The wind stopped and the gate was now fully open.

"Let's get out of here," I said. "This place is haunted!"

As we scurried into the main marble foyer, Director Z came up to us with a concerned look on his face.

"I saw the werewolves run past," Director Z said, "and I heard a terrible racket—is everyone okay? Did you break anything?"

"Oh, man," said Gordon. "We were playing fetch, and—"

"Just got a little too aggressive," Nabila interrupted. "Ben got overwhelmed with the dust and running."

Gordon and Ben looked at her funny, but we let her keep going.

"You probably heard the thunder," she continued. "Wasn't that strange?"

As if to back up her story, another bolt of lightning struck the grounds and shook the manor.

"I see," said Director Z. "Ben, are you okay?"

Ben slumped against Gordon. He tried to speak, but could only cough out a glop of orange boogers—the same color as the vase. He smiled weakly and gave Director Z a thumbs-up.

"I think we need to get him out of here," Nabila said.

"Yeah, let's get him a little fresh air," I said, and headed for the door.

I turned the old brass handle, and an icy chill shot up my arm. The door blew open, knocking me back. As I hit the floor the first thing I noticed wasn't the pain of my rear, but of snow hitting me in the face. A lot of snow.

"Whoa," I said as I slid into Shane, my butt rippling over the marble.

A few Nurses came in and forced the door closed, but even they had trouble finally getting it to shut all the way.

For a moment it was insanely quiet—then my phone rang.

Everyone stared at me as I answered it.

"Hello?" I said.

It was my mother.

"Are you ready, Chrissy?" she asked. "I'll come and get you now."

"Mom," I screeched, still winded from everything

that had happened. "You can't drive in this!"

"Drive in what, honey?" she asked.

"The blizzard. The thundersnow!" I said.

"Chrissy, the sky is blue," she said, sounding confused.

"Well, it's snowing like crazy here. You'll never get over the bridge," I said.

Director Z motioned for me to hand him the phone.

He grabbed it and said, as calm as could be, "Mrs. Taylor, I must admit, I have never seen snow like this before."

He looked out of the window and continued, "It must have started only ten minutes ago, and there's nearly an inch on the ground already. I can't even see past the driveway. I don't think you should pick up the children. The sun sets soon, and the roads must be terrible."

A few *mmmm-hmmm*s later, Director Z handed me back my phone.

"Chrissy, I don't like this," she said. "But if what Zachary says is true, I really shouldn't come out there."

"Don't worry, Mom," I said, trying to be as calm as Director Z. "You'll see us in the morning, anyway."

My cell phone went dead.

"Mom? MOM!?"

With a soft whirring sound, all the lights dimmed and went out.

"Yipppeee!" an old monster yelled from the West Wing.

As the sun set, the snow picked up. I wanted nothing more than to get out of this haunted house.

No-Sleepover

"Looks like we're having a sleepover," Shane said as we watched the snow pile up outside the window.

"Yeah, it should be fun," I added, smiling at Ben, whose breathing hadn't gotten much better. He smiled back, knowing that I was just trying to cheer him up.

"Why don't you sleep in the music room?" suggested Director Z, handing out candles in tarnished old candelabras. "I believe that it's been soundproofed, so the storm might not bother you as much. I'll have the chefs prepare hot chocolate."

"That sounds good for the boys," Nabila said, "but I think it would be best if I slept in my own room."

"Of course," said Director Z. "You can take the room

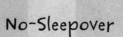

across from the music room when it's time to sleep."

"But, Nabila," snorted Ben. "Will you be okay?"

"I'll be just fine on my own, thank you very much, *habibi*," she said.

"Do you *remember* what happened in that hallway?" Ben whispered with concern to Nabila. "This place is crazy haunted!"

"So far, we only know that there was something mysterious happening with the vase," she whispered back confidently. "I'll be right across the hall."

"Ben," said Director Z, "I'll get one of the witches to brew an antihistamine potion. You certainly look like you could use it."

As Director Z left, we all turned to Nabila. Before any of us could ask her, she replied to the question that she knew was coming.

"I lied about the vase because Director Z said that we would have to pay if we broke anything. Did you see how old that vase was? It must be extremely expensive. Plus, he'll probably never notice. Whatever tried to kill us did us the favor of blowing the mess out into the sky."

"Yeah, but I'm worried whatever *that* was didn't leave with the vase," I said.

"Well, I, for one, am glad that Nabila didn't tell the truth," said Shane. "I don't get enough allowance to buy new nineteenth-century artifacts."

Hours later, after Nabila had gone to her room, Shane, Ben, Gordon, and I sat in the music room. The candelabras rested on the floor, making our shadows jump around the room.

Ben was completely asleep, knocked out from Griselda's antihistamine potion. He clutched his now-empty hot chocolate mug.

"Hey, isn't that the same potion that amped me up?" asked Gordon.

"Yeah," said Shane. "But you had just taken a six-hour nap in a sea worm."

"True . . . true," replied Gordon.

"Okay, guys," I said, blowing out the candles. "Let's get some sleep. We have a big day tomorrow."

We all lay down. The room was insanely dark. And insanely quiet. Too quiet. Nobody said anything for ten minutes, and then . . .

"This place is giving me the creeps," said Gordon. "All I can hear is my heart beating; I think I'm about to go crazy."

"Yeah," I said.

"I dunno," said Shane. "I think quiet is good. Relaxing. Maybe this place isn't haunted after all."

There were a few more moments of silence, and then a harpsichord started to play quietly in the dark.

"Hey, did your mother finally teach you how to play the piano?" Shane asked.

"Noooooo . . . ," I said.

"It's not me," Gordon said.

I tried not to screech as I fumbled for the matches. As I struck the first, I saw we were alone.

"Whew," said Shane, his eyes searching the dimly lit room. "I thought someone was in here."

"You're not worried the harpsichord is playing itself?" Gordon asked.

"Why would I? It's a sweet piece. Probably French. Baroque," Shane said.

Gordon looked under the harpsichord. "It's plugged in or something, right?"

"The power's out," I replied. "Duh!"

I had finally lit the three candles on my candelabra and held it high.

"Gordon, watch out," I yelled.

A guitar floated past Gordon's head—he ducked to avoid it.

It played along with the harpsichord, and both instruments got louder and louder.

"Okay, this isn't so fun anymore," Shane said. "My ears are ringing."

"Let's try to stop it," I said, and lunged toward the harpsichord.

Gordon followed, trying to silence the guitar.

But they got so loud that we were stopped in our tracks, it hurt so much.

"How is Ben sleeping through this?" I asked.

"Let's get Director Z," said Shane. "He'll know how to handle this."

We filed out into the hallway.

"Should someone stay with Ben?" I asked.

SLAM!

The door closed, and all we could hear was the storm, which raged on.

"I guess not," I said.

We rushed down the hall to Director Z's room, but before we could open his door, there was a scream from the foyer.

"That sounds like Nabila," said Gordon.

Forgetting Director Z for the moment, we rushed into the foyer, but didn't see Nabila. We kept moving, jogging into the East Wing, only to find the portrait of Lucinda B. Smythe in a tizzy.

"No matter what I do," she said, "those other portraits keep staring at me!"

She pointed across the hall to the portraits that hung on the wall. They really did stare at you, no matter which way you moved.

"I had a Nurse move me today, but it's no use," she said. "This place is haunted with wicked spirits! They taunt me so!"

"That was you screaming?" I asked Lucinda. "You haven't seen Nabila around, have you?"

"I'm right here," she said, wiping the sleep out of her eyes with one hand and holding her candelabra with the other. "What's going on?"

"Were you sleeping?" Shane asked. "Because our room is a little too haunted for such activities."

"Yeah, can we please sleep in your room?" asked Gordon. "Let's get out of here."

"Where's Ben?" she asked.

"In the music room," I said. "Griselda's potion knocked him out."

"Let's drag him into my room, too," she said.

Before we could head back, a low moan and metallic rattling filled the hall. We looked in the direction of the foyer and saw a suit of armor shake centuries of dust out of its joints and turn toward us.

Someone or SOMETHING was inside the armor.

"Grigore?" asked Shane. "Pietro? Is that you?"

"Waaarrrggghhh," came the garbled reply.

"Really funny," laughed Shane. "Well done."

Gordon, Nabila, and I backed down the hall toward the banquet hall.

With a loud CREAK the armor raised the huge ax that it held.

"Uh, Shane," I said. "I don't think this is a joke."

"Yeah, maybe not," gasped Shane, and we started running.

Behind us, we heard the sound of groaning, clanking metal as the armor pulled its feet off of the pedestal it was nailed to and clanged down the hallway, ax raised high.

"Hurry, Shane!" I yelled. "It's right behind you!"

"GWAAAAAHHHH!" yelled the armor.

Gordon, Nabila, and I ran into the banquet hall and grabbed the two heavy doors, ready to slam them shut.

Shane dashed through and we pushed with all of our might. The doors crashed to a close just as the ax sliced into the wood.

Eventually, there was a clanking of metal as the suit of armor walked away. All we could hear was our heavy breathing and the storm raging outside until . . .

"I told you so," screeched Lucinda from the other side of the door.

We sat huddled in the middle of the banquet hall

around the candelabra, trying to figure out our next move.

"Are we sure there's not another way out of this room?" asked a frustrated Gordon.

"We could climb out of a window," said Nabila.

I peered out of a window and gritted my teeth.

"It looks like the windows are almost covered in snow," I said. "You might freeze before you get to the front door."

"Maybe we can just run past him. His ax is in the door," said Shane.

"Wasn't there an arsenal of weapons hanging next to him?" asked Nabila.

"Right," I said. "But I think we have to try anyway."

Shane walked stealthily to the door, and tried to open it.

"It won't budge. It's either locked or the ax has jammed it, or both," he said.

"Drat," I said, and fell back onto the cold floor.

It was three in the morning, and the snow had completely covered the windows. I huddled in front of a single candle. We were lighting them one at a time in hopes of making them last until daybreak. The others were asleep, and it was my turn to stand guard. I'd begun to nod off when I heard a terrible roar in the hallway. It woke me up fast, and I skittered over to Shane.

"Hey," I said. "Pssst! Wake up. There's something at the door."

BLLLUUUURRG!

Another roar floated into the room from the hallway.

"SHANE! WAKE UP!"

Shane jumped up and swayed on his feet. "Whaytuh?"

"There's something at the door," I said.

Gordon and Nabila were slowly waking up as well.

At the door, the strange creature gave another BLLLUUUURRG and the ax was pulled out of the wood.

"It sounds like a sussuroblat," said Shane.

"Oh, man," said Gordon, his teeth chattering. "I hope not."

The doorknob started to turn.

"Do sussuroblats know how to open a door?" Shane asked.

Gordon jumped over to one of the folding chairs that had been set up for tomorrow's PTA meeting and ran back to the door with it over his head.

"Whhhhhaaaa!" he yelled.

"BLLLLUUURRRGGGHH!" yelled the creature as it opened the door.

Gordon brought the chair down as hard as he could, and—

"Wait!" Nabila yelled. "It's Ben! *Habibi!*"

Gordon threw the chair to the right at the last minute, where it hit the wall with a CRASH.

"Hey, gggggguuysssss," gurgled Ben. "I woke up with a *masssssssiifff sneeeezzzz*, and spent an hour looking for you. Nabila, can I have a handkerchief? I'm dying over here. BLUUUUURGGH!"

Ben walked into the room, and the doors swung shut behind him with a click.

Gordon ran up to the door and grabbed the handles.

"Nooooooo!" he screamed. "It's locked! I gotta peeeeeee!!!"

"Welcome to the party," Shane said to Ben.

PTA Come and Play

The sun rose on a new day at Gallow Manor. We had survived the night, but in the banquet hall, Gordon was struggling.

"Man, if someone doesn't show up soon, I'm gonna have to pee all over this place," he said.

"You could just blame it on the werewolves," said Shane.

"They stopped doing that," I said.

Gordon rushed to a wall and unzipped his fly.

"Gross," said Nabila.

"I have no choice!" Gordon sounded desperate.

There was a click at the door, and it slowly creaked open. Gordon swiftly zipped back up.

Director Z walked in with a scowl on his face.

"What are you doing fooling around?" asked Director Z. "The PTA meeting is in less than two hours."

"How are they even going to get here?" I asked. "There's four feet of snow out there."

"Take a look outside," said Director Z.

Shane and I ran up to the window. The snow had melted enough to look out the very top. Shane gave me a boost so I could have a peek.

"WHOA," I said.

"What?" asked Shane, looking up.

"Dude," I replied. "The snow ends ten feet past the manor. Even the parking area is completely clear."

"I've never seen snow so localized," said Director Z, "and I have a theory about what has caused this. But we don't have time for that now. I must check in with Lunch Lady and make sure the proper preparations are being made."

I opened my mouth to tell Director Z what had happened to us the night before, but he cut me off.

"I suggest you all take showers," said Director Z. "But you'll need to unclog the drains and clean up the bathroom first. Gil decided to take another three-hour-long swamp shower to keep warm last night. There's swamp muck and vegetation everywhere, and we can't let our guests see such a mess."

Frederick, the old stitched-together monster, came

in holding a bizarre-looking metal cylinder with rubber on the tips.

"Here you go, Boss," he said, and handed the cylinder to Director Z.

"Thank you," said Director Z. "Frederick and I have been laboring over this particular piece of plumbing equipment for quite some time, and it should help you out greatly with unclogging the drains. Simply insert the front end into the drain, make sure to hold on to the rubber at the top, and press the red button. It utilizes a quite powerful type of electricity, so please make sure you're not actually *in* the water when using it."

"Got it," said Shane, snatching the electro de-clogger. "Should we expect any alligators?"

"Not this time," said Director Z, and he turned to leave.

"Aw, man," said Shane as we followed Director Z.

We quickly showered and then put on the same clothes we had worn the day before. Ben did his best to clean off the puke and orange boogers.

"Did you find any shampoo?" Ben asked as Shane

walked into the room drying his hair. "I couldn't use anything because of my allergies."

"The only thing I found was the werewolves' flea and tick shampoo," said Shane. "Which is good, because I think they might have given me fleas a few months back, and I'd been meaning to do something about that."

Gordon squirmed on the bench in front of the harpsichord.

"What's wrong with you?" I asked.

"I can't STAND wearing the same underwear two days in a row," Gordon shouted. "It just feels *wrong*."

"Hey," Ben said, squinting. "Is that something green poking out of your butt crack?"

"What?!" Gordon reached back and pulled a huge wad of swamp vegetation out of his pants. "Awwwww, man!"

Nabila walked into the room, looking fresh and clean.

"That's why I always carry an extra pair of underwear in my fanny pack," she said. "You never know. Next time I'll carry a second extra pair for you, Gordon."

"Umm . . ." Gordon looked confused. "Thanks?"

When we got back to the banquet hall, Lunch Lady and a few chefs—men who looked like Nurses, but with chefs' hats instead of nurses' caps—started to bring out the food that Lunch Lady had prepared.

One chef came into the room with a huge bowl of whitefish to spread on the bagels.

"Hey," said Ben, grabbing the bowl, "this is regular fish, right? It's not zombie piranha salad . . . right?"

"Just don't geet any snot in eet," said Lunch Lady. "You really should just lie down, my darleeng."

She grabbed the bowl and put it in the center of the table. Jane the zombie shuffled into the room and was about to grab a handful of the whitefish for a snack when Nabila pulled a bit of vegetable brain out of her fanny pack and jumped in front of her.

"Hungry?" she asked, as she waved the vegetable brain in front of Jane.

The zombie swiped the brain and gulped it down as she shuffled off.

"Hey," said Shane, "you're getting better at handling the zombies than me these days."

"Thanks," she said.

"I'm sure it helps that Ben has got so much snot in his brain that he's part zombie," Gordon said, chuckling.

We shuffled the last of the zombies out of the room just in time for the first parents and teachers to arrive, escorted by Nurses.

"Thank you so much for coming," Director Z said as

each one arrived. "I hope you don't mind being escorted to this room, but our new facility is quite large, and I'd hate for you to get lost."

The parents and teachers were very impressed with the facilities.

"Wow," said one, "this is massive!"

"Hey," said another. "Ms. Veracruz, what are you doing here?"

"Where are the old folks?" asked another.

"Oh," said Director Z, "we didn't feel the need to bother them with your activities, nor you with theirs. They're most likely in their common area, or their rooms."

I stood next to Shane and Gordon, handing out the agendas that my mother had printed up. Nabila was tending to Ben, who was still super snotty.

My mother arrived, took one look at the setup, and gave me a big thumbs-up!

"Chrissy," she said, "I can't believe the snow. We didn't get one bit. It's like it just all dumped on the retirement home. Until I saw it with my own eyes, I thought you'd made it up."

"Totally weird, right?" I replied. "It was a crazy night."

"The food looks great," she said. "How does the lunch lady know Director Z?"

"It's a long story," I said. "I'll tell it to you sometime."

Once everyone had grabbed a little breakfast and settled in, my mother stood up and headed for the podium.

"Good morning, everyone," she said. "It's so great to have you all here. Please refer to the agenda you were handed, and let's get started."

The meeting began, and everything seemed okay. I even started to relax. The five of us sat in the back of the banquet hall in a circle of chairs we had gathered. We played the game of pretending to squeeze the tiny heads of teachers we didn't like between our fingers. Then we saw Mr. Stewart's bushy head of hair and had a fun time squishing his head even though we liked him so much.

The more the meeting dragged on, the more I thought we'd get out of it with no problem.

"Maybe this section of the manor isn't haunted," I whispered to Shane.

"Maybe not," he said. "Nothing happened once we got in here last night."

There was a squeak, and the door swung open.

Murrayhotep walked into the room and looked around.

"Thanks again for the help yesterday," said Shane.

Murrayhotep gave Shane a dirty look, and a few of the parents in the back row SHUSHed Shane as some other parent made a big point at the podium.

"What is that grump doing here?" asked Gordon.

Before we could ask Murrayhotep what he was doing, my mother began speaking from the podium again.

"I just wanted to take a moment to thank Gallow Manor Retirement Home for hosting us today," she said, smiling. "I'd especially like to thank my son and his friends for all the preparations they made over the last few days. They do an amazing job volunteering here at the retirement home. Come on up, guys, and take a bow."

We looked at each other in disbelief and then shuffled up to the stage behind the podium. The audience of parents and teachers applauded.

Murrayhotep stomped his way up the center aisle toward us, his right hand raised.

"An amazing job, my eye! These kids are no good," yelled Murray, and dipped his hand into the bag that he was carrying. "Always bothering us. They—"

Before I could yell at Murray for being such a grump, the mic started to produce feedback terribly.

SCCCRRREEEEEEEEEEE!

We all stood back from the microphone, but it didn't help.

EEEEEEEEEEEEEEE!

Murrayhotep stopped in his tracks.

The audience covered its ears.

My mother tried to move the microphone, but it didn't help.

Nothing helped.

"Where's Zachary?" she yelled, and jumped off the stage—

Just as four terrifying creatures floated down from the ceiling with a bone-chilling roar.

The Fish Sat
Out Too Long

Parents and teachers gasped as four huge, bodiless heads descended from the ceiling. Their long, barbed tongues lashed out from behind sharp tusks.

"I guess this corner of the manor is haunted after all." Shane gulped, dodging the dirty, insanely long and thick black hair that grew out of each head.

Murrayhotep ran back down the aisle in the direction he'd come from. The doors slammed behind him as he left.

"This must be the newest breed of super monster," yelled Gordon. "Murrayhotep is scared to death!"

The creatures growled and slowly circled the five of us as we grouped together on the stage. Drool dripped off of their tusks, and their massive eyes bulged.

In the audience, the parents and teachers chattered nervously. I looked around for my mom, but couldn't find her. Nobody quite knew what they were looking at—or what to do.

"Which action plan?" screeched Nabila. "Which action plan!?"

"Five?" Ben sounded doubtful.

All at once, the creatures opened their mouths with the loudest roar yet. One floated out over the audience, taunting the parents and teachers. Folks were now running to the door.

"It's locked!" someone screamed.

The remaining heads closed in on us on the stage.

"Seven?" Shane sounded desperate. "All of our action plans use old monsters, and they're not here!"

"Just get ready," I said.

"For what?" Gordon asked.

"I dunno—just get ready to defend yourself," I said. "Kick some heads, Shane!"

We were completely cornered, but we had to do something.

"Everyone, please calm down," shouted Director Z as he headed for the locked doors.

Another creature head broke away from the stage and taunted the screaming crowd near the doors.

"WWWWEEEEYYYYYAH!" It moaned and spat.

Shane pulled a few karate moves on the creature heads when they dipped into his space, but they always knew right when to swing out of the way.

"If I keep missing, I'm going to pull a muscle," he said. He finally kicked one right in the jaw, and it flew back onto the floor, a jumble of hair and tusks.

"Waaaa!" squealed Nabila. "One's got Ben!"

Arms had sprouted from the hideous face of another creature, and grabbed Ben, who was now two feet off the ground and rising.

"Guys, help!" he yelled as he rose farther up.

"There. Isss. No. Help. For. YOUUUUU," moaned the head.

"Waaaah," screamed Ben.

Nabila grabbed at his feet.

The head shook Ben violently, and as it did, dust poured out of its long mane. Ben, stuck in the middle of the cloud, took in a huge breath.

"AHHHHH . . .

"AHHHHHHHHHH . . .

"AHHHHHHHHHHHHHHH . . .

"Chooooooooooooooooo!" Ben slobbered and snotted onto the creature's face. I could see a booger stuck on the bulging eye of the creature.

"Ah!" yelled the head as it dropped Ben on the floor with an OOF. "The terrible bogies! My eyes! BLECH! Why, I've never in my life, or my afterlife, seen a snottier sneeze. Dear boy, learn how to cover your mouth! ACK!"

The doors sprang open, pushing the parents and teachers back into the center of the room. The creature that had held Ben floated awkwardly past them and out of the room.

The other floating creatures seemed confused, but quickly followed.

None of the parents knew what to do.

It was deathly silent.

Ben sneezed another violent sneeze on the stage, and was knocked back onto his butt.

We all stood frozen—dumbfounded. Our open jaws nearly touched the floor. For Shane, Gordon, Nabila, and me, it was because we couldn't believe what had just happened. For Ben, it was because he was still choking on the dust. Nabila went over to help him.

The parents and teachers were all dumbfounded as well. They all sat back down, and everyone looked at us with their heads cocked to the side.

I was still standing in the middle of it all, so all eyes were on me. Gordon and Shane backed down from the stage.

"Uhhhhhmmmm . . . ," I said.

Durrrrrrrrrrrr . . . , thought my brain.

Before anyone could say anything, Director Z walked forward from the back of the room, clapping loudly.

"Bravo! Bravo!" he called. A few of the parents turned around and watched him come their way. "What an excellent performance. So gut-wrenching, powerful . . . realistic! Ladies and gentlemen, please give the wonderful St. James Players and many of your own children a round of applause for the amazing theater piece they just performed. What amazing acting!"

"This. Isn't. Act. Ing," Ben coughed.

"Ah, but you are too modest," countered Director Z. He squinted his eyes at me and nodded his head that I should talk.

"Yes," I said. "Ladies and gentlemen, thank you so much for watching our new play: *Horror at Gallow Manor*. We hope we've entertained you this afternoon!"

The room was painfully silent.

I bowed.

Finally, from the very back row, Nabila's parents rose and applauded loudly.

"Bravo," yelled her father. "We knew you had it in you!"

"Oh, you've made us so proud," her mother yelled. "What an amazing cultural experience."

Nabila took a big bow.

The rest of the crowd began to applaud, quietly at first. Then, slowly, they all rose and applauded loudly.

I motioned for my friends to join me on stage, and we all bowed together, poor Ben coughing the whole time. Shane gave him a sharp slap on the back and he finally stopped.

"I think we might win a Tony for this," Ben gasped.

"I think they're just happy to think it wasn't real," Gordon whispered.

"Joke's on them," said Shane. "That was real . . . right?"

"I have an idea," Nabila said. "I think that . . ."

My mother rose—like a zombie—and walked past us to the podium.

"Shhh," I said to the others. "We can talk about it later. I'm just glad we somehow survived."

"Hi, everyone," said my mother to the crowd, her voice shaking a bit. "I think we can hold off on new business until the next meeting. I can't really think straight. All in favor?"

"AYE," the entire crowd responded.

"What about the door prize?" asked one balding father.

My mother grabbed a canned ham and flung it to him, nearly knocking him over.

"It's all yours," she said.

Before Director Z could say "Thank you for coming," the crowd of concerned parents and teachers headed for the door. The Nurse escorts tried their best to walk folks out, but everyone wanted to leave as fast as possible.

"No, no, no," one mother said. "I can show myself out. I insist."

Director Z looked over at me with a concerned glance.

"Gordon," I whispered, "just run ahead and make sure no monsters are lurking on the way to the front door."

Gordon ran off, and my mother walked up to the rest of my friends and me.

"Oh, Chrissy," said my mother, "that was so real. I got really caught up in it. For a minute, I thought maybe the fish had gone bad, because I could have sworn I was seeing things . . ."

"See, I told you something was up with the fish!" added Ben.

Nabila smacked his head.

"Is this why you're always here so late at night, and so stressed?" asked my mother.

I stared at her, dumbfounded.

"Yeah," chirped Shane. "And if you think this is good, wait until you see our karate routine! We'll have it ready for you next month."

"Oh, no," my mother gasped. "That's quite all right. I'd hate to bother all the old folks. It was such a nice gesture that Director Z let us use this space, but I think we'll go back to the Rotary Dinner Hall next time."

"Aw, come on, Mrs. T," said Shane. "This was an amazing performance."

"Well," she said, "I'll think about it."

She turned to leave, still shaking a bit and mumbling to herself.

Once she left, I turned to Shane.

"What were you thinking, inviting my mother back to Gallow Manor after we barely survived this time?"

Shane replied something along the lines of "I dunno," but I could only focus on the creature that had appeared behind him.

"GWARRRRR!" growled the creature.

The Masked
Avengers

"WHA!" I screamed and pointed behind Shane. "It's back!"

Shane spun around and landed in a karate pose.

"Kick its head," I called out.

Then we heard a giggle coming from underneath the horrifying face. I took a closer look to see that Nabila's body was sticking out from under the head. Her fluorescent fanny pack was unmistakable.

She pulled off the monster head and handed it to me.

"I think this is a Balinese mask," she said. "Perhaps with some sort of enchantment on it. There are similar masks in Egyptian tradition."

"It's ugly," said Ben, who grabbed the mask from my hands and sneezed again. "And heavy. Do you think this is real hair? What's up with the mirrors on the tongue?"

"I read in the *The Book of the Dead* that masks are sometimes used to protect the dead," she said.

"This place is obviously haunted," said Shane.

"By 'the dead,' you mean ghosts?" Ben asked.

"The ghosts are just trying to protect themselves?" I asked. "So they're *not* trying to kill us? I think it's time we told Director Z about the vase. We need his help figuring this out, and that's when it all started."

We found Director Z in the front foyer with Gordon.

"I've just escorted the last old parent—or should I say grandparent—out to her car," Director Z said. "She was quite shook-up, but in the end, I think I convinced her that she had just watched a bit of performance art. I think we somehow made it through the PTA meeting without letting out any of our secrets. If anything, it may have drawn their attention away from the residents."

"Director Z," I said. "I have something to tell you."

"Let me guess," he said. "You broke something."

"How did you know?" Gordon asked.

"A major blizzard formed over the manor, for one." Director Z started counting things off on his fingers. "Lucinda was screaming about evil spirits all night. There was a hole in the banquet hall door thanks to an ax. You—"

"You knew?" Nabila gasped. "Why didn't you do anything?"

"I told you that if you broke anything, you'd pay," he said. "I sensed a disgruntled nature in the spirits of this house and I could feel that they were very much upset with our presence. But I also knew that if we just kept to ourselves, and didn't bother them incessantly, they'd leave us be."

"So the house *is* haunted!" said Shane.

"Did you have any doubt after what just happened?" Ben asked.

"I had my theories," Shane replied.

"What was it?" asked Director Z. "What did you break?"

"A vase," we all said at once.

"Not the vase in the North Wing?" asked Director Z.

"That's the one," said Gordon. "Technically the werewolves broke it!"

"It doesn't matter who broke it," Director Z said. "I

believe it held the ashes of one of the matriarchs of the family. You must make peace with the spirits."

"How?" I asked.

"You're smart kids, you'll figure it out," he said. "I'd start with the North Wing. That's where this all started. That's where you should try to end it."

"Hello?" Shane yelled into the North Wing hallway. "Ghosts? We're so sorry. We didn't mean to break your vase."

"Yeah," added Gordon. "We were stupid, and we're sorry. Please stop haunting us now."

"We brought you your mask back," I said, holding up the mask as an offering.

"Come out and get it," said Ben with a sniffle.

There was silence in the North Wing hallway.

Nabila paced back and forth as we waited for some sort of reply.

"All right, I've had enough!" she yelled. "Just because we broke the vase with your old dead mother doesn't mean you have the right to kill us. She was already dead!"

An angry rumble filled the hall.

"If you have anything to say about it, come out here at ONCE!" Nabila finished with a flourish.

"What are you doing?" Ben asked. "You're just going to make them madder!"

A ghostly figure appeared in the hallway and rushed toward us, raising a short sword in the air.

"You fooooools," yelled the ghost, who, as he came closer, looked terribly old. He wore a tattered old uniform.

"I care not about that dusty old vase," he said. "No ashes of a blood relative lay in it."

"Okay, so what's the problem?" asked Shane.

"Those terrible old monsters you've brought into our home," he said, moving closer to Shane, sword still raised. "They snort and snot and burp and barf. They're unclean. I don't want such filth in our house. They disgust me!"

With that, he swung his ghostly old sword at Shane's neck.

"Shane!" yelled Nabila.

It went through Shane's neck but didn't even leave a mark.

"Cool," said Shane.

"Cool?" hissed the old ghost. "I would go so far as to say that my blade is ice-cold."

"No, I meant 'cool' like 'neat' or 'awesome,'" said Shane. "What time period are you from, anyway?"

A ghostly kid appeared and ran toward us. "1897. What year is it now?"

"2014," I replied.

"Wow, I've been dead for one hundred seventeen years. That's thirteen times the amount of time I was alive."

"So you're nine," Nabila said, never failing a math quiz. "We're all eleven and twelve. What's your name?"

"I'm Quincy," he replied. "And this is my great-grandfather, George Stratford."

"That's Lieutenant Commander Stratford to you," he grumbled.

"You'll have to pardon my grandfather," said another ghost as he joined Quincy and George. "He talks so much about these old monsters that sometimes I think *he's* the old monster."

Another ghost appeared out of nowhere. A woman. And then a little girl came into view.

"That's my mother, Mary Stratford, but she likes to be called Lady Stratford," said Quincy. "And my three-year-old sister, Leila."

Five ghosts in total.

"We're so sorry we frightened you," Lady Stratford said. "But we were at our wits' end. When those werewolves destroyed the vase and left such a mess, why, we couldn't help but lash out."

"They can't stand messes," added Quincy.

"But we never would have hurt you," Quincy's father said. "We were just trying to convince you to leave this house."

"It was you in those masks?" I asked.

"Yes," said Quincy's father.

"I collected those terrifying masks from the island of Bali during a tour with the Royal Navy," said George. "They are said to channel the spirit of Rangda—an evil witch who eats small children. I thought they'd spook you out of the house good, but here you are now, standing right in front of me."

"Why are you still in the house?" Shane asked.

"We were trapped in the South Wing when the fire started," said Quincy's father. "We think it was the servants."

"But there is no South Wing," Gordon said.

"Exactly," said Quincy.

"We're sorry," I said. "But I think the old monsters are here to stay. All we can do is ask them to behave. And now that we know you're here, I'll ask them to do that."

"You might want to cover your mouth when you sneeze," said George, pointing at Ben. "It was such a powerful load of snot that it flew through my eyehole and directly into my eye."

All the ghosts shuddered.

"They hate bogies, too," said Quincy. "I once dug one out with my finger, and—"

"Quincy!" Lady Stratford scolded.

"Got it," said Ben.

Quincy waved as the mysterious figures faded away in front of us.

"Um . . . bye?" said Shane.

Mysterious Gifts

Somehow, Director Z convinced us to help out the next night. I think it was punishment for breaking the vase. After we shuffled around school like zombies for the day, we found ourselves standing at the snowy entrance to Gallow Manor once again.

But something was different.

"What's that noise?" asked Ben.

We all put our ears to the massive wooden door.

"Are the monsters . . . laughing?" Gordon said, flabbergasted.

"There's something else," said Nabila. "Scratching and whimpering. It sounds like a puppy."

She concentrated for a moment.

"And a kitten."

We rang the bell, and soon heard the sound of claws scraping down the hall and toward the door.

The door swung open, and a cute little brown puppy waddled out onto the welcome mat and started nibbling on Shane's shoes.

"Hey," Shane said, leaning down and patting the dog, "what's up, dude?"

"I thought your hearing was flawless," Gordon scolded Nabila. "Where's the kitten?"

From the feet of the Nurse who had answered the door, a small black-and-white kitten hissed at the dog.

"Friendly little thing," said Nabila. "I'm still trying to figure out why my ancestors were so in love with cats."

Shane shuffled the dog (and us) inside, and the Nurse closed the door.

"Where did these guys come from?" I asked the Nurse.

"Grigore," said the Nurse.

"Why are you back in your old uniform?" Ben asked. "Your tight uniform?"

"More comfortable," said the Nurse.

"I see," said Shane, thinking about it as the Nurse walked away.

The kitten took off down the hallway toward the East Wing. The puppy gave a sharp bark that echoed in the foyer, and chased after the kitten.

"Careful of the zombies!" I yelled at the furballs, and turned to my friends.

"They'll be eaten alive!" I said.

"I dunno," said Shane. "Everyone loves puppies and kittens."

"Exactly," said Gordon. "Sooooo tasty!"

"I wonder if Director Z knows about this yet," Nabila said.

"Let's go talk with Grigore first," I said.

We found the batty old vampire in the game room with the huge fireplace. He was talking with Grace, the most with-it of the zombies. She moaned in approval at something he said.

"Are you guys agreeing on who gets to eat them?" I asked.

"Oh, no," said Grigore. "Your mother's gift is just vonderful. We vouldn't even think of eating them."

"My mother's gift?" I asked, confused.

"The puppy and kitten," said Grigore. "It vas so nice of them to thank us for using the space."

"The puppy and kitten are from the PTA?" I asked.

"Yes," said Grigore. "They vere at the door this morning. I vas the vone who heard them scratching. They came vith a nice note."

"Oh no," said Ben. "The PTA has no idea what it's done."

"Where's the note?" I asked, not believing that my mother would send a puppy and kitten—at least not without talking to me first.

"I don't know," said Grigore. "I lost it somevhere vhile ve vere playing."

There was a bark in the hallway, and the cat rushed into the room and pounced on Ben. Ben screamed.

"Nooooo!" He grabbed the cat and tried to pull it off of himself.

"Claudine!" Grigore stood up and yelled. "Bad kitten! No, Claudine!"

"They named the cat Claudine?" Gordon asked, chuckling.

"My allergies!" Ben continued screaming as Grigore pulled the kitten off of him.

When Grigore finally got the cat off, Ben was covered in cat hair.

"Get the hair off of me!" said Ben. "Hurry! I'm gonna get hives!"

We brushed the hair off of Ben while Grigore sat down and stroked Claudine.

"Grab my inhaler, Nabila!" Ben shrieked. "Hurry!"

"I'm hurrying, I'm hurrying!" she shrieked back.

She dug around furiously in her fanny pack, and when she finally found the inhaler, she shoved it into Ben's hand.

He pulled off the cap, shoved the inhaler into his mouth . . .

. . . and stopped.

"Why aren't you using it?" I asked.

"I don't think I need it," he said. "I'm usually hacking and coughing and wheezing as soon as cat hair hits my skin, but I feel fine."

"Maybe it's one of those hypoallergenic cats?" Nabila said.

"Hypo-what?" asked Gordon.

"Cats that are less likely to trigger your allergies," Nabila said.

"AHHHH . . .

"AHHHHHHHHH . . .

"CHOOOOOO!" sneezed Grigore, and his dentures flew into the fireplace. They jumped out of the flames and chattered out into the hallway, most likely heading down to Grigore's coffin in the dungeon.

"Guess not," said Shane.

Before we could come up with any more theories, there was a scream from the hallway.

"You MONSTERS," said an otherworldly voice. "WE WILL DESTROY YOU!!!"

Cute and Cuddly
Poop Machines

The room shook violently. A chandelier fell on top of the chessboard, flinging Howie the werewolf and Jimmy the Moth Man back onto the dusty carpet.

The fire blew out in the fireplace.

A great roar thundered down the hallway.

"What is it?" asked Gordon, covering his ears.

"It's got to be—" I said.

"GHOOOOOOOOSTS!" Grigore finished.

The half dozen old monsters in the game room got up as fast as they could, knocking into one another as they shuffled around the shaking room.

"Why are you guys scared?" asked Gordon. "Didn't

Director Z tell you what was going on with our ghost friends?"

The puppy flopped into the room, frightened out of its mind, and right into Nabila's arms.

"Yip, yip, yip, yip," it barked.

"GET THAT THING OUT OF MY SIGHT!" A voice rattled our teeth, and Quincy's father floated into the room.

"Very angry ghost friends," said Gordon.

"Father! Father, stop!" Quincy yelled as he floated in after his father.

But Quincy's father didn't stop. He headed right toward Grigore.

"Noooooo!" Grigore cowered in the corner, holding the kitten tightly. "I don't even have any teeth. You vouldn't harm a helpless old vampire vith no teeth, vould you?"

"Helpless old vampire?" huffed Quincy's father. "You were the one that brought them into the house. These evil little things."

The kitten hissed from Grigore's arms as Quincy's father leaned in closer.

The puppy growled in Nabila's tight grip.

"Whoa," she said. "Settle down." She tried to calm the dog, but it bit her. "OUCH!"

She dropped the yipping puppy, and it scurried out of the room.

"Father," Quincy tried again. "Leave them alone. You're worse than Great-Grandfather."

"Yeah," I said, moving next to Quincy. "What's the big deal! It's just a puppy and a kitten!"

"Don't tell me how to act, boys!" he shouted. "I'm defending our house! Our honor. How dare they bring these creatures into our home . . ."

His ghostly face turned demonic; fangs poked out over his lips, his eyes glowed red, and he roared into Grigore's face.

"Please, sir," whimpered Grigore. "Please don't drain me of my juice. Please."

"He can't hurt you," I yelled at Grigore. "He's just upset that you're in his house and you let the dog and cat in."

"I can most certainly hurt him," hissed the demon ghost. "I will scare him until he's demented."

"Too late," Gordon said, giggling.

"Gentlemen, gentlemen," Shane said.

He moved between the quaking vampire and the upset ghost. The kitten saw the perfect moment for escape and bolted into the hallway.

"We can work this out," Shane said in his calmest Zen master voice. He turned to Quincy's father with his hands up in surrender.

"I know that you're upset . . . um . . . ," he said, "what's your name?"

"RICHARD," roared the ghost.

"And you have every right to let your feelings be known, Richard," Shane said calmly. "But I'd ask that you calm down just a little, otherwise Grigore will only hear that you're screaming, not that you're saying something."

Richard roared again, this time blowing Shane's hair back.

"Okay, thank you for listening," Shane said calmly, and then turned to me.

"Richard, we didn't have time to tell the monsters about you," I said. "I'm sorry. But we were pretty tired yesterday, thanks to your big show at the PTA meeting."

"That was fun," squealed Quincy.

"Har, har, har," said Ben.

"Grigore," I said, "go find Claudine and Sir Kibblebreath. I'll have to bring them back to my mother—if it really was the PTA that brought them into the house. They can't stay here—not if you want to live in this place without being haunted every day."

Grigore slowly limped out of the room, and Richard didn't stop him. The other old monsters followed, Grace the zombie taking a swipe at Richard's face with an upset groan. His face returned to normal. Well, normal for a ghost, anyway.

"Now wait a minute," Lt. Commander Stratford said as he floated into the room. "I don't think we should be too hasty, Grandson."

"Do you really want those beasts strutting around this house?" asked Richard. "You said yourself these old monsters would rain ruin upon our house—letting those terrible creatures into it is certainly a step toward that."

"I think, Grandson," Lt. Commander Stratford said, waving his short sword around the room, "that those beasts will end up doing more harm to the old monsters then they will to us, or our house."

"What do you mean?" I said.

"Oh, I don't know," said the old ghost. "I just think they've got something in them."

"Yes, they've certainly got a lot in them," said Lady Stratford as she entered the room, Leila in tow. "And quite a lot of it has come out onto our carpets. Disgusting."

The puppy and kitten scampered into the room again, and Quincy backed away.

"I think they're scary," said Quincy. "And they make my nose feel funny."

Just thinking about it, Quincy sneezed, and snorted up a huge, glowing booger. He went to pick it, when—

"Quincy!" his mother screeched. "WHAT IN HEAVENS ARE YOU DOING?"

"Ma," said Quincy. "Why are you always ruining my fun?"

"Fiddlesticks," said his mother. "You should really

use a handkerchief! It's completely uncouth."

"This is what's going to happen," I said, scooping up the dog. "We're going to get these guys out of your hair. Then, we'll introduce you to the Director, and you guys can set some ground rules about the old monsters in the house. Everyone's gonna be happy, I swear it. Shane, grab the cat."

"It was a terrible idea, anyway," added Ben. "Quincy, let me get a look at that booger . . ."

"I'll search the house for stained carpets, and do what I can to scrub up the mess," Gordon said.

"Great," I said. "Nabila, could you help Gordon?"

Nabila sat in a chair staring off into space. A long string of drool hung from her mouth.

Nothing to Sneeze At

"NABILA!" screeched Ben. "What's going on?"

"It bit me," she mumbled. "So badly."

"What?" I asked.

We all rushed over. Her hand was red and swollen.

"She's having an allergic reaction to the dog bite," said Ben, and he unzipped Nabila's fanny pack. "I just need to get my rash cream, Nabila. And an allergy pill."

The Lt. Commander floated over. "See, I told you that there was something special about these mangy little furballs," he said.

I looked down at Sir Kibblebreath, and wondered if there was something special about him. He shook his little head in my arms, and some hair floated up into my nose.

"Ah, ahhhh, ahhhhhhh . . . CHOOOOO!" I sneezed so hard that the glass on the fallen chandelier shook a bit.

"Yes," said Richard. "There is something 'special' about these animals. Which is exactly why we need to get them out of our home immediately. They're making me itchy just looking at them."

"We'll leave you to help out your friend," said the Lt. Commander. "We'll be back for an update. Unless we see your friend first."

"See our friend first?" Gordon asked.

"Oh, you mean if she dies?" Shane asked.

"Exactly," wheezed the old ghost.

"Great-Grandfather!" squeaked Quincy. "You're so mean!!!"

"I'm. Not. Goingtodie." Nabila gasped. "Feeling better . . . already."

"Come on, Grandfather," said Richard. "They've had enough." Richard sneezed himself out of the room with a huge ACHOOO.

"And so have I," came Richard's voice from the hallway.

"Where do they go, anyway?" I asked as the rest of the family floated into the hall, some through the open door, and some through the walls.

Shane sneezed.

"What the heck is going on?" Ben said. "I'm feeling better than I have in weeks, and everyone else is sneezing or having allergy attacks—even the ghosts!"

"Okay, everyvone," Grigore said as he entered the room with a basket. "I've found vone of our furry little friends."

"Wait, what?" I asked. "We've already got Claudine *and* Sir Kibblebreath."

"Huh . . . ," Grigore said as he put down the basket. "But . . ."

We all peered into the basket to see . . .

Another kitten!

"What the . . ." Gordon was astonished.

Grigore sneezed, his dentureless lips flapping like a whoopee cushion.

"Were there two kittens when they arrived?" I asked Grigore.

"No," he said. "Just vone. Of each. Two in total."

Grigore scratched his bald head, trying to figure it all out.

"Are you sure?" I asked.

"Gentlemen," said Director Z as he stormed into the room. "Are you responsible for the puppy which is currently in my office?"

"Nope," said Shane. "We're just responsible for this one."

"That one looks exactly like him," said Director Z, pointing at the puppy in my arms. "Yes, that's the one. How did you get him out of my office? I just locked him in there so he wouldn't be eaten by the residents."

"So there must be two of each," I replied.

"What?" asked Director Z, annoyed. "Please tell me what's going on here. I don't think it wise to have animals at this facility."

"We're not sure what's going on," said Shane, "except that Grigore found a puppy and kitten at the door, with a thank-you note from the PTA. And he brought them in."

"Just two, though, I svear!" Grigore said.

"But then how are there four animals now, Grigore?" demanded Director Z.

"I don't know," whined Grigore.

"De. Mented," chirped Gordon.

"Stop it," Ben said, and kicked Gordon in the shin.

"Yeah, you show him," said Nabila.

"Feeling better?" I asked Nabila.

"What happened to Nabila?" asked Director Z.

"That little beast bit me," said Nabila, pointing at the puppy. "And I had a very bizarre allergic reaction."

"We'll have the witches take a look at that," said Director Z. "Or would you like Leech Lady to take a little blood from the wound?"

"I'll go see the witches," said Nabila, and she made her way out of the room.

"Chris, I need you to get these animals out of the house at once," Director Z said.

"Okay," I said. "I'll tell my mother she needs to pick me up early. Maybe we can take them back where she got them. Shane, can you help?"

"Sure thing," said Shane. "The sooner the better. I'm starting to get hives."

"Gordon and Ben," said Director Z, "can you please help the chefs prepare dinner? It's taco night, so things might get messy, between the olives, onions, eye-of-newt, and other toppings crawling all over the place."

Director Z, Shane, and I were left alone.

"You swear you didn't have anything to do with this?" he asked.

"Why would I?" I replied. "Feeding baby animals to old monsters is just not a hobby of mine."

"Have you had a chance to speak with the ghosts?" asked Director Z.

"Yeah, and we were able to chill them out, until the puppy and kitten showed up," Shane said.

"That old ghost loves the animals for some reason," I said. "Do you think he brought them?"

"I'm not sure," said Director Z, "but I don't like them. They—"

Director Z stopped and quickly pulled out a handkerchief.

"Don't like who?" asked Shane.

Director Z paused with the handkerchief in front of his nose.

"I think he means the puppies and kittens," I said.

"AAAAAAACHOOOOO!" Director Z sneezed. "Get them out of here, boys."

When she picked me up, my mother confirmed that she hadn't sent any pets to the retirement home.

"Although that does sound like a good idea," she said. "I wish I had thought of it. I hear animals really help old people stuck in retirement homes feel happy."

I wondered for a moment if Grigore was lying about where the puppy and kitten came from, but didn't think about it long. They'd have a new home soon.

Luckily, my mom's friend Barbara runs a rescue shelter. As we drove there, Shane and I tried to contain the animals as they raced around the inside of the car.

"WHHHHAAAAAACHOOOO!" I sneezed.

A huge wad of green snot broke into booger chunks on the windshield. It looked like a bird had eaten split pea soup and relieved itself on our car.

My mother turned on the windshield wipers with an EWWWWW.

"No, Mom," I said with a snort. "That's on the inside."

"WELL, COVER YOUR NOSE NEXT TIME," she screeched as my boogers dripped onto the dashboard.

Lunch Lady
Liaisons

Ben and I were sitting in Mr. Bradley's social studies class when I *thought* I saw someone's face in the door window, staring right at me.

I couldn't be sure. I was still suffering from the aftereffects of being trapped in the car with the cats and dogs the day before, and was feeling a little foggy. The good news—I couldn't smell Mr. Bradley's breath today.

My nose dripped all over my Social Studies book. I was running out of tissues and I had given up trying to catch every bit of nose ooze.

"Looks like you've flooded the Great Wall of China," Ben said, pointing at the open chapter on Chinese culture. "I thought that was impossible."

"I can't even think straight right now," I said.

The door to the classroom opened up, and Lunch Lady poked her head into the room.

"Meester Bradley?" she said.

"What do you want, Ms. Veracruz?" asked Mr. Bradley.

"I want those two boys," she said, pointing at Ben and me. "They have to answer for the chicken casserole all over my cash register."

Ben looked at me strangely, but we knew not to say anything.

"Why doesn't the principal have a word with them?" Mr. Bradley asked, confused.

"Oh, that's where I'm breengeeng them," said Lunch Lady. "Right to thee principal."

"All right," said Mr. Bradley.

Lunch Lady quickly pulled us out of the classroom and rushed us down the hall into the janitor's closet.

As she closed the door behind us, I said, "You can't just pull us out of class like that."

"Actually, you can pull us out of Mr. Bradley's class any time," said Ben. "His breath is the worst. Though the barf water in the janitor's mop bucket comes in a close second."

"What if Bradley checks in with Principal Prouty?" I asked.

"He's too lazy to check my story," said Lunch Lady. "And this is *muy serio.*"

"What if the janitor shows up for a mop?" I asked.

"I gave heem some cheecken Parmesan to eat—hees favorite," Lunch Lady sighed, and then quickly snapped back to attention. "If you're worried about thee janeetor, shut up and leesten!"

"Okay, okay," I said. "What is it!?"

"There are more aneemals running around Gallow Manor," said Lunch Lady. "A lot more! The Director has geeven me thees letter to geeve to you." She held it up. "You are to get your friends, give eet to thee principal, and hope she dismeesses you early for thee day."

"What does it say?" Ben asked and went to tear open the letter.

"Don't touch eet!" said Lunch Lady, smacking Ben's hand. "Eet has to look official."

"Please tell me it doesn't have a glowing signature," I said.

"Just geet your friends, and geet the letter to thee principal," growled Lunch Lady.

It was 2:00 and we found ourselves lined up in the principal's office.

"From what I hear around school," Nabila said, "only bad kids end up in the principal's office. I don't like this."

Principal Prouty sat at her desk, eyeing the crusty old letter, which she had taken out of the sealed envelope. The smell of mold filled the room.

Shane sneezed. Gordon tried to stop his nose from snotting.

"Those poor creatures," Principal Prouty mumbled as she read the letter.

She put the letter down and stared at me.

"Sooooo . . . ," I said nervously.

"Well," said Principal Prouty. "You have to go help them with the outbreak. Zachary says it's pretty bad."

"Yesssss . . . ," I said, wondering what exactly Director Z had told the principal.

"So, you know Zachary?" asked Shane. "I mean, the Director?"

"We have an ongoing business relationship, yes," said Principal Prouty simply.

She stared at us.

We stared back.

Nabila finally broke the silence.

"All right!" she chirped. "Let's get out of here, then!"

We all stumbled awkwardly out of Principal Prouty's

office, like we were spooked old monsters and she was an angry ghost.

My mother reluctantly drove us to Gallow Manor. It took a bit to convince her that Director Z had arranged some of during-school-hours volunteering with the principal.

As the sound of her car faded into the distance, we could hear strange new sounds coming from the manor.

BRRRRAAAACK.

SLLLLUUUUUURRROOONT.

HAAAAAAA-CHOOOO!

WAAAAAAAAAAA!

"They're all sick!" said Nabila.

The door swung in to reveal a very sick-looking Nurse. He sneezed in our faces with a spray of boogers and then passed out. His head hit the mat outside of the door with a thud.

"Nurse Ax?" I yelled, getting down to check on him.

"Nurse Ax?" Shane slapped his cheeks.

"Are you sure that isn't Nurse Inx?" said Ben.

"Nurse? Nurse?"

We were all bent over the Nurse when another

figure appeared in the doorway. The even-gaunter, even-whiter figure of Director Z. He looked insanely sick. He stared at us with his red eyes, loosening his always-perfect tie. He swayed in the doorway, about to collapse.

"Children," he said. "Help."

Nothing to Sniff At

"Director Z!" I screamed.

Shane and I rushed up to him to make sure he didn't fall.

"Don't forget about me," said the Nurse, but his face was smashed on the welcome mat, so it came out, "Don forgt ba me."

"Yes, yes," said Director Z, "I'm fine. I just got dizzy. Help Nurse Ax out."

Gordon and Shane bent to pick up Nurse Ax, and with a huge grunt from all three of them, he was back on his feet again.

"What's going on?" asked Nabila.

Director Z opened the door wider, and presented

the foyer with a flourish.

Inside, dozens of puppies and kittens were running around like crazy. Up to the North Wing. From the West Wing.

In the East Wing, Lucinda B. Smythe screeched, "Oh, heavens, there's just so many of them!"

"There are *too* many of them," said Director Z. "Just when we think we've cornered them all in one room, a monster screams from another part of the manor."

"Scream?" Gordon asked. "Why would the monsters be afraid of them?"

"I think the sheer numbers," said Director Z, "and the fact that they're multiplying so fast may have something to do with it. Not to mention, I've never been more allergic to a creature in my life."

Director Z sneezed so hard that snot flew through the fingers of the hand he had placed over his mouth.

"I hear that," I said, and my nose started to twitch. "This place is swarming with fur."

"I have something to show you," he said, and beckoned us down the West Wing hallway.

"They're everywhere," said Ben as we made our way to the werewolves' room.

"Kittens swatting at each other," Shane said. "Puppies rolling over one another. Normally I love this stuff—when the puppies and kittens aren't multiplying like freaky amoebas."

"Clearly something unnatural is happening," said Nabila as we entered the bedroom.

"Clearly," said Director Z, pointing at a curled-up old dog on a chewed-up mattress.

"Who is it?" I gasped.

"It's Howie," said Director Z sadly. "And he's suffered a severe monster juice drainage. He passed out here after peeing all over the harpsichord. Did you know that before he played accordion, he played the harpsichord? It must have been the only thing he recognized in this place. So sad."

Director Z looked tired and zoned out.

"The puppies and kittens did this to him?" asked Gordon.

Howie's leg twitched, and Nabila bent down to stroke it.

"It's okay," she said. "It's just a bad dream."

A banshee screamed past the open door to Howie's room, chased by a half dozen dogs.

"This is no dream," Director Z snapped, regaining some of his energy. "The puppies and kittens did do this to him, and I'm still trying to figure out how. But a few of the residents and I have come up with a theory.

"These animals give off toxic allergens—that much we know. Even for us, the living, they have an effect."

"AAAAACHOO," Gordon sneezed. "Yep."

Gordon turned to Ben.

"Dude, I'm sorry I made fun of you for your allergies," Gordon said. "This totally bites."

"But I believe that, with the residents, the allergies are actually something worse," continued Director Z. "Something far, far worse. I believe that the puppies and kittens are absorbing monster juice. They get their victims ill, and then, when their monster juice escapes, they're there to absorb it. Not by biting, or eating, just by . . . being in the area."

"Little monster juice sponges," said Shane.

"Once they have too much monster juice to handle, they split in two—or three or four, who knows—and they absorb even more. My guess is there were a few more kittens and puppies in the manor last night when you took the first four away with your mother. There are so many places to hide in this massive manor. The dungeon alone . . ."

"Let's talk with the ghosts," I said. "They'd probably be able to float easily through the house and see into places where we can't see. We'll need their help to get all of them out of here."

"No, we have to keep them here," said Director Z. "They're too ordinary-looking. If we turned them out into the wild, they might find owners, and who knows what else they're capable of."

"Oh no!" Nabila said. "What about the kittens and puppies at the animal shelter?"

"I don't think we need to worry about that for the moment," said Director Z. "They barely had any exposure to the monster juice here, and there's no monster juice present at the shelter—at least none that I know of—so they should remain weak. We must first focus on the issue at hand."

"What if we just . . . ," Gordon said, and motioned cutting his throat with his thumb.

"Gordon!" Shane gasped.

"I thought about that," said Director Z, "but again, they might not die if killed. They might grow stronger. No. We need to gather them all into one room. And, Shane, you have to stop seeing them as cute little cuddly-wuddlies and realize that they are the new threat to monsterdom!"

"Man, this is just so sad," said Shane.

"We need to work quickly!" said Director Z. "Luckily, we aren't filled with monster juice to drain, but we can get sick, and if we have severe allergic reactions, we could all die. The Nurses and I have already been exposed too much. I need you gentlemen and lady to set things in motion while my staff and I walk the grounds and try to air out our sinuses. First things first. Talk with the ghosts."

Covered in Boogers

"Ha-ha-haaaa!" Lt. Commander Stratford's chuckle filled the North Wing hallway. "You want us to help YOU! I'm having too much fun watching those old monsters suffer. I haven't been this happy since my dear sister was still with me."

The old Lt. Commander stood atop a small spiral staircase that led to a number of small rooms on the second floor, as well as the balcony that surrounded the wing.

"You nasty old fart!" Gordon yelled up the staircase. "No wonder your sister ran away. Where are the nice ghosts? I want to talk with the nice ghosts!"

"She didn't *leave* me," he said. "She was a ghost like

me, but her energies were drained and I lost her. I'd do anything to get her back. And I'd do anything to get rid of those old monsters."

Quincy, Leila, and their parents slowly materialized next to Lt. Commander Stratford.

"Teeheehee," said Quincy. "Great-Grandfather, you just got called an old fart!"

"I disagree, Grandfather," said Richard. "I'd do anything to get rid of those nasty animals. We must help these children.

"And, in return"—Richard pointed a ghostly finger directly at my head—"you WILL get the old monsters to behave. And they will stay away from the North Wing. And we will stay away from them. Agreed?"

"Agreed," we all said.

"Poppycock!" yelled the old ghost as he raised his sword. "My family might have an agreement with you, but I, most certainly, do NOT. CHAAAARGE!"

He floated swiftly down the stairway, sword pointed at our heads.

"I really wish he'd stop doing this," said Gordon.

"I think it feels pretty cool," said Shane.

WHOOOOSH!

With a roar, the old ghost shot through our bodies and into a supply closet at the bottom of the stairs.

"Dreadfully sorry about that," said Richard. "He always has to make a point."

The closet door shot open and a dozen puppies and kittens tumbled out with the old ghost, who was coughing and hacking and moving much slower now.

"Can't. BREATHE," he wheezed. "Get. Them. Away!"

"Ghosts breathe?" asked Nabila.

George slowly floated up the staircase.

"Well, don't bring them up here!" said Lady Stratford.

But, before the ghosts could float away, they began coughing and sneezing as the animals, and all of their dander, came floating up the stairs with the old Lt. Commander.

"Great. Grand. Father," coughed Quincy. "Are. You. Okay?"

The puppies and kittens jumped around inside the forms of the ghosts, which were frozen at the top of the stairs.

"Guys! Guys!" yelled Ben. "Are you okay?"

HACK, COUGH, SNORT!

"We've got to get the puppies and kittens away from them," I said, and we rushed up the stairs.

Halfway up, each ghost, in unison, leaned back with an "AAAAAHHHH . . .

"AHHHHHHHHHHHHH . . .

"CHOOOOOOOOOOO!"

A shower of glowing, emerald-green snot—filled

with boogery chunks—showered down on us from the top of the stairs, pouring out of each of the ghosts.

We slipped and stumbled backward, falling down the stairs with the animals, which had all been thrown down with us.

When I finally was able to get up out of the muck, I realized I couldn't hear out of my right ear. I pulled a huge booger out of my ear hole.

"Oh man!" I yelled, looking down. "This is disgusting."

"Well, the good news is, I feel much better," said Quincy. "Whew, that felt great! How about you guys?"

The other ghosts nodded.

"And we've got a good batch of animals," said Shane.

"All right, everyone, grab 'em, I guess!" I said.

"I need to take a quick shower," said Ben. "I'm sort of grossed way out over here."

"We don't have time," I said. "We've got to move fast—monsters are getting sick."

"We'll float around the house and let you know where we find them," Richard said.

It was a long, hard afternoon of animal wrangling that had turned into a rougher evening. We stood snotting and wheezing in front of the banquet hall, which was filled with nearly fifty puppies and kittens.

SNORF!

SNORRRRT!

SNAAAARRRRF!

"I feel like my clothes are turning into armor with all of these drying boogers," said Gordon.

"All of the animal hair doesn't help, either," said Shane. "It just sticks right on. AHHHHCHOOO!"

A Shane booger hit my temple.

"Uggggggh," I grunted, and wiped off the fresh, hot booger.

"Ack!" yelled Nabila. "You tossed it right at me."

She in turn tossed the hot booger, and—

"How dare you!" yelled Lucinda B. Smythe.

Shane's booger sat on her portrait in a way that made her look like she had lost a tooth.

"Wow, she looks like a hockey player," said Gordon, laughing.

"That's *not* funny," said Lucinda.

Quincy floated up behind Nabila and leaned in close to her.

"PSSSSST," whispered Quincy.

"Wahhhhh!" screamed Nabila. "AAAHHHCHOOO!"

"I scared a sneeze out of you," Quincy said, giggling.

"It's better than a fart." Gordon snickered. "AAAACHOO!"

"Sorry, I couldn't help it." Quincy kept giggling. "I just came to tell you that we can't see any puppies or kittens hiding anywhere."

"Yeah, well how do you like this?" asked Nabila.

She pulled a crusty chunk of boogery hair off of her shirt and tossed it at Quincy. It hit his head and floated around a bit.

"Ah, ah, ahhhhh . . . " Quincy shook his head. "SCHPLOOOOOOO!"

Quincy shot up through the ceiling, showering emerald-green boogers down on us and Lucinda—now it looked like she had lost several teeth.

"EEEEEWWWWWWW," we all said.

A door to one of the empty rooms in the East Wing swung open, and Murrayhotep stuck his head out. He eyed us through his wrappings.

"Would you cretins please shut up?" he growled. "I'm concentrating in here."

SLAM!

"Well, it looks like the monsters feel better already," said Shane. "At least that monstrous old monster."

"Well, then, I think we're finally done. Even if we're not done, we're done," I said, exhausted. "I'm done. Are you guys done? It's the Nurses' turn."

As we walked to the foyer, a sick zombie collapsed

in front of us. A froth of snot bubbled up through his mouth and nose, and he spasmed violently on the floor.

"We've got to get him to a Nurse," said Nabila as she bent over to pick him up.

We saw more sick monsters as we dragged the zombie through the foyer.

"Clarice, you don't need to use that anymore," I said, pointing at her walker. "It's gonna be a while before my mother comes back for another visit—if she ever comes back."

"But I actually need it now," she wheezed.

We passed the zombie off to a Nurse and headed for Director Z's office in the West Wing. There was moaning and groaning like we hadn't heard since the days of Raven Hill.

We passed by Old Bigfoot's room on the way to Director Z's office.

"Help," he screamed and coughed. "Helllllp!"

I grabbed the door handle.

"It's locked," I said. "Gordon?"

"Got it," he said, and busted the door open with his shoulder.

Inside there was a pitiful sight.

"He's been pinned to his bed," Nabila said, pointing, "by a kitten?"

Shane snatched the kitten off of the beastly, hairy man, whose snow-white fur—which had been gray just a few days ago—was a devastated war zone of snot around his neck.

"You look terrible, Roy," said Shane. "How long has this been going on?"

"I don't know." Roy shook and coughed. "I woke up with it on my chest. ON MY CHEST. WHAAAAA-CHOOO!"

We were once again showered in boogers.

"I'll rush this one to the banquet hall," said Shane.

There was a loud POP, and Shane suddenly was holding two kittens.

They both looked up at him with a "mew."

"I mean I'll rush *these* to the banquet hall," said Shane. "I'll ask Murrayhotep what his secret is—he's the only one doing okay right now!"

"WHAAAACHOOO"—Shane sneezed his way down the hall.

"I feel terrible," Roy said. "Get. Me. A. Nurssppplloorrfff!" Roy began to choke on his own snot, writhing around in the bed for a moment, and then going deathly still.

"Roy!" I screeched. "Roy!"

Gordon put his ear down to Roy's twisted mouth.

"Get a Nurse!" yelled Gordon. "He's barely breathing!"

Ben snagged a Nurse from the hallway, and the Nurse ordered us out.

"What's going to happen to him?" asked Nabila as the Nurse slammed the door in our faces.

The SLAM echoed through my swollen head.

"My head!" I yelled. "It's bursting with snot."

"My mother just texted to say I could stay later," said Ben. "I feel great, and Director Z and the Nurses could use my help. You guys get out of here. Get some rest, or you'll end up like Roy. I'll let Director Z know."

Later that night I sat up in bed. No matter what position I tried, I couldn't keep myself from feeling like I was drowning in snot. I grabbed my phone off of the nightstand and texted Ben.

How are things going?

Not good. But I have an amazing idea.

What is it?

We need to get a monster to eat boogers. Ghost boogers.

Ghost Boogers

The next day at lunch, Gordon, Shane, Nabila, and I sat with tissues shoved up our noses to stop the snotting. We forced down our lunches. I had spent the morning either snotting, or trying desperately to not fall asleep.

"The monsters aren't getting much better," said Ben. "Roy's still in a coma. Lots of them were even older-looking than when you left."

Ben stopped to chomp down on a Grilled Scream and shoved a handful of French Flies into his mouth.

"I feel bad for the monsters, but oh, man, this is the most I've tasted in months," he said, energized.

"Good for you," grunted Gordon. His eyes were crusted shut and his nose was practically raw from blowing it so much. "I had to skip practice this morning. I can already feel my muscles shrinking."

Some kid tried to sit down at the end of our table, so Nabila pulled the tissue out of one of her nostrils. After a small shower of snot landed on the table, the kid walked away.

"Aw, thanks," said Ben. "I just really don't feel like barfing today."

"So, tell me again about the ghost boogers," said Shane.

"Wait," I snorted. "You were for real last night? I thought you were joking."

"No, I think it might actually work," said Ben. "Director Z is waiting for some 'removal crew' to come in from the Canadian retirement home network and take away the cats and dogs, but things are still so bad—leftover allergens and stuff—that he was thinking about moving the old folks."

He shoved another handful of greasy French Flies into his mouth.

"Careful, dude," said Shane. "You'll spew."

"Naw, not today," Ben said. "Anyway, I had a flash of inspiration. I was feeling so good, I realized that my body had somehow formed an immunity to whatever it was the puppies and kittens were exposing us to."

"What does that have to do with ghost boogers?" Nabila asked.

"Like me, they aren't as affected by the puppies and kittens. Except for when they're overexposed. Then they explode in snot. But I think it's some sort of ghostly immunity defense."

"So you're saying eating the boogers would make the monsters immune, too?" asked Shane. "Like a vaccine."

"Like the way vaccines are made from the viruses they fight?" I asked.

"Maybe, and yes," said Ben. "I think it might power them up for a bit—not necessarily cure them. I told Director Z, and he agreed—if one of us tested it."

"You mean we have to eat boogers?" asked Gordon.

"Well, one of you guys needs to, since I'm not sick. He's worried that if we test it on a monster and it backfires, it could really do some damage," said Ben. "And he can't test it, because he can't be knocked out with an allergy attack."

"What about a Nurse?" asked Nabila.

"Same thing," said Ben. "They're just too important. Look, it's just a handful of boogers. If it works— awesome—we have a whole staircase of snot to chisel off and pass around to the old monsters. If it doesn't, I'll be standing by with my inhaler, creams . . . all sorts of stuff."

We reluctantly headed to Gallow Manor after school to test Ben's theory. None of us were too excited about the idea of eating boogers. We all knew it had to be done, but no one—other than Ben—was looking forward to it.

As we entered the East Wing, the smell of the puppies and kittens coming from the banquet hall was overwhelming.

"AHHH-AHHH . . ." I struggled with a sneeze.

"CHOOOOO!" Nabila finished my sentence.

"This is bad," Gordon said with a snort. "But I feel like eating ghost boogers is going to be worse."

"Oh, finally," said Lucinda as we stepped in front of her boogered face. "It took you a full day, but you're finally back to clean me up."

"Well, we'll start with one," said Ben. "And then we'll see what happens."

"You do it," said Gordon to Shane.

"No, I think our fearless leader should do it," said Shane. "Chris, lead by example."

"If this works, you're all going to be eating boogers," Ben said. "So—just do it!"

"Fine," said Nabila, and she reached up to the portrait to pluck off the biggest booger.

"Make sure it's not mine," said Shane. "The one you flung, remember?"

"It's not yours," said Nabila, and she stared at her snack. "Okay. Here we go. I'm doing it."

She plopped it into her mouth.

The sound of Gordon dry-heaving beside me only made the situation worse. There was no way I was going to be able to do this.

"Dear child, what are you doing?" screeched Lucinda.

"I'd suggest chewing on it," said Ben. "You know, grind it up good."

Nabila took Ben's advice, gritted her teeth, and started to chew.

CRUNCH, CRUNCH, CRUNCH.

"Sounds dry," said Shane.

"Uggghhh," Nabila said through her closed mouth.

Her eyes started to water. A little sweat formed on her forehead.

CRUNCH, SQUISH, SQUISH.

A trickle of green drool dribbled down her chin.

"That's good," coached Ben. "Just like that. Now swallow."

Nabila swallowed hard . . .

GULP!

. . . and turned a boogery-green color.

"Oh no. Oh man," she said. "Whuuuurp!"

She gagged.

"You have to keep it down," said Ben. "Keep it down."

"Huhhhhhh." She dry-heaved a little but nothing

came up. "Okay. I'm okay."

Then she took in a huge breath of air through her cleared nasal passages.

"Yes! It works!" screamed Ben, giving Nabila an awkward bear hug.

Gordon, Shane, and I looked at each other. We knew what had to happen next.

"Perhaps being sick isn't so bad," said Gordon. "Maybe I don't need to play sports or be fit."

"Just do it," said Ben. "It isn't so bad, right, Nabila?"

"Isn't so bad? I just ate a giant booger," she replied. "It was disgusting. But I do feel much better."

Shane plucked a booger off of Lucinda.

"Looks like we might clean you off yet," he said.

"Well, hurry it up," said Lucinda.

"Mmmmm," Shane said as he popped it into his mouth, though his eyes said, "Blarrrf!"

I peeled more boogers off and handed some to Gordon, who reluctantly took them from me.

"Good luck," I said, and chomped down on a handful of boogers.

Gordon slowly pushed his boogers past his lips and into his mouth.

We choked down our snot snack and breathed deeply for the first time in days.

"Wahooo!" Shane yelled. "Let's grab a few green ones and feed them to an old monster."

We rushed back to the West Wing and Director Z's office with a good handful of boogers.

When we got to his office, Pietro was there, talking about the flea infestation that had come along with the puppies and kittens.

"We're sick *and* we're itching like crazy," Pietro said, a large string of snot falling out of his nose.

Even though he was in human form, he took off his shoe and started to scratch behind his ears with his foot.

"How'd you like to feel better?" asked Shane.

I held out my hand to Pietro.

"It worked?" asked Director Z.

"Sure did," said Ben.

"What is it?" asked Pietro.

Nabila replied, "They're boo—"

"Bound to make you feel better," I cut Nabila off. "Just eat it."

Pietro crunched and munched on his treat, and swallowed hard. "Ewww . . . what is this stuff?"

"We'll tell you, but first tell us, how do you feel?" asked Ben.

"Pretty good, actually," he said, and then breathed in deeply.

"Hoooooooooooowl," Pietro said, rattling the windows in Director Z's office. "Wow, I feel really good."

He stood up and stretched.

"He's still gray and wrinkly, but he looks good," said Nabila.

"He would probably just have to eat more to get more energy back," Ben said.

"Eat more what?" asked Pietro.

"Boogers," said Director Z. "Ghost boogers. Amazing."

"Ghost boogers?" Pietro gagged. "Is this a joke?"

"You feel great, right?" I asked.

"Yeah, I suppose," said Pietro. "Just a little disgusted."

"Awesome," I said. "Then maybe you could help us collect all of the boogers in the North Wing that the ghosts left behind."

"I'll get the old monsters prepared," said Director Z.

Pietro stared at the stairs, scratching his bushy werewolf-hair head.

"Boogers?" he asked. "What boogers? I don't see any boogers."

"I don't, either," said Ben.

"The stairs are now the cleanest part of the house,"

said Shane. "They almost sparkle."

He put down his rusty metal booger-collecting pail that Director Z and the Nurses had scrounged up for each of us, and called out, "Quincy! Quincy!"

"Hey, guys!" Quincy appeared at the top of the stairs. "Don't the stairs look great?"

"Ghosts can clean?" Nabila asked. "Why was this place so dusty when we first got here?"

"I told you that my parents hated bogies," Quincy said. "As soon as you guys left, we cleaned it all up. Why are you so upset?"

"Believe it or not, we think that your boogers are the key to saving the old monsters from the effects of the puppies and kittens," I said.

"Oh . . ." Quincy thought about it for a minute. "Well here, then."

Quincy dug into his ghost nose with his ghost finger and pulled out some green gold. He handed it to Pietro.

"Thanks, kid," he said over a boogery crunch.

"But I think we're going to need a lot more than that," Ben said, and held up his bucket. "Buckets and buckets."

We all held up our buckets.

"Quincy," I said, "you and your family have to help us. You need to fill these buckets for us."

"Impossible," said Lady Stratford, who materialized suddenly to his right. "You ask too much of my family. We just want peace."

I was about to plead our case, when Quincy did it for me.

"Mom," said Quincy, "if we don't help the old monsters, they'll just get older. And louder. And dirtier. It will just be worse for us."

The rest of the family appeared at the top of the stairs.

"Plus—remember when you and Dad were worried about who was going to move in here? Well, these old monsters don't even care we're here. In fact, we can float about freely. If a stuffy old rich family moved in here, we'd have to hide."

"I guess you're right . . . ," said Lady Stratford.

"You're not really thinking of forcing yourself to sneeze like you did before, are you?" Richard said.

"We have no choice, dear," Lady Stratford said. "Your son is right. He's sharp as a tack, just like his father."

"Fiddlesticks," said the Lt. Commander. "They can all go to—"

"Grandfather!!" everyone screamed.

"Okay," said Richard. "What do we need to do?"

Buckets of Boogers

Once again we stood in front of the door to the banquet hall—this time with the ghosts.

"Will someone *please* finish cleaning this mess off of me?" screeched Lucinda B. Smythe.

"Free boogers!" said Gordon. "Go for it, Pietro."

Pietro walked over to the portrait and began to lick the remaining boogers off of Lucinda.

"Oh. Stop. No," said Lucinda. "Not like this. Ack! Your breath is terrible. Be careful! I'm an OIL painting!"

"Hey, who was it that hacked into the door with the ax?" asked Ben.

"I'm loath to admit it, but that was me," said Richard.

"Well, we have the perfect tool now," said Ben. "You

can stick your head into the banquet hall through the ax hole to soak up all the animal dander you need and then one of us will be holding on to a bucket for you."

"We're ghosts, son. A locked door is no problem for us," Richard said as he shoved his ghost head through the door.

I stood steady with my bucket.

"AHHHHHHH . . ."

The butt cheeks in his finely pressed pants raised up once.

"AHHHHHHHHHHHHHH . . ."

Twice.

"AHHHHHHHHHHHHHHHHHHHH . . ."

He pulled his head out from the door and aimed for my bucket with bug eyes.

"CHOOOOOOSHLURBSCHLURBSCHLURP!"

His ghost nostrils flared, his lips flapped, and out poured the snot.

And he kept going!

"My bucket's almost full," I yelled. "Shane!"

Shane pushed his bucket above mine, and Richard filled it halfway up.

"Yeah!" said Ben. "Awesome. Nice snottin'!"

Lady Stratford was next, followed by Quincy. We were up to four buckets.

"I don't think we need to force any snot out of Leila," I said.

But she walked over to the bucket Quincy had just filled, dug deep into her little ghost nose, and picked out a surprisingly large booger.

"Bogie for you," the little three-year-old said with a smile.

"Oh, Leila, how sweet!" cooed her mother. "That's so nice of you."

"Nice," said Quincy, and he dug into his nose.

"Tut-tut." His mother slapped his ghost finger out of his nose. "That's enough for now."

We headed into the dining room of the West Wing, where Director Z and the Nurses had gathered every resident.

HAAAAACHOOO!

GWAAARRRFFF!

SNOOOORRFFFF!

Everyone in the room was sick. The table was covered in a layer of monster snot, and with each AHCHOO the layer got thicker. In some places, it dripped off of the tables.

"They're so much older than before," said Nabila.

"I can't take it!" screeched Griselda. "I'm itching everywhere. The *inside* of my body itches." Griselda fell to the floor, writhing in agony. She began choking, and a Nurse swiftly pulled her up and slapped her on the back.

Murrayhotep leaned back in his chair, giggling.

"Why is Murrayhotep so happy?" asked Ben. "Why isn't he sick?"

Before anyone could answer, one of the old vampires sneezed himself off of his chair. When a Nurse picked him up, he was oozing boogers.

"I'm. So. Tired!" he wailed, and passed out.

"We'd better just hurry," said Shane, helping Griselda.

"Yes, the residents are getting delirious," said a very concerned Director Z. "I really want to administer this treatment as quickly as possible."

"Let's make sure everyone gets the same amount," said Nabila, and she grabbed one of the soup ladles on the table.

"Yeah, and make sure we get some," said Gordon. "I'm already feeling sick again."

"We can always ask the ghosts to make more," I said. "Although I'd rather not, if we don't have to."

The old monsters stared at us strangely through their weak watery eyes as we scooped out sloppy, goopy snot with booger chunks.

"What is that?" Clarice the banshee asked.

"Pietro said this was ghost snot," replied Frederick.

"I don't believe a thing Pietro says," said Clarice, and she ate a spoonful. "Ugh, this is terrible!"

"So it is ghost snot?" asked Queen Hatshepsut, the oldest of the mummies in residence. "Oh, I can't do it."

She pushed her plate back.

"You have to eat it," said Shane. "You guys are going to feel better."

The old zombies had a stronger reaction to the boogers than the other old monsters did.

"Garrrrrr!" yelled one, and threw his booger bowl at Director Z's face.

"People, people!" yelled Director Z, green chunks dripping down his face. "Please, remain calm. I know that everyone is exhausted, but Ben assures me that eating this will help you. Just ask Pietro."

"Oh, this stuff is disgusting!" yelled Pietro. "It wasn't this bad the first time."

"Maybe because it's so fresh?" I wondered out loud.

The old monsters that could were starting to stand up and walk away from the tables. A Nurse shoved a spoonful into Griselda's mouth, and she immediately hacked it up.

Director Z caught a booger that crept down his face with his tongue and almost gagged when he started chewing.

"Oh my," he said. "This actually is pretty bad."

Shane sucked down a spoonful and almost immediately barfed up the green goodies.

"Terrible," he shrieked.

More monsters were throwing booger bowls.

"Wait, wait!" I said, scooping up handfuls of snot

134

off the raggedy old carpet. "Stop doing that! We'll figure something out. Don't waste it! It's magical, I swear."

"Vell, it's not magical if ve can't eat it," snorted Grigore.

"Well, VHAT do you VANT me to do, cook you a booger pie?" I asked, frustrated.

"Hey," said Shane. "That doesn't sound like a bad idea."

"Booger sauce over pasta?" asked Ben.

"Booger pâté?" offered Nabila, and then, "No, no, it's too hard to cook."

"Fresh garden salad with booger bits?" Shane tried.

"Booger casserole with chicken and noodles?" I asked. "Wait, even better—Mac 'n' Sneeze!"

"Real-life Mac 'n' Sneeze," chuckled Gordon, then the visual of it hit him. "Oh, I think I'm going to hurl."

We looked at Director Z.

"All right," he said. "Let's have a dinner party! The Nurses and I will try to calm down the residents as much as we can."

He wiped off his face with a handkerchief and handed it to me.

"Here," he said. "For your booger pie."

Hungry for Boogers

Once we had gathered as much of the snot as we could, we instructed the chefs in the kitchen on how to perfect our creations.

"The boogers should be super crispy," said Shane to one chef. "Nice and crunchy, so it really complements the bacon in the salad. Fry them hard, and don't be afraid of oversalting."

"Hmmmm," said Gordon, peering under the arm of another towering chef, as he mixed furiously. "Maybe we should throw the cheese sauce in a blender before adding the macaroni. It's a little chunky right now."

I was about to tell my chef to add more eggs to my

booger pie, when Director Z came into the room.

"Chris, can I have a word with you?" he asked, adding, "in private?"

"Sure," I said. "You guys need to figure out a main course. Maybe roast chicken with herbs and boogers?"

"So, not 'original recipe'?" Shane giggled.

"I think the walk-in refrigerator will be the perfect place to speak," said Director Z, and opened the door for me.

I'd been having a great time in the kitchen and had almost forgotten about our situation. As the door shut, I began to get worried.

"What's going on?" I asked.

"Chris, I fear that the puppies and kittens are more powerful than we think," he said. "Or they're just a precursor of something worse."

"What do you mean?" I asked. "Once the monsters eat dinner, we'll be good to go!"

"Maybe," said Director Z. "Or maybe not. I'm still trying to figure out how the puppies and kittens got here in the first place, and I fear that it may be the work of someone on the inside."

"You mean a traitor?" I gasped. "One of the old monsters is a traitor?"

"I just don't know," said Director Z. "In addition, the team sent to investigate and deal with the puppies and kittens is no longer communicating with me. I fear they may have been destroyed. I have a very bad feeling about this."

"What do you need from me?" I asked.

"I need you to carry something for me," he said, loosening his tie.

"Your pendant?" I asked.

"Indeed," he said, and pulled a chain out from under his shirt. A piece of bloodstone hung from the bottom.

"I had two of these in my possession—mine and one that had belonged to my old mentor," he said. "And now the other one is gone. I thought I had hidden it well enough in this old manor, but apparently I was wrong. Someone has gotten to it. If this is all the work of a traitor, they'll most likely be after this one as well."

He handed his pendant over to me. It was strangely heavy.

"I cannot stress enough how important this task is that I'm about to give you," he said. "Humans have only just recently begun wielding pendants. It used to be only senior monsters that held them—those that were tasked with saving their kind. The second pendant—the one that I spoke of before, the one that was stolen—was the last to be worn by a senior monster Keeper. He was a wonderful Cyclops by the name of Percy. I had been meaning to find a Keeper to replace him, but quite frankly, we've lost so many residents that there was no need for a new facility. Percy's pendant would have been much safer off this property . . ."

Director Z looked off into the back of the cold, refrigerated room, lost in thought.

"Director Z?" I asked. "Should I hide this one? Maybe I could give it to the ghosts?"

"No," he said, snapping back to attention. "No, you must hold it. At this point, I don't trust anyone, especially that old cutlass-wielding ghost who has it in for my residents. I don't trust anyone but you, Chris."

I started to put the necklace around my neck.

"Wait," said Director Z. "Keep it on you, but don't wear it. It would be too easily seen."

"Okay," I said, and I put the pendant in my pocket.

"You are a Keeper now, Chris," said Director Z. "If anything happens to me—"

"What's going to happen to you?" I said, afraid.

"*If* anything happens to me," he continued, "you'll be in charge. The Nurses will follow your every order. The residents will have no choice but to fall in line under the power of the pendant."

He pulled another pendant out of his suit coat pocket.

"Wait, I thought you said you lost the other one," I said.

"Oh, I did," he said. "This one is a fake. If someone comes looking for the other pendant—my pendant—I want them to think I still have it. And you have to play along with me. No matter what happens—"

"What's going to *happen*!?" I said, really upset now.

"No matter what happens," continued Director Z, "you must play along that this is the real pendant. Understood?"

"Understood," I confirmed.

Within an hour, the family-style booger feast was ready. We helped the chefs carry out our crazy creations.

"It looks so good, I just drooled a little," said Gordon. "I don't even feel like hurling. Do I like eating boogers now? Have I become that guy, the booger eater?"

"This is going to be amazing," said Ben. "Amazing."

"I dunno," I said. "They might not even be hungry for real food—they all look terrible. Three more have passed out. We're going to have to hand-feed some of them."

A few of the old monsters reached out and grabbed spoonfuls of food and put it on their plates. The sounds of sneezes and snotting still filled the air, and a few of the older monsters that hadn't already passed out kept falling out of their chairs. Nurses held a few in place and not-so-gently shoved spoonfuls of food into their mouths.

"I wish we had made a big soup," Shane said. "Split-pea. The boogers would have blended right in and the weaker monsters wouldn't be having such a hard time."

We gathered around a large plate of food to share. We didn't want to eat too much—the monsters needed it the most.

"Man, I'm pretty proud of us," I said. "I don't think anyone would think all of this was made with ghost boogers."

"I feel great, too," Nabila said. "In fact . . . "

She sniffed a long, hard sniff.

"I think I can smell!" she said. "Barely . . . but I can smell!!"

"No way!" we all yelled.

"This is amazing," she said, and hugged Ben. "What's that smell?"

"Um . . . ," Ben looked down nervously.

"That's what is known to those who can smell as 'stinky armpits,'" said Gordon through a mouthful of salad.

"That's what those smell like . . . ," she said, a sour look on her face.

"Sorry," said Ben. "But, since you couldn't smell, I didn't spend much time scrubbing in the shower. And I sort of ran out of deodorant."

"Just wait until you smell his barf," I said, chuckling.

The noise level rose in the dining room as the old

monsters slowly came back to life.

"I vant more!" yelled Grigore, and he plunged his spoon back into the Mac 'n' Sneeze.

"Grrrrrrr," growled Pietro and Howie as they fought over a chicken leg.

"Look," said Ben. "Even the older ones are starting to get into it."

Instead of holding up weak old monsters, the Nurses were struggling to get food on plates fast enough.

Old Bigfoot was chowing down on my booger pie, and with each bite, his fur glistened a little more. He stood up straighter.

"It's working," said Ben. "It's really working. Roy's back!"

"Ow!" shrieked Grigore. "There's something under my dentures. Vhat did you put into this?"

I rushed over to Grigore with Shane.

"Just take them out," said Shane. "I'll take a look."

Grigore pulled out his dentures.

"No way!" yelled Shane. "There are teeth under your dentures."

"Vhat?" Grigore gasped and put a finger into his mouth. "Ouch! They're sharp. I love it!"

"Look," I said to Shane. "He's getting his hair back."

Grigore reached up to his head, which was sprouting fuzzy black hair.

"Stop bothering me—I've gotta eat!" he cried with joy.

Up and down the table, the monsters were getting younger by the second.

"This is amazing," said Director Z. "Gentlemen, you've done it again! The residents look healthier than they have in years!"

"Mmmmm," shrieked Murrayhotep, and he jumped up onto the table. "This tastes amazing! OM NOM NOM!"

He shoved handfuls of whatever he could grab into his mouth.

"Hey!" shrieked Clarice as Murrayhotep snatched a meatball and strands of pasta from her plate. "What are you *doing*?!"

"Murray, stop that this instant!" yelled Director Z.

But Murrayhotep kept going, on his hands and knees, down the long table, eating and screaming and flinging food everywhere.

"What's gotten into him?" wondered Shane. "He was the only one that wasn't sick."

"Murray, this is my last warning," said Director Z.

In response, Murray grabbed the roast chicken in the middle of the table and flung it as hard as he could at Director Z, knocking him back.

"NURSES!" yelled Director Z from the floor, and the Nurses moved in to detain Murrayhotep.

"You just try and get me, you brainless oafs!" he yelled.

"Get back," yelled Pietro, and not-so-old monsters jumped back from their chairs and away from the table.

A Nurse grabbed Murrayhotep by his leg, and he came crashing facedown on the table.

He quickly turned right-side up and smashed his foot into the jaw of the Nurse, who went down hard onto the floor.

"Ha-ha-haaa!" yelled Murrayhotep. "Serves you right."

"Where is he getting the energy?" asked Gordon.

"He just ate half of the food," I said.

Two Nurses moved in on either side of the table and reached up to grab Murrayhotep.

"INUM-RA!" yelled Murrayhotep as he flung his hands outward. There was a flash, and the Nurses were flung to either wall.

Director Z, who was wiping boogery chicken off of his suit, stood up and faced Murrayhotep.

"This is preposterous!" yelled Director Z, so loudly that the dining room windows rattled.

"This *is* preposterous!" Murrayhotep yelled back. "Our kind is nearing the brink of extinction, and *humans* have been put in charge of our safekeeping? I've had enough!"

Murrayhotep raised the palms of his bandaged

hands toward Director Z. Everyone stood in shock.

"*OSIRIS-MUN-RA!*"

Thousands of scarab beetles buzzed out of Murrayhotep's palms, descending upon Director Z, who fell to the floor, screaming.

"Feast, my precious ones!" yelled Murrayhotep. "Feast until you taste bone!"

Your Mummy Doesn't Love You

"KHEPRI-RA-ATUM," yelled Nabila, her hands held high.

A great wind blew through the dining room. The chitter-chattering scarabs were blown off of Director Z and back onto Murrayhotep.

He dropped onto the table, flailing wildly, trying to fight off the beetles.

"Where did you learn to do that?" Ben asked.

"I'll tell you later," Nabila replied, running to Director Z, whose face was pockmarked with tiny bites.

As we helped the Director up, he turned to Nabila.

"Thank you," he said.

"That was AWESOME," yelled Shane.

"*RA-MUN-OSIRIS!*" yelled Murrayhotep, and the scarabs flew off his body and exploded, a thousand small pops. He ran off of the table in a flash.

"Get him!" I yelled.

The entire room got up and rushed to the door—not-so-old monsters, kids, and all. Murrayhotep stopped in front of the doorway, his tattered wrappings flapping slightly, his breathing heavy.

"I will not run from you," said the old mummy with a wild look in his eyes. "It is *you* who shall run from *me*."

We all stood facing him, a large angry wall of monsters and kids, ready.

"You sure about that?" asked Shane. The monsters behind him growled and bared their teeth.

Murrayhotep raised his hand and displayed his huge gold ring for a moment, before grabbing the black gemstone in its center and turning it with a click.

"What are you doing?" I asked.

"Something I should have done long ago," said Murrayhotep. "Taking control of my afterlife. Doing something worthwhile."

"What are you getting out of this?" I screamed. "Eternal life? And you would throw away all of your friends here?"

"I was promised that I would be reunited with my sister," he said. "And I would do anything for her. You would have been destroyed in good time, anyway."

Lt. Commander Stratford entered the room, his gnarled, ghostly hand gripping his short sword tighter than ever.

"ALARM! The beastly animals are on their way down the hallway to you," he yelled, swinging his sword around.

"What?" gasped a few not-so-old monsters.

"Why would you care?" I asked the old ghost. "You've had it out for the monsters since they got here."

"Now that I know *who* brought them here," said the Lt. Commander, "I can focus my energies on him. I took the liberty of floating into his room and peeking at his papyrus diary. Luckily, I can decipher hieroglyphs—thanks to my time with the British Expeditionary Force in Egypt. I'm talking about you, you whippersnapper!"

He raised his short sword at Murrayhotep's head.

"You brought the animals?" asked Director Z.

"It's true," Murrayhotep said, and hundreds of puppies and kittens filed behind him as he raised his golden ring again.

"Then you have betrayed us." Director Z spoke gravely.

Murrayhotep turned the ring once more.

"EEEEEEEEEEEEEE!" The animals screamed and thrashed on the floor.

"What's wrong with them?" screeched Nabila as she covered her ears.

The werewolves howled along in agony with the tiny animals. The banshees screeched.

"Ha-ha-ha-haaaaaa!" yelled Murrayhotep. "Be free, little ones, be free!"

And with a great SPLUNK, black, leathery wings burst out of the backs of the puppies and kittens. The screaming turned to screechy laughing as the animals' heads stretched out, fur exploding into long, lizard-like faces with sharp, sharp fangs. Their jaws stretched and their teeth clamped together as they transformed.

"I knew those little guys had something in them," screeched Lt. Commander Stratford, and he floated out of the room. "I'm going to get help!"

"What are those things?" Ben asked.

"Meet the sangala!" hissed Murrayhotep. "The bringers of your doom!"

The leathery lizard animals took flight, their wings WHAPWHAPWHAPing, and hovered behind Murrayhotep. Some of them began drooling a hot, sticky drool that sizzled and hissed as it hit the floor.

We stood face-to-face with the newest monster juice–drinking enemy. The monsters lined up behind us hissed and swatted at the air.

"Attack Formation Delta Four!" screamed Shane.

The vampires all turned into bats and floated high up to the wooden beams of the dining room.

"Wow, they got so big," marveled Gordon. "Those

boogers really worked some magic."

"Did they work enough magic, though?" Ben wondered.

Moth Man soon followed the bats into the eaves. The werewolves turned into wolf form and padded out in front of us, teeth exposed. The tallest monsters, Frederick and Roy, headed to the front. The rest did their best to make sure the oldest monsters were mixed in with the strongest.

"It's going to be hard to deal with the fact that these nasty things can fly," said Gordon as we formed a circle. He turned to Shane. "I'm glad you insisted on the buddy system for the older, weaker ones."

The witches threw up a protective charm in front of us and then rushed to the kitchen to prepare for the wounded. Half of the Nurses stood near the kitchen, to help wounded monsters into the makeshift infirmary. The others headed up front with the tallest monsters.

The Director stood next to us and raised the same metal cylinder he had given us to clean out the drains. He powered it up, and a bolt of electricity flashed out of the front like a whip. He swung the electro-whip over his head.

"Whoa," said Shane, wide-eyed. "He didn't tell us it could do that!"

"It's your move, old man," said Director Z.

"Destroy them," Murrayhotep commanded the

animals, "but leave the Director unharmed. He is mine!"

The sangala swarmed.

Director Z, with a crack of his electro-whip, began knocking down sangala one by one. Nurses rushed up to crush the flopping creatures on the floor with their massive boots. Werewolves stood at the ready to tear apart the ones the Nurses missed.

One werewolf jumped off of the dining room table and snatched a sangala in its mouth as it came tumbling down to the ground.

CHOMP.

Murrayhotep ran up to Director Z, knocking him down onto the ground.

"Ooof!" yelled Director Z as he hit his butt hard. His electro-whip turned off as it fell from his hand and rattled into the crowd of clashing monsters and sangala.

Director Z's fake pendant came up around his neck and dangled in front of his tie.

"YESSSSSS!" screeched Murrayhotep, and he lunged for Director Z and his prize.

"Not so fast, Hotep," yelled Gordon, tackling Murrayhotep.

He wrestled Murrayhotep to the ground, pinning him in place.

"Arrrgh!" yelled Murrayhotep, who struggled, then pinned Gordon. They were stuck together—a crazy, sweaty pretzel.

Director Z headed into the battle with the monsters and sangala, searching for his weapon.

"My children," Murrayhotep croaked from under Gordon, "come and help me."

A dozen sangala, who were battling the vampire bats up above, swooped down toward the struggling Gordon and Murrayhotep.

"Karate shield!" yelled Shane.

Shane, Ben, Nabila, and I stood around Gordon and Murrayhotep and began karate-chopping down sangala as they floated in. They snapped and snarled, flapping their wings like crazy.

SCREEESCREEESCREEE!

Our hands hit their faces with leathery THUMPS.

"Aaaahhh!" yelled Shane, and he clutched his right hand. "Watch their fangs!"

"Your hand is smoking!" screeched Nabila, knocking back another sangala.

"It hurts!" cried Shane. "We need help over here! Zombies!"

From the crowd, which was beginning to fill with the screams of now-old monsters, Director Z pushed a few zombies toward us.

"Scream if you need more," he said, and then raised his electro-whip in time to avoid being dive-bombed by a sangala.

They karate-chopped their way toward us.

On the floor, Gordon and Murrayhotep continued to struggle.

"Let me loose now," hissed Murrayhotep, "and I promise to leave you children unscathed."

"Yeah, right!" said Gordon, and he twisted Murrayhotep's arm.

"Waaaaaargh!" Murrayhotep cried. "You'll pay for that!"

The zombies joined us, surrounding Murrayhotep and Gordon. They weren't very accurate, but they made for a good shield, constantly chopping at whatever was in front of them.

They were followed by a severed arm, walking on two tiny claws, the hand swaying back and forth.

It skittered past us and out the door.

"What was that?" asked Ben.

"Pay attention to the sangala," I said, ducking just in time to save my nose from a juicy, fangy SNAP.

"Aaaaaah," an old monster screamed.

Then a huge hairy leg, also walking upright on two tiny claws, skittered past.

"What was *that*?" asked Shane, pointing into the crowd. "Ugh, is that going to happen to me?"

I looked into the crowd to see Bigfoot with one less big foot.

I looked at Shane's hand, which was raw, bruised, and still smoking.

"Stick it in the booger pie," I said.

Shane ran over to the table, and we kept swatting off the sangala. One of the zombies missed his target, and a sangala bit into his arm, zombie blood and sangala drool flying everywhere.

His arm turned green and tore itself from his body, landing on the floor. It sprouted two small claws, jumped up, and ran off.

"My arrrrrrm!" the zombie moaned.

"You have another arm," I yelled. "Don't just stand there!"

The sangala attack intensified, and arms and legs swarmed past us and out the door in droves.

"I can't hold on much longer," grunted Gordon.

"Get OFF!" yelled Murrayhotep.

"The booger pie worked," Shane screamed. "Everyone, eat the leftovers for a power boost."

A few legless monsters hopped over to the table and began to chow down.

Almost immediately, new legs grew back into place with a POP.

"Wow, that's amazing," yelled Ben.

A few sangala swooped past the stunned Ben to bite Gordon and help their master.

"Wah," Gordon yelled, and flipped Murrayhotep on top of his body, shielding himself from the sangala, which could not hurt their master.

Murrayhotep jumped up, triumphant, and headed toward the main battle.

"*ANUBIS-MAR-DUN*," screamed Nabila.

Murrayhotep stopped in his tracks and turned around to face Nabila.

"How DARE you," he hissed.

"What did you do?" I asked.

Before she could answer, Murrayhotep's wrappings started unwrapping themselves.

"Arrrrrggh!" screamed Murrayhotep.

The wrappings flew up into the air and rained down on us. The sangala flew away, dodging the wrappings.

SHRRRRRRRPPPPP!

They seemed to go on forever, until the ends finally floated down on us.

Murrayhotep stood before us, completely naked.

He ran out of the room, his frazzled, dried mummy butt shaking slightly as he flew down the hallway.

"A mummy with no wrappings has no power," said Nabila.

We cheered, still covered in the wrappings.

"Amazing," said Shane, and high-fived her. "Ow . . . my hand still hurts."

"More booger pie?" I asked.

Shane looked over at the table.

"It's all gone," he said.

A half dozen more arms and legs ran past us and out of the door.

"Help, gentlemen, help!" screamed Director Z.

He was the only one left standing in the room aside from us, swatting at the two dozen sangala that flew just above his head, trying desperately to keep them at bay.

Old monsters writhed on the floor, and arms and legs were popping off everywhere. From the kitchen, more screams could be heard—the wounded and dying.

"Oh no!" yelled Nabila.

The sangala swooped down on the monsters.

Let's Wrap
It Up

"CHAAAAAAAARGE!" yelled a voice, and Lt. Commander Stratford appeared with his family, Leila and all, to swoop down on the sangala.

"SNOOOOOOOOTTTTT!" he yelled again, and each of the ghosts floated to a sangala . . .

SNIFFFFFFFFFF!

. . . and sneezed.

SNOOOOOOOOORRRRFFFFBLLLLL!

Delicious glowing green boogers rained down on the monsters.

"Eat!" yelled Richard. "Eat, my friends."

But the monsters couldn't eat. They were overwhelmed by the sangala, who continued their furious attack. Director Z couldn't lash them back fast enough, and the ghosts couldn't do anything but snot more.

"I have an idea!" yelled Nabila. "The wrappings! The sangala left us alone once they landed all over us. Maybe they still think the wrappings are their master."

"Wrap yourself in one," I yelled, and wrapped myself in one long piece of cloth. "Ew, I can smell Murrayhotep's BO."

The others quickly did the same, bundling up in Murrayhotep's stinky old wrappings.

"WAAAAAAAAH!" We ran at the battleground in the dining room, screaming our heads off to scare the sangala.

The sangala kept chewing on the monsters until we ran into the crowd. They floated up, confused to see five Murrayhoteps. The ghosts floated through the sangala and sneezed once more, another booger shower.

"Sneeze on the monsters in the kitchen, too," I yelled at the ghosts.

"Snot on us! Snot on us!" they chanted from the kitchen.

The monsters on the floor ate and licked and guzzled boogers and snot, fighting for their lives. Arms and legs popped back into place. The vampire bats circled above us.

"Grigore," I yelled, and one of the bats, now a little

grayer, flew down to me. "Let me wrap this around you."

I ripped off some of my wrappings and wrapped them around Bat Grigore.

"Let's use the wrappings to lead all of the sangala into the walk-in refrigerator," I said. "It's a much smaller space, and we can finish them off there!"

The monsters all rose, stunned, old, and busted—but with all of their legs and arms in place.

"Grigore!" I yelled. "Keep them from flying up too high!"

We slowly stumbled forward, pushing the sangala toward the kitchen. Bat Grigore did a great job of keeping them lower, and we got them through the door.

A werewolf, newly revived from the boogers that the ghosts had rained down in the kitchen, lunged up to grab a low-flying sangala, and a few broke off and back into the dining room.

"Wait, wait!" I yelled at the werewolf. "We have to wait until they get into the walk-in refrigerator."

"I'll handle the few that went back into the dining room!" yelled Director Z. "Nurse Inx, Nurse Grob—come with me."

They headed back into the dining room as we pushed deeper into the kitchen. Monsters noshed on boogers in preparation for the final battle in the walk-in refrigerator.

The sangala spat and snarled and snapped at us and

Bat Grigore, but had no choice. They couldn't harm us, and we wouldn't let them get past us.

"Just a little farther!" I yelled. "Steady!"

We pushed them all into the walk-in refrigerator, and they smashed into jars and snarled at boxes of food as they looked for a way out.

But there was no way out.

"All right," I yelled. "Get 'em, guys!"

We stepped out of the doorway, and dozens of zombies, werewolves, vampires, and more spilled into the room, crushing, crunching, and grabbing.

SCREEEEEEEEEEP!

The sangala's screeches were cut off as the last one was crushed between the jaws of Pietro.

"Yeah!" we all yelled, jumping around with relief.

We peeked back into the walk-in refrigerator.

"Ew," said Ben.

"Gnarly," said Gordon.

The room was covered in the green guts and leathery parts of the sangala.

The monsters all roared with happiness.

And then there was a great BOOOOOM from the dining room.

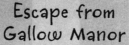

Escape from Gallow Manor

We rushed into the dining room to find two Nurses lying on the floor, and a newly wrapped Murrayhotep leaning over a disarmed Director Z.

"Is that toilet paper?" asked Shane. "I hope it's double-ply, or it won't last for long."

"The pendants shall be mine!" yelled Murrayhotep, and he grabbed for the chain on Director Z's neck.

BLURRZZZZZT!

Murrayhotep was thrown off of Director Z.

Director Z stood up boldly, strolling toward Murrayhotep.

"Did you really think I hadn't put a protective charm on it?" yelled Director Z.

Murrayhotep slowly stood up, his toilet paper wrappings drooping a bit.

"Well, then," Murrayhotep snarled, "I guess I'll have to kill you."

"If I die, the pendant loses its power," Director Z said.

The still-drained-but-at-least-they-had-all-their-limbs monsters came into the room. They snarled and clawed the air, upset to see Murrayhotep again.

"I don't have time for this!" Murrayhotep screeched. "I'm taking you to him! He'll know what to do!"

Murrayhotep raised his arms: *"AMON-RA-NAMAN!"*

Director Z collapsed like a sack of potatoes.

"Noooo!" I screeched, and ran toward Director Z. I threw myself down on the floor and grabbed his face.

"The moon's face is the perfect place for record keeping," said Director Z, and then he passed out completely.

"Get back, you dog!" Murrayhotep yelled, kicking me with his toilet-papered foot.

I slid all the way to the wall, clutching my belly. I felt like I was going to throw up—blood.

"Are you okay?" asked Shane.

"Let's just *get* him," I gasped.

But Murrayhotep had a head start. He had already

thrown Director Z over his shoulder and was running down the hall.

Shane yanked me up to my feet, and we thundered down the hall with our friends and the older-again monsters.

Murrayhotep ran into the North Wing, opened the small iron door on the wall, and sent the gate crashing down. We slammed against the gate, monsters pushing us up against the bars.

"Everyone stop pushing!" I grunted. "You're gonna crush us."

"He can't take the Director," screeched a banshee.

Old Bigfoot pushed his way through the crowd and grabbed the bottom of the gate.

"RAAAAAWWWWRRR!" he grunted, and the gate slowly rose.

There was about a foot of room from the floor to the bottom of the gate.

"Gooooooo!" he said. "Can't. Hold. For. Long."

Ben, Shane, Gordon, Nabila, and I slid through, and the gate came crashing down again.

"Shane and Nabila," I yelled. "We have to catch up with him. Ben and Gordon, open the gate for the others."

The three of us rushed down to the end of the hall, where a mysterious open door led to the grounds.

"Hey, where did this door come from?" Shane asked as we burst through and could see Murrayhotep in the moonlight up ahead, running for the forest.

"It's too far for me to throw a spell on him," Nablia said, gasping.

"Hurry," I huffed.

We had almost caught up to Murrayhotep when he hit the forest.

"I can't see anything," I said as we entered the thick, tall trees.

"Over there!" yelled Shane.

"Is he bringing him to a tree trunk?" I said. "That tree is huge."

"It's not a tree," said Nabila. "It's a spaceship. A huge rocket."

"No way!" I gasped.

Murrayhotep ran up to the tall, oil-black, shiny ship, and placed his hand on the door. A light shone into the forest as the door slowly hummed open. Inside the opening, monster arms and legs walked around.

"So that's where they were running to," said Shane.

Murrayhotep rushed inside, and the door began to close.

"Go!" I yelled. "We can make it!"

We rushed up to the door, just as it slid back into place.

We slammed into the cold hard metal.

"Noooooo!" I yelled, kicking the ship.

A great vibration shook our feet.

"No time for anger," Shane said. "This thing's gonna take off!"

We ran back toward the grounds of the manor. At the forest's edge, monsters started to zoom past us.

"Guys, no!" I yelled. "Get back to the manor!"

The monsters, who normally never listened to me, turned back and ran with us.

There was a great roar, and a bright light, as the ship took off, blowing us all over the grounds in a burst of hot wind. I rolled until I hit the bush shaped like a raven and watched the ship take off into the night.

The
Moon's Face

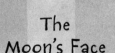

We rushed to the West Tower of the manor, and I swung up my telescope.

"Where is he going?" asked Nabila.

I focused on the ship and then pulled back a little. The ship was tall, with strange spines jutting out of the sides, and a green glow propelled it through the atmosphere. It was so black, I shouldn't have seen it, but its surface shone like crazy.

"The moon," I gasped. "It's headed right for the moon."

"No way!" said Ben.

"The moon . . . ," I said, trying hard to think.

"What?" asked Shane.

"Before he passed out, Director Z said, 'The moon's face is the perfect place for record keeping.'"

"What does that mean?" asked Gordon.

"I have no idea . . . ," I said, staring again through the telescope at the moon's face.

The moon winked at me.

"Huh?" I said, shocked, pulling my face back. "It's like the moon has a real face . . . just like . . ."

"What!?" Nabila screeched, dying of anticipation.

"Just like the face of the moon in that weird room I saw." I gasped. "Guys, follow me!"

We rushed downstairs to the dining room.

The stronger monsters were helping the Nurses clean the dining room, though most of the monsters had gone to bed to get some rest.

"It was this door," I said, stopping in front of the weird room. "This is where I saw it!"

I turned the handle . . . and the door opened.

We rushed in, and I pointed up to the grainy old photo.

"See?" I asked.

"Totally cool," said Shane.

Gordon closed the door, and we found ourselves in a small library, with a model of the solar system hanging from the ceiling. The planets were all metal balls. I opened a closet to find a metallic space suit with a glass helmet.

"I just need to figure out what kind of records we're looking for," I said, biting my bottom lip.

"Well, there are plenty of books here," said Ben, pulling one out of a bookshelf with a puff of dust. "This one's on the effects of zero gravity."

"This one's about the great wars of the Andromeda Galaxy," said Nabila, opening another.

"What's this?" asked Gordon, holding up a small black cylinder.

"I think that's an old record," said Shane. "I saw one once in a museum."

"A record!" I said. "'The perfect place for record keeping.' Director Z must want us to listen to that record."

"Didn't we see an old phonograph in one of the rooms?" asked Shane.

"Yeah!" replied Nabila. "But which one . . ."

"The music room?" Gordon said.

"No," said Ben. "The bear-rug room?"

"No," I said, frustrated. "This place is too big! It doesn't matter. We all remember seeing one. Let's go find it."

We found it in the game room, tucked behind the chessboard in the corner.

"How do we work it?" I asked. "Any guesses?"

"Well," said Shane, grabbing the cylinder. "It looks like the cylinder fits here."

He clicked it into place.

"I think you crank this handle," said Gordon, and started to crank.

"Put the needle on the record," said Nabila.

"It looks like it's going to scratch it like crazy," I said.

"Just do it!" said Ben.

I put the needle down on the cylinder, and a great scratching sound came out of the huge cone at the top of the phonograph.

SCHHLLLRRPPHHHSCHHLLLRRPPHHH!

"I think we broke it!" I said.

Then, out of the scratching, came a voice.

"Journal entry dated July 24, 1892. Today, my work is finally finished. The Stratford family has been kind enough to endure all of my late-night madness and the strange clanking from deep below their dungeon. I will have to thank them for the use of their manor for years to come. But it is finally complete. A fully functional spaceship, capable of transporting over one hundred souls, set on a course to the moon. Unfortunately, I have lost my previous creation, Frederick, a monster crafted of human flesh and brought to life by electricity. He escaped from his home weeks ago, and I would have hoped to have found him by now. For only he can sit in the captain's chair and power the great ship into the cosmos with his strange electrical energies."

"Did Frederick make it through the sangala attack?" I asked.

"I think so," said Ben.

"Well, it sounds like all we need to do is get him into the captain's chair of that ship that's hiding somewhere deep below the dungeon," I said, "and we can save Director Z."

"On the MOON?" asked Nabila. "I can't go to the moon! I have to ask my parents' permission first."

"I'd like to see *that* conversation," Ben said, snickering.

"I don't think this is the kind of thing you ask permission for . . . ," I said.

"This is crazy," said Gordon. "We're going to the moon."

"To the MOON!" yelled Shane.

"My dream come true!" I yelled, suddenly insanely excited.

"Was your dream to go to the moon with a ship full of monsters?" asked Nabila. "Because we're going to need them for whatever's up there. We can't do it alone."

"Ah, so you're ready to go now?" asked Gordon.

"Monsters in space," said Shane. "I think I saw that movie when I was a little kid."

"Oh no!" I said, slapping my forehead.

"What is it?" asked Nabila.

"The moon," I said. "Because of the lunar cycle and the time of day, I think . . ."

"What?" Shane asked, pulling my hand off my forehead.

"Oh, man . . ." I didn't want to tell them until I was sure.

I pushed away from Shane and rushed to the bookshelves, pulling out books like a madman. "This isn't what I'm looking for," I screeched, tossing dusty old books to the floor.

"What is it?" yelled Ben, upset that I was so upset.

I ran over to a large table, which was piled high with charts and diagrams. I frantically dug through the pile, finally finding what I was looking for: a dusty, yellowed old launch-window chart.

"Yes!" I yelled, and held it up for closer study. "NO!"

"WHAT IS IT!?!" yelled all four of my friends.

"The current window for launch to the moon is going to close in"—I looked at my iPhone—"forty-five minutes."

"Okay, so we'll wait a few days," said Nabila. "I need to think up a story to tell my parents, anyway."

"No," I said, studying the crusty document. "It could be more than a few days—even a week or two before the next window opens. Who knows what they'll do to Director Z before then. We have to go NOW!"

"All right," said Shane. "Let's find Frederick. Then

we've got to find the ship. And then we'll blast out of here!"

"All right, all right," said Ben and Gordon.

"Fine," said Nabila. "But we're all going to be in huge trouble."

"Not as much trouble as Director Z is in," I said. "We've got to move fast."

Must. Find.
FREDERICK!

"The East Wing is clear," said Gordon. "No sign of Frederick?"

Monsters shuffled into the foyer from different parts of the manor.

"Nothing," said Clarice.

"Where did he go?" asked Medusa. Her snakes hissed sadly.

"FREDERICK!!!" Roy's voice boomed through the foyer. All of us—monsters, boys, and girl—waited for a sound.

NOTHING.

"Now that I think of it," said Pietro, "I don't seem to remember seeing him after the battle. Maybe his head

173

came off and ran into the spaceship."

"Ew," I said.

Nabila shuddered.

"No, no, no," said Shane. "I'm sure that I saw him."

"Pietro," I said to the old werewolf. "We've only got twenty minutes left. Come with the five of us to Frederick's room, and give it a good sniff."

"I'm no bloodhound," said Pietro.

"You are today," said Gordon, who slapped Pietro on the back. "Maybe your nose can tell us something."

Pietro turned into a wolf and padded down the West Wing into Frederick's room. We followed.

Sniff, sniff, sniiiiiiiff!

Pietro sniffed around the old stitched-together monster's room. Then he pushed his snout out of the room and sniffed the hallway.

"Anything?" asked Ben.

"Grrrr . . . ," grumbled Pietro, shaking his mangy head *no*.

"Wait," I said, walking over to the laundry basket in the room. "I think this will help."

I opened it up, and used the tips of my fingers to grab a dirty pair of Frederick's tighty-whities.

"Ick," I yelled, tossing them at Pietro.

Sniff, sniff . . . HOOOOOOWWWWL!

Pietro was off, racing down the hallway, back toward the foyer.

"Hurry!" I yelled, running after him. My friends followed.

In the foyer, he took a sharp left toward the North Wing, and then with a great SCREEEECH of nails, changed his mind and decided to go down the East Wing instead.

"Don't you DARE lick my face again," Lucinda B. Smythe screeched as Pietro ran past.

We burst through the huge doors and followed Pietro to the organ keyboard at the back of the banquet hall.

Pietro stopped in front of the keyboard, barking furiously.

"What's next?" Ben knelt down and asked the werewolf. Drool sprayed into his face. "Is he behind the keyboard? Can't you change back to human form and tell us what's happening?"

"WAIT!" I said. "He might be naked. You never know—sometimes they lose their clothes when they change."

"Don't!" yelled Gordon.

I held my hands over my eyes, but Pietro just kept barking. Then he lifted a paw up onto the organ, and three sour notes echoed through the huge, empty room.

"You want us to play it?" I asked.

"Look!" said Nabila, pointing at a key. "This one's more worn than the others. And this one. That one, too."

She pushed the frothing werewolf to the side, and pushed down on all three keys at once.

With a great creak, the organ keyboard jerked forward, throwing Nabila on her rump. Then, with a great scrape of wood and stone, it slid to the left.

"A secret stairway!" Nabila said. "I knew it!"

With another bark, Pietro jumped down spiraling stairs.

"Are you sure we should—?" Ben tried to ask, but the rest of us followed Pietro.

"Okay, okay, I'm coming," huffed Ben.

"This reminds me of going down into the vampire crypt at Raven Hill," said Shane. "Ah, the good old days."

"Don't talk," said Gordon. "I'm getting dizzy."

Candles on the wall gave us a little light, but there was something brighter at the bottom.

We made our way to a locked iron door with torches at either side. Pietro started barking like crazy again. We jiggled at the handle, and pushed the door, but . . .

"Nothing!" I grunted. "Ugh! We've got ten minutes left! How are we going to get behind that door, find Frederick, and then find the ship?"

"I can help," Quincy said from stairs. "Let me see what's on the other side."

"Oh, Quincy!" yelled Nabila. "That's a great idea. How did you know we were down here?"

"I've been following you this whole time!" he said.

"This is the most fun I've ever had in the manor."

"If Frederick is on the other side, tell him to open the door," Nabila said.

"I will!" said Quincy, and he floated through the door.

Pietro finally stopped barking, and it was silent at the bottom of the stairs.

After what felt like an eternity, Quincy popped his head through the door with a "Boo!"

"Wah!" yelled Nabila. "Stop doing that to me! What's the news!?"

"Frederick is on the other side," said Quincy, "but he's in bad shape. He's on the floor, rolling around and moaning."

"Oh no!" I said. "We've got to get in there."

"There's a latch on the other side of the door," said Quincy. "But I can't lift it."

Gordon was inspecting the door frantically.

"Hey, look at this," he said, sticking his finger through a small hole in the door.

"It's not near the latch," Quincy said.

Gordon's brow furrowed. "Unless . . ." His eyes lit up. "Quincy, go get Medusa as fast as you can!"

"Aha!" Shane said, immediately realizing what Gordon meant to do.

Two minutes later, Medusa came down the stairs. She stood in front of the door, scratching her head.

"Which one of you is the longest?" she asked.

"I am," hissed one snake.

"No, it's ME," hissed another.

"I'm long enough," another said. "Let me try."

"Just hurry!" I yelled. "We're running out of time."

Medusa quickly put her head up against the door, and after a few more seconds of shoving and hissing, one snake went through quickly.

CLICK!

"Got it!" I yelled, pushing the door forward.

"Hey!" yelled Medusa, who was dragged forward with the door. "Give Jimmy a chance to slither back out of the hole!"

"Sorry!" I yelled. "The clock's ticking."

We rushed down a dark stone hallway and then popped out into a huge cave—with a rocket ship sitting in its center.

"Whoa!" I gasped.

"Awesome," said Shane.

"Why didn't you tell us the spaceship was in here, Quincy?" Gordon asked.

"You never asked," he replied.

I was stunned. It looked more like a funky skyscraper than a spaceship—all glass and metal.

"Look up there, you can see the stars," said Ben, pointing to a huge hole in the roof of the cave. Forest vegetation poured over the side.

"Look at the bottom set!" Nabila pointed at Frederick, slumped against the ship, motionless.

"Frederick. FREDERICK!"

The Final Countdown

Shane rushed over to Frederick. "Are you okay?" he asked.

Frederick woke up from a daze and slowly got to his feet.

"Whew!" said Nabila.

"No, I'm fine," said the giant monster. "This is a safe place for me. This was my home when I was first created by my father. After the sangala attack, I decided to retreat here."

"Why were you moaning and rolling around?" asked Gordon.

Frederick stared up at the huge ship, a tear in his eye. "This wonderful monument makes me miss my father."

"It's all right," said Shane, patting Frederick on the back. "Let it out."

"NO!" I screeched. "Let it out later! We've got to go in five minutes, or we'll have to wait for weeks! Director Z might not even be alive then."

Frederick looked shocked, but he pulled himself together.

"Quincy, go get the other monsters," I said. "Tell them to get down here immediately. NOW!" I turned to Frederick. "How do we get into the ship?"

"Ship?" Frederick asked.

"Yes," Shane said, pointing up. "The rocket ship."

"You called it a monument," said Ben. "Don't you even know what it is?"

"My time here was short," said Frederick, "and I was confused in my first weeks. That's why I ran away from my father. Without thinking. By the time I remembered where he was, I couldn't get back. But I always had the image of this magnificent structure in my mind. I couldn't believe my luck when we moved here."

"Neither can we," I said. "That ship is going to take us to the moon, but we have to leave in the next four minutes. How do you open it?"

"How should I know?" Frederick said, frustrated.

"But you're the engine that powers it," said Gordon. "Maybe you have some special power to open the door."

"Don't worry about it," said Ben, standing at the

base of the rocket ship. "I think we just pull this lever."

He pulled the lever, and the stairway slowly came out of the bottom of the rocket, clinking and clanking.

With a great SCREEECH, it came to a stop . . . two feet above the ground.

"This thing is pretty old," said Nabila. "Are you sure we want to do this?"

"Yes, I'm sure," I said. "Now, where are those monsters? Frederick, come with me onto the ship. We've got to figure out how you power it up as soon as possible."

I helped him reach the first step, and then we both rushed up the stairs. As soon as Frederick was inside, small bulbs lit up. We could see more metal and glass.

"Where would the engine be?" I said.

We ran deeper into the ship, passing large mazes of crisscrossing pipes. I noticed that most of them led to the same place.

"Let's go that way," I yelled, and we turned down a tight hallway, filled mostly with the pipes, that led to . . .

"The engine room!" I yelled.

Insanely large generators lined the walls, and in the center, surrounded by glass, was a metal chair with a metal helmet hanging above. It looked ominously like an electric chair.

"I think you're supposed to sit there," I said to Frederick. "Get strapped in, quick! We've only got three minutes."

Frederick sat down in the chair, and the metal helmet lowered onto his head.

CRACK. SNAP. SNIP! CRACK!

Lightning shot through Frederick, leaving dark marks on the glass.

Now I know why that glass is there, I thought.

The lightning got stronger, and Frederick spasmed in the chair.

"YARRRRGGGGHHH!" he screamed, shaking and sputtering.

"Frederick, are you okay?" I yelled over the cracks.

"This is amazing!" said Frederick. "Finally, something that utilizes all of my energies! It's absolutely thrilling."

His body shook, and the lights on the ship glowed brighter. The generators hummed softly.

"I'm running to get the others," I yelled. "Keep it going!"

I jumped down the stairs of the rocket, forgetting the last step was two feet off the ground. I fell, but caught myself and rolled. I stood up to find all of the monsters there.

"ALL RIGHT!" I yelled. "There's a cargo hold in the second level—everyone pack in!"

"There's no way I'm going into space," cackled one of the witches.

"We've just recovered from a major attack," added Roy.

Half the crowd erupted in protest.

"What are you going to do?" yelled Shane over the crowd—and the growing hum of the rocket ship.

I reached in my pocket and felt the bloodstone there. I could feel its power as I rubbed it.

"QUIET!" I yelled.

The monsters were quiet, but I still needed to yell over the roar of the engine.

"Director Z needs our help. ALL of our help. We've got two minutes to get on the ship. Let's get going. I COMMAND IT!"

That was all it took. The monsters rushed aboard, the stronger ones helping the older ones onto the busted staircase.

"Gordon and Ben," I said. "Stay with the monsters and get them into the cargo hold. Shane and Nabila, we've got to find the bridge."

Between the roar of the engine and the screams of the monsters, my head spun. There was only one place I hadn't seen on the ship, so I ran there, my friends following.

"Here it is!" I said, bursting onto the bridge.

"It looks like the bridge of an ocean liner," said Shane.

The room was filled with levers and switches, and in the center was the biggest lever of them all, next to the ship's wheel. It was labeled QUARTER THRUST, HALF THRUST, and FULL THRUST.

"But how do we start it?" I asked.

"Wait, over here!" Nabila said. She pointed at a huge red button. "This has to be it."

"Unless it's the self-destruct button," said Shane.

"No time," I said, leaning forward and pushing the red button.

The whole ship shook violently, rattling our teeth.

"Guys," yelled Ben as he came in. "There wasn't enough room! We're all on, but not everyone fit into the cargo hold."

Twenty old monsters came in after him, crowding the already-small bridge. Two zombies blocked the massive lever in the center.

"Move to the side, guys," I said, and pulled the lever as far as I could. "I can only get it to half thrust!"

The stronger monsters pushed through the small crowd that had formed on the deck to help. Grigore, who still had real teeth and black hair, jumped forward and pushed down . . .

CLICK.

The lever was now at full thrust, and the ship began shaking even harder.

Nuts and bolts flew down from the ceiling.

"There's got to be something that starts the liftoff sequence," I yelled. "Shane, try that lever."

Shane pulled a lever. NOTHING.

Nabila pulled another lever.

A metal panel exploded from the wall, showering sparks over Howie the werewolf. His hairy neck caught on fire. Shane jumped on him to put it out, while Roy, trying hard not to singe his fur, put the panel back in place.

"Look!" yelled a witch.

She pointed at a small clock on a panel on the right side of the bridge.

It was at T-minus fifteen seconds and counting.

"Okay, hold on, everyone!" I roared, and grabbed the wheel.

Ten seconds.

The ship sounded like it was falling apart. I could hear Frederick screaming.

Five seconds.

A crack formed in the glass in front of us.

"Wa-hoooooo!" hooted Shane.

Three seconds.

Two . . .

One . . .

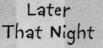
Later
That Night

"Hello? Helllooooo?!"

Chris's mother knocked furiously at the front door of Gallow Manor.

"Open this door this instant!" she insisted. "I know that you're in there, Chris! Shane!"

She paused for a minute, and a worried look washed over her face.

"I hope you're in there!" she said. "It's so late! You should have been home hours ago."

The headlights of a car flashed into her face, as it came up the road. It stopped in front of her, and the principal of Rio Vista Middle School stepped out of the driver's seat.

"Thank goodness you're here," said Chris's mother. "I couldn't think of who else to reach out to. I wasn't ready to call the police and make a fuss . . . not yet!"

"I'm sorry I'm so late," said Principal Prouty. "I volunteer at the animal shelter after school, and we've been having a problem with overpopulation. And my allergies have been terrible. What seems to be the matter here? Surely somebody must be home?"

"No, and I've been knocking for the last half hour," she shrieked.

The door slowly creaked open. She and the principal looked at each other.

They both headed to the entryway, but were pushed back by a ghostly old figure in what appeared to be a naval officer's uniform. He glowed strangely in the moonlight.

"Why are you at my door?" asked the old man.

"I demand to speak to Director Zachary!" Chris's mother screeched. "Or a nurse. Or anyone! Where is Chris Taylor?"

"They've all left," said the mysterious old figure.

"All of them?" asked the principal.

"What do you mean, 'they've all left'?" asked Chris's mother.

"I mean exactly what I said!" hissed the old man. "Nobody's home. They're all gone. And I have no idea when they'll be back. Satisfied?"

The door slammed in their faces.

"How could they all be gone?" asked the principal. She looked confused and sad. "We've got to find them. Right away."

"Your concern for your students is touching," said Chris's mother.

"It's not just the students I'm worried about," said the principal.

Chris's mother gave her a questioning look.

"I'm also worried about my grandfather."

Burpstronauts

by M. D. Payne

Grosset & Dunlap
An Imprint of Penguin Random House

To Francesco, for giving me the chance

Prologue

The pale, gaunt man could no longer stand. A guard held him up by his armpits. The front of the pale man's suit was splattered with blood. A hooded figure, shrouded in darkness, leaned in close to the man.

"Where. ISSSSS. IT?!" The hooded figure's voice boomed. "I will not ask again."

The pale man's words came out as a mumble. "It's somewhere safe." His teeth were stained with blood. "I can assure you of that."

"Safe? Soon *nowhere* will be safe," the hooded figure hissed. Black spittle shot out from the hood. "It's just a matter of time. Still, I would rather not wait." He leaned in closer. "Tell me where it is . . . and it would be best if you answered my question this time. You should be very afraid indeed if you force me to ask again."

"Show me your face," said the man calmly. "Then perhaps I shall answer your question."

The hooded figure pulled away and clutched his hood closer around his head.

"Who I am is of no consequence to you," he said, his voice growing loud with anger.

"It seems I'm not the only one suffering from fear," said the man. He laughed through his pain, showering blood deep into the hood of the figure.

"THE PENDANT!" yelled the hooded figure, his voice echoing around the massive throne room. "It shall be mine—no matter how hard you protest. I shall find a way into that feeble mind of yours and extract the answer. Where is the real pendant?"

The hooded figure held up a pendant, waving it in front of the pale, gaunt man's face. "How dare you try to trick me with this *fraud*!"

He then crushed the bloodstone like a corn puff from a sugary breakfast cereal. It turned to powder with a CRUNCH.

"How dare I?!" asked the man, still laughing. "I would have been insane to hold on to the power once I realized you sought it. Oh no, I put it somewhere you would never, EVER think to look, you insane, broken creature. How dare *you*? What are *you* of all people going to do with all eight pendants? You haven't the strength in you, Cord—"

The hooded figure cut off the pale, gaunt man with a gloved fist to his stomach.

"OOOOOOF!"

The man fell to the floor in pain, too out of breath to scream. The guard leaned down to pick him up, but the hooded figure waved him away.

"Never speak that name here," hissed the hooded figure.

When the man got his strength back, he stared into the terrible red eyes of the hooded figure, spat a wad of blood on the floor, and laughed so hard that dust began to fall from the ceiling of the throne room.

"So it *is* you!" said the man. "Ha-ha-ha!"

"ENOUGH! Another kiss from my latest creation will dry up your laughter and loosen your tongue," said the hooded figure. "Oh yes, it shall break your spirit . . ."

He clapped his hands together. The guards at the door backed away slightly as a small man in a white laboratory coat pushed a large tank into the room. Dark water sloshed around, spilling out of the tank.

The man calmly watched as the tank approached.

The hooded figure pulled a slimy black serpent out of the tank and slowly brought it toward the mouth of the man. The serpent crackled slightly with a pulse of electricity as it came closer.

"Not quite yet, my sweet zapeel," the hooded figure cooed. "Be patient."

Two guards moved to the man, one on either side. One lifted him up, and the other grabbed his mouth, forcing it open.

"Argggglllll," gurgled the pale man, more blood oozing down his chin. He was trying desperately to pull his tongue deeper into his mouth.

The mouth of the serpent opened to reveal sharklike rows of teeth.

The hooded figure leaned in and latched the disgusting creature onto the pale man's tongue.

"AAAAABLLLLLRRRRSHHHH," the pale man screamed.

The hooded figure let go of the zapeel and backed away. A jolt of electricity zapped through the writhing black creature into the pale man's mouth.

The door to the throne room flew in with a BOOM, startling the slimy black serpent, which fell to the floor with a FLAP.

"Master," said another guard as he rushed in. "We've heard reports—"

"HOW DARE YOU INTERRUPT ME?" yelled the hooded figure. "I have almost broken him!"

"I'm so sorry, Master," the guard said, bowing, his voice shaking with fear. "Once I tell you the news, I'm sure you'll understand."

"Well, speak, you idiot, speak!" the hooded figure said. He picked up the zapeel and held it over the tank. It angrily flopped into the water with a SPLASH.

"Don't worry, my pretty," said the hooded figure, leaning in and tapping the glass lovingly. "You can feast on this fool if his story is not worthy of this interruption."

"A ship has crash-landed a mile from here, in the Gorgon Rift," the guard finally spit out.

"Has it now . . . ," said the hooded figure, turning to the man. "Looks like this new development has spared your pitiful life . . . for now." He moved his fiery glare back to the guard. "And *you* will live to disappoint me another day. Send the Andromedans to greet our newest guests."

The guard ran out as quickly as he could.

"Meanwhile," the hooded figure said, motioning to another guard, "the Director here is doing a better job of holding his tongue than I thought. He's going to need a few more sessions with the splurtsar and its delicious truth serum. Fetch Murray."

"Murray?" asked the guard, confused.

"The mummy! Now, be quick!"

As the guard ran out, he said, "Murray's just not a mummy's name . . ."

The pale, gaunt man snickered.

Earlier That Night . . .

The huge iron ship lurched—Frederick, the old green patchwork monster, was straining as he used the electricity that gave him life to power the engines. Slowly the ship lifted toward the hole in the ceiling of the massive cave.

The giant wooden steering wheel spun out of control, knocking me back. It looked like something you'd see on an old pirate ship.

"Come on, guys, help me steer," I yelled as I scrambled back to my feet. "If we can't get above ground, we're totally toast!"

Grigore the vampire and Gordon ran over, and we grabbed the wheel as hard as we could together.

"To. The. Right," I said through gritted teeth.

Grigore and Gordon grunted along with me as we slowly turned the wheel to the right. It shook so hard in our hands that my body was vibrating.

"My teeth hurt," yelled Gordon, his bulging muscles straining the sleeves of his Rio Vista Middle School Athletics T-shirt. "It's like I ate too much sugar on a freezing cold day."

CHATTER CHATTER CHATTER!

Shane and Roy, the Bigfoot, ran over to help us.

"We're not gonna make it," wheezed Ben, staring bug-eyed out the cracked window. He took a giant hit off his asthma inhaler. "The ship's gaining speed, and we're about to hit the ceiling."

The other monsters huddled together for safety, grabbing on to anything that looked like it wouldn't fall off the ancient rocket ship.

I pressed all my weight against the wheel. "As hard as you can, guys," I yelled. "PUUUUUUUUSHHHHH!"

The zombies stared blankly as we struggled with the wheel.

SCRAAAAAAPE!

The nose of the rocket dragged along the craggy, rocky ceiling, making even more cracks in the window.

Everything vibrated and shook. It seemed unlikely that the rusty old rocket would hold together much longer. Then suddenly, the shaking stopped and the ship lunged forward, knocking us all to the floor. We were out of the cave!

Once we lifted above the earth, the sounds of the engine quieted to a level just below mind-numbing. Then we started to accelerate.

"Aw yeah!" yelled Shane. "We did it."

There were cheers throughout the bridge.

He lifted his hand off the wheel to give me a high five.

"Um, not a good time," I said.

"Oh right, we should probably keep our hands on the wheel," said Shane.

The ship really picked up speed when we hit the clouds. It felt like we were being pulled into the floor of the bridge, then—

BOOM!

—we hit turbulence and bounced off the wheel, sliding in all different directions.

"We've got to keep the rocket going straight," I yelled. "Otherwise, we're never going to make it."

I struggled to my feet for a moment, but was forced down onto all fours by the insane g-forces. I crawled over to the wheel on my belly. Roy struggled to stop himself, but the hairy monster couldn't keep from sliding farther away.

"My fur!" he yelled. "Too slippery!"

I had to roll to the side to make sure the Bigfoot

didn't crash into me as he slid across the floor.

"The ship's at the wrong angle! I think we're heading back down," I yelled as I tried to grab ahold of Roy. There was no way we could keep the ship on the right course without the burly Bigfoot to help us steer. Even Grigore wasn't that strong.

"I can't . . . ," the Bigfoot gasped again, his teeth rattling just like ours, ". . . get a grip."

The ship began to descend back to earth, and Roy slid even farther from the wheel.

"Oh man," moaned a green-looking Ben. "I'm going to hurl."

"We need to help Roy get up here!" I yelled, struggling along with a group of monsters to hang on to the wheel. "I can't believe we rushed onto the ship without the Nurses! We could really use their muscle."

"Wait," yelled Nabila, who was pressed flat against one of the rusty metal walls of the bridge. "I've got an idea!"

"What is it?" I asked. "Hurry!"

"Grigore!" Nabila yelled as we picked up speed, plummeting toward the earth. "Call the other vampires from the cargo hold with your mind. Bring them to us. Bring them to us as bats."

Grigore began to concentrate, his eyes wandering away in a daze. But his strength at the wheel held.

Soon, three vampire bats awkwardly flapped into

the room, their confused squeaks saying, *Wait, why are we here?*

"Nibble all the fur off Roy!" said Nabila.

"WHAT?!" yelled Roy. "No way!"

The bats squeaked in confusion, flapping hard to avoid the flying glass as different meters and gauges exploded.

"Just do it!" I yelled to the vampire bats.

"Nooooooo!" yelled Roy.

But the vampire bats swarmed Roy and did as I commanded.

BZZZZRRRRRPPPPP!

Their little fangs worked fast, as fast as the fastest electric razor. In a flash of fur, a very pink and very naked Roy appeared.

"Get over here! We need your monster strength," I yelled, and an embarrassed Roy crawled up the floor and grabbed the wheel.

"Arrrrrggghhhhhh," we grunted hard as we turned the wheel, and we could feel the ship rise into the air once again.

Once Roy had helped push the wheel down, he gave me an angry glare.

"You could have just had them take the fur off my paws, you know," he said.

"It wasn't *my* idea," I retorted. "Nabila?"

We looked over to the spot on the wall of the bridge

where she had been pressed, but she was gone. Looking down, we saw a pile of tangled brown hair, a fanny pack, and glasses.

"Better safe than sorry," she mumbled.

The ship blasted even faster into space, higher and higher, until . . .

"Why is it so quiet?" asked Ben, turning even greener. "My stomach feels like we're still climbing. Ugh."

"Look!" said Nabila, pointing out the window.

"We're in space!" I yelled. "We made it! The autopilot should take us from here—the crazy inventor said in his message that the rocket was already set on a course to the moon. The moooooooooooon!"

I relaxed my grip. Shane and the monsters shared worried looks as they all slowly let go of the wheel.

The ship kept moving along its trajectory.

There was a great cheer on the bridge.

"Chris, look!" Nabila said, pointing at my feet. "You're floating!"

"You too!" said Gordon, pointing at Nabila.

I pushed my feet down onto the floor, and shot up toward the ceiling. "Weeeee're innnnnn spaaaaaaaaaaaace! Wahoo!"

The Monsters and Me in Zero-G

"Aw, man, this is AWESOME!" I yelled, corkscrewing through the air. "I can't believe it! We're going to the moon! THE MOON!"

Landing with an OOOF on one of the control panels, I looked up at all the doodads and whirligigs.

"I feel like I'm in a dream," I said.

"It looks more like a *nightmare*, with all of Gallow Manor's monsters on board," said Nabila. She'd spent the previous twenty minutes attempting to clean up the shattered bits of the ship and chewed-up Bigfoot fur that floated around the bridge.

Shane high-fived a passing zombie.

The zombie cartwheeled backward off the bridge.

"Stop messing around," said Nabila. "We've got to figure out what we're going to do when we get to the moon. We don't even know where Murrayhotep is taking Director Z. 'To him,' Murrayhotep kept saying."

"I know," I said. "And it freaks me out to think of who—or what—we're going to find on the moon. But we should have enough time before we get there to figure it all out—how to get Z and the pendant back. I know we should be worried, and I am, but this is by far the greatest moment of my life. So just give me a few minutes to take it all in."

Shane pushed off a wall, grabbed Nabila, and twirled her around in the middle of the room.

"Okay, fine!" she said, giggling. "But then let's get serious."

Ben's face was smashed against a glass porthole. He stared out at the blue planet that was slowly receding behind us.

"Wow," said Ben as the ship rocketed deeper into space. "Earth is so small."

"Dude, you realize you're upside down, right?" asked Gordon.

"Right-side up, upside down, it's all the same," Ben said.

"If we don't remember which way is which, I think something bad will happen," said Gordon, who had strapped himself into a chair next to a burned-out panel.

"I hope we didn't need any of these controls."

Behind me, I heard Pietro and Howie, two of the old werewolves, discussing how fun it was to transform in zero-g.

"This is great," said Howie with a crooked grin. "It's so much easier. Fast. Like . . . POOF! But how do you transform into a wolf without crashing against a wall?"

"Push yourself away from a wall just before you start to transform," replied Pietro. "Watch . . ."

Pietro kicked off the bridge of the spaceship with a "YEAHHHHOOOOOOWWWWWL" as he transformed.

"Wait for MEEEEEEHHHHHOOOOOOWWWWL," Howie said, transforming with ease as he followed.

"Watch it, furballs!" someone screamed.

"Get out of your chair, Gordon," Nabila said, pushing off Gordon's face to fly toward me. "You're missing out."

"Whatever, Crazy Hair," Gordon said, pointing at Nabila's head, which, thanks to the zero-g, was a huge, floating, jet-black mess.

"Sorry," she said, "I didn't have a chance to pack a hat while we were rushing dozens of monsters onto this Victorian-era spacecraft."

"This is unbelievable," gasped Shane, who had joined Ben at the porthole.

"How far have we traveled?" asked Nabila.

"I really wish that I could make sense of these

controls," I replied. "It's unlike anything I've ever seen on *Star Wars* or *Star Trek*."

"*Star Blech* is more like it," said Gordon.

"Boy, zero-g makes you really cranky," said Shane.

"I just don't trust anywhere I can't play football," Gordon said.

"Just wait until we get to the moon," I said. "Even *I'll* be able to throw a fifty-yard pass there—just one-sixth the gravity of Earth! Oh man, it's going to be *great*!"

"Once we rescue Director Z from some form of evil that waits to crush us," said Ben. "Then you can have your football game."

A few of the old witches walked onto the bridge, dodging everyone and everything floating past them. "Everyone's safe down in the cargo hold," said Katherine, the oldest of them. "One of the zombies fell to pieces with all the shaking, but we took care of her before all the parts could float away."

"How are you walking!?!" asked Shane.

The three gray old ladies cackled, and Griselda walked in holding up a jar of gooey . . . something.

"What is that?" I asked. "I bet there's some essence of spiderweb and eye of newt in there . . ."

Gordon practically leaped out of his chair in excitement, but grabbed it quickly again to keep from floating away. "Hey, Griselda, bring some of that newt juice over here."

"Oh, it's not anything but marmalade," said Griselda.

"Why do you always think the marmalade is something gross?" Shane asked me.

I had no answer.

Griselda slathered a generous amount of marmalade onto Gordon's shoes, and he was able to stand on the floor once again.

"Anyone else?" asked Griselda.

"No, we're having too much fun," replied Nabila, who was spinning like a top while looking out the big window at all the stars.

"Suit yourself," said Gordon. "But you'll be sorry. Griselda, are my muscles less likely to shrink now that I'm walking? Chris, how long until we reach the moon and some gravity?"

I turned to one of the many gauges that slowly, creakily turned on the massive control panel, when I was struck in the face with a squeaking furry object.

"Aw, get off!" I yelled.

The bat bounced off my face, scratching me slightly with its rough wings, and corkscrewed wildly into . . .

"My hair!" Nabila screamed. "Ahhhhhh! Get out! Get out!"

She reached up to try to untangle the bat, but it just squeaked louder and got even more tangled.

"Judging by the squeaks, I think that's Grigore," said Ben as he kicked off Shane's rump to float over to Nabila.

"I don't care *who* it is!" she screeched. "Just get him out of my hair."

By the time Ben reached Nabila, Grigore's mad flapping was dragging her through the air in the opposite direction.

"Wait!" said Ben. "Stop flapping, Grigore!"

"I think he's panicking because he doesn't know how to fly in zero-g," said Shane. "But Ben will be able to untangle him as soon as he stops flapping and Nabila calms down."

"See," said Gordon. "This is why I'm sticking to the floor. Literally."

A helmet from one of the space suits floated past Gordon, and he snatched it up.

"Extra protection," Gordon said. "So how long is this going to take, Chris?"

"Hmmm," I said, trying to ignore Nabila's screams as Grigore dragged her off the bridge. "I'm not sure . . ."

I gazed up at the gauges that had survived the voyage, and scratched my head.

"We're going to get there in ten hours!" I said.

"Aw, that totally sucks!" yelled Gordon.

"What do you mean, 'totally sucks'?" I asked. "It took the first Apollo astronauts four days, bonehead. This is amazing! We might even have to slow down before we hit the moon. The moon! I might pass out from the excitement."

"Are you sure it's not the zero-g that's going to make you pass out?" asked Shane.

We stared at the moon as it grew larger in the window. "No, it's definitely the excitement," I said. "I just never thought I'd actually go to the moon. I mean, I had hoped and dreamed. But this is amazing! It's unbelievable. It's like I've been training for this moment for my entire life. I just always thought it would be with NASA—"

"I hope this tin can we're flying in protects us from solar flares and cosmic rays," added Shane.

I shivered at the thought of cosmic rays blasting through my body.

"I've got to admit," said Gordon, "I always thought you were pretty dorky for staring at the moon all the time. But all that dorkiness really paid off. Because I have absolutely no idea what cosmic rays are."

The sound of retching floated up the stairs into the bridge.

"Aw, man," Ben moaned as he spun into the room. "This is worse than the Barfitron."

"He got sick chasing Grigore and me around the ship," Nabila said, floating in behind him.

"Plus," Ben said, "I inhaled some of Roy's hair, which is floating all over the ship."

"I did the best I could," said Nabila. "There was more hair than I could handle!"

"Just burp a little," said Shane. "That always makes you feel better."

"That's a good idea," said Nabila, floating over to help him.

"WAIT," I yelled. "There's no such thing as burping in space!"

But it was too late.

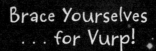

Brace Yourselves . . . for Vurp!

Ben tried to burp, but ended up blowing a pretty good collection of multicolored chunks all over the bridge.

"There's no gravity to push food down and air up in your stomach," I said, swatting a few chunks away. "The astronauts call it a 'wet burp.' I call it a 'vurp.'"

Just the sound of the word made Ben gag again. He closed his mouth tight, and two jets of wet vurp shot out his nose, spinning him backward a bit.

"Ugh, keep it in, dearie!" screeched Griselda, who was slathering a second coating of marmalade on Gordon's shoes.

"Sorrggggbbbllllllrrcchhh," said Ben, and let it loose

all over a zombie who had floated onto the bridge at the worst possible moment.

"Get it off me!" the zombie yelled. "Oh, it's terrible. Now I know what a sussuroblat feels like."

He shimmied and shook it off his rotting body.

"I've never seen a zombie move so fast," said Shane. "And I know some fast zombies."

The zombie's arm flew off and directly into the open mouth of Pietro in werewolf form.

GLLUUURP!

"That will make a tasty snack," said Shane.

But the arm was shaking so violently that it gagged Pietro.

He WHARFED up the arm along with a hairy wet mess.

"Oh man, a werehairball!" said Gordon. "Those are the worst. Pietro, I thought I told you to stop licking yourself so much!"

The mass danced around, started to growl and shake, and then got pulled apart by the lack of gravity.

"Bet everyone wishes they had a helmet on, huh?" taunted Gordon.

The bridge was now filled with a disgusting cloud of Ben's dinner, Roy's hair, and Pietro's hairball.

"Wait, why was the hairball growling so loudly?" asked Shane.

I peered out the window in shock.

"The moon!" I yelled. "It's so much closer than it should be! We're going insanely fast. Like, a hundred thousand miles per hour!"

"ARGGGHHH!" a scream came over the intercom, and the lights flickered.

I floated through the cloud of barf-hair and slammed my fist down on the intercom.

"We're coming in too fast!" I yelled. "You've got to reduce your energy, Frederick."

Bells began ringing through the ship, clanging like a large alarm clock.

The ship shook violently, and Nabila crashed onto a control panel, crazy hair first.

"OOOOOOF," she yelled as her head crunched down on a button.

"Nabila!" yelled Ben, swiping away the barf that was orbiting around his head. "I'm coming."

But Ben wasn't going anywhere—he couldn't get any footing.

Gordon kicked Ben in his butt, and Ben finally went flying over to Nabila.

"Oh, I'm okay," she said weakly as he crashed into her. "I think I inhaled your barf. I'm officially grossed out."

Ben grabbed Nabila and kicked off the control panel, just as another violent shudder caused it to spark and catch fire. The zombie floated over and began slapping the control panel with the arm he had lost, to put out the flames.

Frederick's "ARRGGGHHHHH" was even louder now.

"Frederick!" I yelled over the screech of the ship. "I know you're in pain, but you have to turn off your power completely, or we're going to come into the moon's orbit too fast and crash-land. But you need to give me one last burst of power when I tell you to. Can you do it?"

"YARRRGGGHHHHHH!" he yelled back.

"I'll take that as a 'yes,'" I said. "Wait until I say NOW!"

I turned to the monsters at the wheel. Roy had used his entire body to bear down on it, and I was suddenly glad that Nabila had had the vampire bats take off all his hair.

"Keep it steady!" I said. "When Frederick gives us the burst, you've got to turn it clockwise!"

"We're at five thousand feet and plummeting," yelled Shane from the altimeter.

"GET READY TO PULL THE NOSE UP!" I yelled.

"Four thousand . . ."

"Three thousand . . ."

"NOW, FREDERICK," I yelled.

The ship careened to the right, pushing every floating friend and monster into the back left of the bridge. Roy was able to hold on tight by sticking his pasty-pink arm under the spoke of the wheel when it turned back to the left.

"Arrrrrgh!" he screamed.

"ARRGGGHHHH," Frederick screamed over the intercom.

Shane was still clutching the altimeter and shot off the changing altitude as quick as a machine gun.

"Five hundred . . . four hundred . . . three hundred . . . two hundred . . ."

"HOLD ON!" I screamed.

"Hold on to what!?" Gordon yelled as his marmalade failed and he dropped onto the pile of monsters in the corner.

SCREEEEEEBOOM!

Houston, the Eagle Has Belly Flopped

"Hwaaaa!" I gasped for air, convinced the hull of the ship was wide open.

I could breathe...but pitch-black silence surrounded me. And because I could breathe, I could smell the mix of barf and wet monster hair. I was actually pretty glad I couldn't see it.

"Frederick?" I yelled. "FREDERICK!?"

No response.

"Guys?" I asked.

Soft moans floated up from the room. I couldn't tell where they were coming from. I couldn't even tell if we had landed right-side up.

"I don't even know where *I* am," I said.

"BUUUUUURP." Ben burped and sounded greatly relieved. "Well, I'm not vurping, so we must be on the moon. Did we land on the dark side?"

"That would be impossible. I think we crashed deep into the lunar surface and got buried in moon rock," I said.

"It's getting hotter by the second," said Nabila.

"This gravity feels so weird," Gordon said. "But at least we're not floating around uncontrollably anymore."

"Lights would help, though," said Shane. "Did we lose Frederick? What happened to the electricity?"

"I'm so glad all of you made it," I said. "I wouldn't have forgiven myself if you had died."

"No, I wouldn't have let you forgive yourself," Shane said. "Because I would have haunted you for all eternity."

"Like Quincy?" I asked.

"No, I'd be a cooler ghost than that little stinker," said Shane. "For one thing, I'd be older and wiser for all eternity."

"Yeah, by a whopping two years!" screeched Nabila. "Can we get on with it? We have to do something. I'm burning! What on earth are we doing?!"

"You mean, 'what on moon' are we doing," replied Ben.

"You know what I mean," she said. "Don't try being smarter than me, it's just never gonna happen."

"She's right," I said.

"Hey!" said Ben in protest.

"No, she's right that we need to move fast," I said. "Without the power cells to run the climate system, we'll get pretty toasty in this old tin."

"Why?" asked Gordon.

"During the lunar day, it can get as hot as two hundred fifty degrees," replied Shane.

"Oh right . . . ," said Gordon. "Yeah, of course, why didn't I think of that?"

"But not even that will last long," I said, "with sunset coming soon."

"Sunset?" asked Ben. "Now I'm confused. You said we weren't on the dark side of the moon."

"The dark side of the moon is only dark when looking from Earth," I said. "In actuality, every part of the moon gets two weeks of sunshine and two weeks of darkness."

"So, we're about to experience two weeks of darkness?" asked Shane.

"Yep," I said. "Well, darkness along with earth- and starshine."

"Uh-oh!" said Shane.

"Then we'll have to deal with the cold," I said. "So either way, we need to figure out the climate system."

From outside the ship, thunder rumbled.

"It vas a dark and stormy night . . . ," Grigore said, giggling.

"That's not possible," I said. "There's no weather on the moon."

"Then it must have been something else," Gordon said.

"But what?" Nabila asked.

BOOOOM. Again the sound of thunder.

"Now it's even closer," said Ben.

"Do you think they know we're here?" asked Shane.

"Who are 'they'?" Gordon asked.

"Guys, I'm frying!" yelled Nabila. "We've got to do something!"

"All right," I said. "I've got an idea, but I need to feel my way down to Frederick."

"I could use my night vision to guide you," said Grigore, and a clammy, dead hand wrapped itself around mine.

"On a dark and stormy night on the moon, the old vampire grabbed me in the dark," I said, and now I was the one who was giggling.

Grigore, despite his amazing vampire abilities, was still a goofy old man, and he just couldn't handle the low gravity. It had taken us far too long to get down into the darkness to speak with Frederick. It was getting really, really hot in the ship.

"I'm *melting*," Frederick moaned from his electric chair.

"Don't worry, buddy," I said. "I don't think you'll melt until at least eight hundred degrees."

"Okay, but I'm *thirsty*," he said.

"That, I can help you with," I said. "Grigore, go get some water from the supply closet."

"And get the werewolves," said Frederick.

"Werewolves?" I asked.

"I need a charge," he said.

"Oh of course!" I said, understanding what needed to happen.

While we waited in the hot darkness, Frederick gave me a status update. Since he had been plugged into the ship, he was the eyes of the ship as well as its energy supply.

"Oxygen levels dropping," he wheezed while I rubbed his back to comfort him. "My power near zero. Climate-control system overloaded. Find the control panel on the bridge, this big." He used his hands, which sparked slightly with electric charge, to show me how big. "Hit it and pull the short lever to turn it back on. I can't turn on the lights to help you find it. May be too much of a power drain, even with the werewolves' static charge. I'm so sorry."

"You did a great job," I said. "We made it! I'll figure out the climate control. You just charge up."

In the dark, I could hear the werewolves pad into the room. I moved away from Frederick and heard the sound of their dry old fur rubbing up against Frederick's legs and the legs of the electric chair he used to connect with the ship. After a while, there was a soft glow coming off of Frederick, and I could see the werewolves rushing around in a circle, their tongues almost dragging on the floor. Their eyes bugged.

Frederick leaned back with a sigh, taking in their static charge.

"Take breaks, guys," I said. "Or you'll pass out."

The werewolves stopped every once in a while and nuzzled his leg, a great spark flying from their wet noses into him.

CRACK!

"Ah!" yelled Frederick. "Stop it!"

CRACK!

"That tickles!"

CRACK!

"I mean it! Stop it!"

The werewolves laughed a growly laugh.

"Play nice," I said. "He's had a rough ride. Grigore, give Frederick his water and then help me down to the cargo hold. I have an idea."

Down in the cargo hold, the monsters were buzzing with anticipation.

"Did we make it?" one asked in the dark.

"Are you dead, now, too?" asked another.

"Yes and no. But I can't answer any more questions until later," I said impatiently.

Once I heard from Frederick that his batteries were too low to power the lights, I knew what I had to do.

"All the zombies, gather around," I said.

I heard shuffling and heavy breathing, and was suddenly surrounded by the six zombies of Gallow Manor Retirement Home. I could tell because of the outrageously rotten smell, a stink made even worse by the heat.

"Okay, guys, maybe just back off a little," I said. "I'm still breathing, you know?"

There were a few moans, and then the zombies obeyed, backing away and making the room smell "somewhat funky" as opposed to "insanely barf-inducing."

"Sorry, Boss," said one of the zombies. "We ran out of the breath mints you gave us pretty early in the trip."

"It's okay," I said. "I need you guys to use the air lock at the back to exit the spaceship, then walk up to the front of the ship and clear away all the moon rocks that are covering the bridge's viewport."

"You got it, Boss," they said. "Just tell us what to do."

"Feel your way to the back of the cargo hold and pull the lever," I said.

There was some shuffling as the zombies searched for the lever, and then a loud clank. With a metallic SCREECH, the door rolled open.

I could hear them shuffle into the air lock, so I walked over with Grigore to close the door behind them.

"Wait until we close this door before you open the second one," I said to the zombies.

Grigore waited with a hand on the lever. "Use your strength," I said to him, and with a grunt, he clanked the door shut.

I pressed an ear against the door and could hear the zombies open the second door.

Air WHOOOSHED out of the air lock, and then there was silence.

The utter silence of zombies in space.

"We're cooked if they can't find their way," I said to Grigore. "Let's go back to the bridge and wait."

If the Moon
Were Made of Cheese,
It Would Melt

"So, what's the deal?" said Shane. "I hear a lot of the monsters calling you 'Boss' these days. Even I can't get the zombies to do much, no matter how many brains I bribe them with."

"I'm only telling you because I trust you," I said, grabbing his sweaty shoulders and pulling him toward me. "You can't tell the others, and you can never let the info loose, not even under torture."

"Okay, okay!" he said. "What is it?"

"I'm holding a pendant," I whispered directly into Shane's sweaty ear. "I'm an astronaut . . . and a Director."

"What?!" Shane yelled.

"I'll explain later," I said. "But we just have to hope

this works first. You're sweating. And you never sweat."

"Is Frederick dead?" asked Nabila. I jumped in the dark, wondering if she had heard my secret.

"No, but he tells me that he only has enough power for the climate system. We just don't have enough light to see what we're doing and fix it."

"Why can't he turn on the lights?" asked Shane.

"Because that would use up what little power he had, which we need—"

"—for the climate system, got it!" Shane said, finishing my sentence. "Whew, it's hot in here."

"What's the plan?" asked Ben.

"I'm hoping that before the sun sets on our part of the moon, the zombies can remove all the moon rocks that are covering the viewport. Then we'll use the light to fix the climate system with Frederick's instructions."

"Aren't the zombies gonna get cooked?" asked Gordon.

"I don't think so," I replied. "I'm more worried about them wandering off looking for moon brains."

"And if they do get cooked or wander off?" asked Shane.

"Then we'll most likely freeze in the hull of this ship, when the sun sets," I said.

"Goooooo, zombies!" he yelled.

We waited and waited and waited, frying like little chicken drumsticks, until . . .

"Wait, what is that sound?" croaked Pietro between pants. Circling Frederick had made his throat dry.

"I don't hear anything," I said.

"Scraping . . . ," said Pietro.

I listened hard and heard it!

With a big scrape, part of the viewport was exposed. A zombie with a very big grin peered in and gave me a thumbs-up.

The rays of sun took Grigore by surprise. He threw up his hand to cover his eyes, but the rest of him began to smoke terribly.

"Arrrgh," he wailed. "I'm just not as old as I used to be!"

"Gordon," I said, "drag Grigore out of those rays. Grigore, you've got to go down to the cargo hold. The sun is extremely strong on the moon—there's no atmosphere to shield it!"

Soon the rest of the viewport was exposed, and I took a quick few seconds to look out at the moonscape.

"Wow . . . ," I said. "I can't believe it."

I was so excited, I drooled a little.

"Believe it!" yelled Nabila. "Look at the sun!"

She pointed at the sun as it sank quickly behind one of the moon's many peaks.

"We don't have much time," I said, jumping back into the room and stumbling across the shards of metal, barf, and hair that covered the floor. The witches, who had all been napping, suddenly woke up.

"Are we there yet?" one of them cackled.

The glow of the sun was already starting to fade as I scrambled frantically to look for the control panel that Frederick had described.

"We need to find a panel the size of Herr Direktor Detlef's fish tank," I said. "But I just don't remember seeing anything like that in here."

Ben pointed to the wall above one of the control panels and said, "It's over here! I remember barfing on it."

I ran over the metallic debris in the middle of the bridge, trying not to trip over the larger chunks or slip on the wet barf and werewolf hair.

"How do we get it open?" Shane asked.

I slammed my fist against the far right side, and it swung open.

My eyes crossed as I looked deep into the massive control panel. It was huge mess of levers, metal pipes, wires, glass tubes, and strange dials. You'd need to have an engineering degree from the 1800s to make sense of any of it.

"Uhhhhh . . . ," I said to nobody. "Frederick said to look for the shortest lever, but these all look exactly the same size!"

"What happens if you pull the wrong one?" Nabila asked.

"I have no idea," I said. "But I'm assuming it would be terrible."

The rays of sun that had been pointed at the panel disappeared.

I looked up to the window and saw that there was more dirt and rock that could be cleared away.

"Shane, keep the zombies there!" I said. "Get them to clear out that last bit of debris!"

Shane waved madly at the zombies. They wandered back to the window, and he started to pantomime what he wanted them to do.

"MOVE. THE. ROCK," he said. "MOVE. THE. DIRT."

"They can't hear you," I said, peering once again into the ancient control panel.

"It helps me figure out how to move my body," said Shane. "DOOOOO. IT."

Soon, a little more light shone into the control panel, and in the very back, past a tangle of wires and pipes, I could see . . .

"The short lever!" I yelled, and reached in to pull it down.

The hiss of air conditioning sounded through the bridge.

"Oh, it's sooooo good," said Nabila, and she rushed over to a barfy pile of scrap metal, pushed it aside, and shoved her face in the vent that was there.

All over the ship, monsters and kids alike sighed a collective "ahhhhhhhh . . ."

A loud banging sounded throughout the bridge.

BOOM BOOM BOOM.

A few of the zombies stood at the window, pounding furiously.

"They're freaking out," said Ben. "Why are they freaking out?"

Soon, all the zombies were going crazy. They pushed up frantically against the window.

"What are they trying to yell at us?" asked Nabila.

Some had their backs squished against the glass, looking out toward the dark.

"Is something out there with them?" asked Ben. "Oh, please tell me there's nothing out there with them."

Three huge figures rose above the six zombies—they looked like massive, swollen heads, throbbing with green goo, mouths filled with razor-sharp teeth. Tentacles floated below the heads, swaying softly in front of the zombies.

"Oh man, there *is* something out there with them," yelled Ben.

"RUN!" yelled Nabila.

But the zombies were too terrified to notice, even if they could have heard her.

Vurp Invaders

The zombies stood frozen in front of the bizarre, disgusting aliens, who gnashed their teeth and reached out their tentacles to probe their prey.

"Gah, they're disgusting!" yelled Gordon. "Like the worst zit times a hundred. Is that green stuff in their heads pus? Ugh!"

"I was really hoping I wouldn't run into an alien on this trip," said Ben.

"I figured aliens would show up," said Nabila. "I mean, we've pulled a whole bunch of old monsters into space. It was bound to happen."

The aliens began oozing fluorescent green and yellow from their mouths, forming a cloud around the zombies. Five of the zombies ran, but one was left in shock, staring.

The creatures' big bulbous heads began to palpitate and squirm. Somehow, I swore that I heard burping.

The trapped zombie turned away from the creatures and looked at us through the glass. There was literally nothing we could do.

"Help me!" he screamed.

"How can we hear that?" I asked.

And suddenly, BOOM, another great peel of thunder sounded on the ship, just like the ones from before.

Waves of sound rippled through the zombie, liquefying him and spraying a blast of blood and guts all over the window. He looked like a fly that made the mistake of buzzing in front of a Mack truck.

Soon we could hear a slurping noise, and all the zombie's parts were lifted off the viewport and into the waiting mouths of the creatures.

Satisfied with their meal, they pressed up against the glass, feeling the window with their tentacles.

Howie the werewolf transformed and ran right up to the viewport, snapping his dog teeth and scraping at the window with his paw.

"What are you doing?" I said. "You probably shouldn't let them know that we're in here!"

"GRRRRRRRRR BARK BARK BARK."

"They're starting to notice us," warned Shane.

The heads closed in and started exhaling the green goo once again. It hung in front of the ship, and for sure this time I could hear a gentle BURP BURP BURP sound. Suddenly, their tentacles suctioned up against the glass and pulled.

"HOW IS THAT POSSIBLE!?!?" I screamed. "They shouldn't be able to do that."

"What do you mean?" asked Gordon.

"The moon exists in the vacuum of space," replied Nabila. "And in a vacuum, the suction required to grab the glass just isn't possible."

"I think they're vurping a cloud around them that is capable of transmitting sound in space," said Shane.

"Space Vurp?" I asked.

The strange aliens leaned back hard, and the crack in the glass that had started at takeoff got a little bit bigger.

"BARK BARK BARK BARK BARK."

"Stop it, Howie!" I commanded. And Howie HOWWWWWWWWLED.

The ship shook, and the aliens backed away from the glass as more moon rocks and moondust poured over the viewport. Somewhere, someone laughed a deep, gut-trembling laugh. The laughter shook the ship even further and we were tumbled onto our butts. Shards of barfy metal tore into our jeans.

"OW!"

The bridge was dark and silent again.

"Sorry if I did that," wheezed Howie. "I was just really upset."

"No, I think you did good," said Shane. "I'm just not sure you did it alone."

"What do you mean?" asked Gordon.

"I have a theory—" said Shane.

"Now I'm freezing," said Nabila, cutting him off.

"Oh, just please, please, please tell me we didn't break the climate system," I said.

There was a soft whirring sound, and the climate system and lights came up again. There was a loud pop of static from the intercom.

"Chris." The staticky voice of Frederick came over the intercom. "Oxygen levels normal."

There was more static, and then . . .

"You really need to come down to the cargo hold," Griselda's voice cut in. "You are not going to believe this."

I could hear the excited grunts of monsters.

We entered the cargo hold to see the monsters gathered around a massive tear that had opened up in the metal floor. A thin canyon made of moon rock could be seen below it.

"What in the world?" I asked.

Nabila replied in her usual way. "You mean, 'what in the moon?'"

"You know what I mean," I said.

"After Howie howled," said Griselda, "this crack opened up in the floor."

"I guess that's what shook us up so badly," I said.

"The air is slightly smelly," said Medusa, who leaned down near the crack.

A snake from her head slithered into the crack.

"But it's totally breathable," hissed the snake.

"Thanks, Bruce," said Shane.

"That must be where the oxygen is coming from," I said. "Incredible."

Shane walked over to the crack and got on his hands and knees, trying to poke his head into it.

"Be careful it doesn't close back up!" said Gordon.

"The crack is too thin for me to see anything. Can you see anything else?" Shane asked the snake.

"No," hissed Bruce. "But there is a light coming from down there . . . somewhere."

"I think we've got to explore this," said Shane. "We know what's up on the surface of the moon, and it's not good."

"But how can we, if it's too thin to crawl into?" I asked.

"Maybe we chisel away at the rock and try to make

it wider?" suggested Gordon.

"Give it a try," Nabila said to Roy.

Roy walked over to the crack and lifted his naked arm.

WHACK!

The ship shook again, but nothing happened.

"Ow," said Roy, and he cradled his hurt hand. "I miss my fur."

"Oh dearie," said Katherine. "I might have packed something that can help you. Come over here with me."

"Maybe we shouldn't try to widen it until we figure out where it goes," said Nabila.

"How can we figure that out?" I asked.

"Let's send out some scouts," Nabila responded.

"Scouts?" asked Gordon.

"A fleet of vampire bats," said Nabila.

There were three loud pops behind us. Grigore, Vlad, and Camilla, in the form of vampire bats, fluttered in front of Nabila.

"Vhat do you vant us to do?" they asked.

"See where the crack leads. Observe and report back to us. If you see anyone or anything, don't let them see or hear you. Got it?"

"Got it!" they squeaked, and swooped quickly into the crack.

"Now we wait," I said.

"Guys, I think I know why the crack opened in the

first place," said Shane.

"What's your big theory?" asked Gordon.

"The moon opened up the crack," said Shane confidently.

"What!?!" the entire cargo hold of monsters and kids said in unison.

"Wait, hear me out," said Shane.

"Go on," I said.

"Remember, back on Earth, the huge map of the moon in the space room where we found the phonograph record that led us to the ship?"

"YES!" the entire room responded.

"I don't think it was a map of a moon that looked like it had a real face," said Shane. "I think it was a picture!"

"A picture of the real man in the moon?" I asked. "But he doesn't really exist. There's not a man in the moon, just like it's not really made of cheese."

"Or is it . . . ," asked Gordon, staring at the rock.

"Did you see Roy just hit that moon rock?" asked Nabila. "I think it's safe to say the moon isn't cheese."

"Agreed," said Shane. "I knew just from the landing that the moon wasn't made of cheese. It's too hard. But that's not the point."

"What is the point, Shane?" I asked, flabbergasted.

"The point is, Howie howled, and the moon responded," Shane said. "Howie, what were you feeling when you howled?"

"I was howling for protection," responded Howie. "I was howling for help."

"And we got both," Shane said. "Those nasty creatures aren't bothering us anymore, and we might have had the next path in our quest to save Director Z open up right in front of us."

There was a scraping, flapping noise, and the vampire bats flew out of the crack under the cargo hold. Covered in moondust, one by one they transformed back into vampires with loud POPs.

"Ve must hurry," said Grigore, rushing over to me. "Ve have seen Murray and Director Z, and Murray is going to kill him!"

Finding Z

The monsters freaked out.

"Director Z!" A werewolf howled. "No!"

"That murderer!" screamed a banshee.

A few of the monsters started clawing at the crack, desperate to make it wider.

"Wait," I said. "Slow down. What's happening? You saw Murray and Director Z?"

"Yes," said Grigore. "The crack leads to a system of caves. If you follow the glowing globes down far enough, you'll find a prison. Ve saw Murray . . ."

"Murray the mummy?" asked Shane. "You mean Murrayhotep?"

"Yes, our Murray," responded Grigore. "Ve saw

Murray drag Director Z out of his dirty underground cell into a room with a disgusting creature that burps out a tarry ooze."

"I think he called it a 'splurtsar,'" interrupted Vlad with a shudder.

"Yes, that vas it," said Grigore. "I think the ooze is meant to control Director Z's mind and make him give up all our secrets! A disgusting truth serum! The vile creature burps it up directly into the mouth of Director Z."

"So he's not trying to kill Director Z?" I asked.

"I don't know!" said Grigore. "I think so. Murray said, 'I don't care vhat Master says. I'm going to kill you and say it vas an accident. He'll thank me later.' But he might have been just trying to scare Director Z."

"Either way," I said, "we need to get down there as quickly as possible."

"It von't be easy to get down there," said Grigore. "Ve vere lucky ve made it. There vas a strong laser barrier that ve had to fly through. I singed my fur!"

Grigore turned around, and there was a burn mark up the back of his head.

"Let me help you with that," said Shane. He licked his fingertips and put out the pieces of hair that were still smoldering.

"But we've got to try," I said. "You heard what Murrayhotep said! What if he actually means it?"

"What do we do?" asked Ben.

"The first thing we need to do is figure out how to widen this crack," said Nabila.

"The werewolves should howl," said Shane. "They should howl asking the moon for help. They should howl asking the moon to open up this crack so we can actually fit into it."

"All right, then, do it!" I commanded the werewolves.

"HOOOOOOWWWWWWWL!"

The room shook. With a blast of moondust, the narrow entrance in the floor of the cargo hold opened up into the moon caves below.

I rushed up to the newly widened crack and could see that there were craggy moon rocks jutting out along the way to the first glowing globe that Grigore had mentioned.

"We should be able to climb down now," I said.

"So, what's the plan?" asked Shane.

"We shouldn't bring everyone down there," I replied. "Just a few. The humans, the vampires, and the werewolves. Otherwise, Murrayhotep will hear us coming from a mile away."

"Well, let's get going then!" yelled Nabila. "We don't know how much time we actually have."

She jumped into the crack and started navigating her way deeper inside.

"All right," I said. "Let's do this. Vampire bats in the lead . . ."

With a POP, the vampires turned back into bats.

". . . werewolves take up the guard in the back. Nabila, slow down!"

We all made our way into the crack. I looked up to see the werewolves pad down after us, and the faces of concerned monsters surrounding the entryway.

"Somebody go see if Frederick needs anything!" I yelled, and added, "And the zombies are probably scared to death in the air lock. Let them in—I almost forgot them."

We reached the first glowing globe, which was connected directly to the moon rock with a crude plug. It swayed slightly in the gravity of the moon.

"I wonder what that is," said Shane.

"I have no idea," I said, putting my hands in front of the glowing globe. "It's not hot."

One of the werewolves nipped at Shane's pant leg.

"All right, we're going, we're going!" insisted Shane.

We followed the vampire bats deeper down into the moon.

"The deeper we go, the warmer it gets," said Nabila.

"And the stinkier," Ben added.

"And the stickier," I said.

"Maybe the moon is made of cheese after all," said Shane.

We all listened to our sneakers SCHLOOP, SCHLIP, SCHLOPP as we walked deeper, passing globe after globe.

Suddenly, the greenish glow on the moon rock turned to red as we rounded a corner, revealing a tunnel crisscrossed with lasers.

"A security barrier!" I said. "That's what singed your fur?"

One of the bats fluttered down to me. I could see the small burn mark on its head.

"Yes!" it squeaked.

A loud scream echoed through the tunnel from the other side of the barrier.

"Sounds like we found Director Z," said Shane.

"We've got to hurry!" I said. "Werewolves, can you try howling again? Ask the moon for help!"

The werewolves raised their heads and opened their muzzles. Immediately, the vampire bats flew down into their necks, choking them.

"What are you doing?" I asked.

"If we can hear Director Z's scream," said Nabila, "whoever's with Director Z will hear them howl."

"Of course," I said. "Sorry, guys."

"Now what?" Gordon asked.

With a squeak, Grigore floated over to a small

numeric pad set into the wall of moon rock, ten feet or so in front of the laser beams.

Ben rushed over to have a look.

"This must turn it on and off," he said.

He leaned in closer to the pad.

"Three numbers are crusted in moondust," he said. "Three, five, and seven. Those must be the three numbers you type in to turn it off!"

"Well, give it a try," I said.

Ben typed in 3-7-5.

With a soft electrical hum, the lasers moved a few feet down the tunnel toward us.

"There are five other combinations of the three numbers," said Ben. "I'm going to try again."

Ben typed in 7-3-5.

A soft electrical hum.

The lasers moved down the tunnel again. Now they were only six feet in front of us. The werewolves backed down in fear.

Ben typed in 7-5-3.

A soft electrical hum.

Four feet away.

Ben typed in 5-3-7.

A soft electrical hum.

Two feet away.

Everyone moved back. Everyone but Ben.

"Only two more possible combinations," said Ben.

He put his finger up to the three.

"Be careful, Ben!" screeched Nabila.

3-5-7

We could hear the hum of the lasers as they moved past the keypad.

Ben jumped back and, with a SQUISH, landed on the floor of gooey moon rock.

Nabila ran over to help him up.

"Maybe we should let the werewolves howl after all," I said. "It might be our only chance."

"Wait!" Ben said. "There's only one combination left, and I can reach my hand through the laser beams."

He rushed back over to the keypad.

"What if you're wrong?" Nabila yelled. "What if there's another number?"

"Then I'm toast," he said. "But I'm sure of it."

He slowly moved his arm in between two of the beams and reached up to the keypad. Nabila rushed toward him, but he held up his other hand.

"Stop," he said. "If I'm wrong, we don't both have to die."

She stopped.

The werewolves whimpered.

Ben looked at me and winked.

Ben typed in 5-7-3.

A soft electrical hum . . .

. . . and with a soft *click*, the lasers turned off.

"Yeah," I said, and ran up to give Ben a hug. "I'm so glad you were right."

The others dog piled us in joy . . .

. . . when another scream from Director Z pierced the air.

"Let's go!" said Ben.

Saving Z

We ran down the tunnel, and with every step, Director Z's screams got louder.

"Is this the way?" I asked Grigore as we came up against a wall with a small passageway crudely drilled down the center.

He fluttered down and turned into a human again.

"I'm sorry, Boss," said Grigore. "I forgot about this part. I vas so worried about Director Z."

I scrambled up into the passageway, but was barely able to wiggle my shoulders in, even if I crawled. It was insanely hot and sticky inside.

"Not even the werewolves are going to be able to fit into that," I said, pulling my head out of the hole.

Another scream came through the passageway.

"How far is Z?" I asked Grigore.

"He's just through this passagevay and around the corner," said Grigore.

"What if we covered ourselves with this moon juice?" said Shane, swiping at the ground.

The werewolves didn't wait. They started rolling around on the ground, their fur squishing into it with a SQUELCH SQUIRCH SQUALTCH. They jumped up and squeezed into the passageway one by one. When the last paws disappeared, I looked over at Shane.

"Great idea," I said, and reached down to grab some moon muck. I slathered it on my arms.

"We don't have time!" said Shane, and he dropped to the ground and started to roll around just like the werewolves had.

We all followed his lead.

I looked over to see Ben's face even whiter than usual, covered with the liquid moon.

"Let's hurry up before it dries," said Shane.

The bats flew into the passageway, and Shane jumped up to follow.

All my friends were able to squeeze through, and it was finally my turn.

I put my shoulders in again, and this time they slipped through. I crawled and clawed through the darkness, barely able to breathe because of how tight it was.

I stopped to take a break, overwhelmed by the intense heat in the passageway.

"How much farther?" I hissed, starting to panic.

But before anyone could answer, Nabila, who was ahead of me, POPPED through the other side, and the strange glow of another globe came through the passageway.

I went to move again, but was stuck.

"Nooo," I said, and dug my nails into the moon rock, sliming forward like a deranged, trapped snail.

Shane grabbed my hand and pulled me through with a wet . . .

POP!

I tumbled to the ground, and Ben put his finger up to his lips. "*Shhhhh.*"

"Do do do it it it," Director Z's voice echoed from around the corner. "Go ahead. Feed me to the splurtsar."

"I wonder what this splurtsar's going to look like?" Gordon asked.

"Something tells me we're about to find out," replied Shane.

"*Feed* you to the splurtsar?" chuckled Murray. "I will feed his black nectar *to you* until you choke."

"Gwarrbbllebll," Director Z said. It sounded like he was already choking.

"Wow, Murrayhotep sounds young," said Gordon. "Really young."

"And angry," Ben added.

"Well, that's nothing new," said Shane.

"Shhhh," Nabila whispered. "Lower your voices. We don't want Murrayhotep to hear us."

"Everyone get close," I said. Everyone leaned in, and the bats flitted quietly overhead.

"Whatever this splurtsar is, maybe we can use it to our advantage. Bats, I want you to fly in to distract Murrayhotep. Once his attention is on you, squeak really loud. Pietro and Howie, when you hear the squeaking, rush in and tackle Murrayhotep. Don't hurt him, just pin him down and chew on his neck a little. We need to ask him who he's working for, and why he betrayed us. We'll pull the splurtsar off Director Z."

I looked at everyone and asked, "Ready?"

Everyone nodded.

"All right," I whispered. "Let's do it."

The bats flitted away.

For a few moments, we couldn't hear anything but Director Z's drinking and choking.

BLURGH. BLACHOUGH. BLUURGH.

"Hey!" yelled Murrayhotep. "Get out of my face, you flying rats!"

I couldn't hear any squeaking, but I was pretty sure Murrayhotep was distracted. I slapped the werewolves on their haunches, and they took off around the corner.

Murrayhotep was halfway through calling for a

guard when his yell was cut off by the werewolves. "GUA—OOF!"

"Good boys!" I yelled, and ran around the corner along with my friends.

Murrayhotep struggled with the werewolves on one side of a small cave. On the other side of the cave, a rotten little creature with red eyes stared at us as it filled a bug-eyed Director Z with black goo. It was the size of a pig, but with the trunk of an elephant. The trunk wrapped around Director Z's neck and into his mouth.

GLURP. BLURP. BLORP.

"The splurtsar!" I yelled.

"You?" yelled Murrayhotep. "Not *you*!"

"Wow, you are lookin' good, Murrayhotep!" said Shane. "Doesn't he look fitter? Not so dusty?"

Murrayhotep struggled under the werewolves. They tightened their toothy grips, but I knew they wouldn't harm him. I'd given them very specific orders.

But Murray didn't know that, and he held still.

The splurtsar tightened its grip on Director Z, dug in its stubby feet, and suctioned onto Director Z's mouth and nose.

We rushed over to Director Z, who flailed under the uninterrupted flow of black nectar. I yanked at the trunk, but it was sealed into place with a mucousy suction cup.

"Ugh, Gordon," I said, pulling at the trunk. "Grab the splurtsar! Hurry!"

The splurtsar let out an annoyed SQUUUUUUEEEE through its trunk when Gordon grabbed it, spraying black nectar all over my face. It snapped its little teeth in anger.

"I vouldn't get that in your mouth!" yelled Grigore, now back in human form. "Don't even sniff it in! Remember, it's a truth serum."

"Ugh," I yelled. "It smells like sewage. Gordon, get ready. We can use that black goop to get Murray to tell us who he's working for."

Nabila, Ben, and Shane knelt down next to Director Z, helping him cough out some of the black nectar.

Gordon brought the squirming, squeeing splurtsar over to the struggling Murray. I shoved its trunk over Murray's mouth, but nothing happened.

The splurtsar struggled, shaking its head.

"He obeys no one but me," growled Murrayhotep.

"What do we do?" I asked.

Gordon squeezed the gross little space pig.

Nothing.

He slapped its pig butt.

It just SQUEED.

Murrayhotep laughed.

Gordon flipped it over onto its back.

I held the trunk tight and asked, "What are you doing?"

He jumped onto the pig, pushing his knees into its stomach.

SQUEEEEEEEEBBBBLLLLUUUURRRRP!

I pinched Murray's nose as the black nectar came pouring out faster than before.

GULP.

And Murray stayed still.

I pulled the splurtsar's trunk away from Murray's drooling mouth, and Gordon rolled the splurtsar back over onto its stomach.

It stood up, took two steps, and crashed trunk-first into the moon rock, dead.

Long-Distance Phone Call

"Director Z?!" I screamed, slapping his face. "Director Z!"

The black ooze that poured out of his mouth was now mixed with blood.

"Ugh," said Shane. "That doesn't look good."

Director Z writhed and moaned on the ground. He must have been in extreme pain. He coughed a mix of blood and black nectar onto my face.

"Oh man, I just wiped the other stuff off," I said, slowly starting the process again.

Director Z gave one last raspy breath and lay still.

"What? No!" I screamed. "This can't be happening."

"Should we do mouth-to-mouth?" asked Shane, leaning down.

"No, wait!" I yelled, pulling him back. "Listen." I put my ear directly over Director Z's mouth. "He's still breathing."

"Not for long, you fools," moaned Murray from beneath the werewolves. "You've killed the splurtsar, and your lame duck Director's only chance for survival."

"What do you mean?" Nabila asked.

Before he could answer, a strange jingling sound came from Director Z.

"What now?" I said. "Does Director Z have an alarm? Does this mean he's dying?"

"Oh, you don't need an alarm to tell you that," chuckled Murray.

"Shut it!" I yelled. "Just because you *can* tell the truth doesn't mean that you *have* to. Maybe we should fetch the witches. Grigore, can you go back and get Griselda?"

Grigore flapped back toward the ship. The jingling sound continued.

"It's his cell phone, you fools," laughed Murrayhotep. "And I hate you all."

"Okay, on second thought," said Shane, "keep telling the truth, Murray."

Shane and I leaned down over Director Z, pawing through the pockets of his perfectly pressed suit, which was stained with the black nectar. The stench of the dead splurtsar already filled the dank cave. I was worried Director Z would be next.

"Got it!" yelled Shane, and he pulled out a thin silver phone. "How's he even getting a signal on the moon?"

"Maybe it's communicating directly with the ship?" said Ben.

Shane flipped it open and said, "Um hello? Oh hi, Lunch Lady, how are you? Yes, I—"

"Gimme that!" I yelled, snatching the phone from Shane. "Lunch Lady, we have a situation."

"What is it?" she said. "We've been talkeeng with Deerector Z the entire trip, but he hadn't respondeed in so long, we decideed to risk calling. Is he . . ."

"Dying?" I said. "I think so. He was poisoned by a splurtsar."

"An overdose of splurtsar?" asked Lunch Lady. "Oh my. You must hurry. Geet the splurtsar and feed it some gassy food. Beans, cauleeflower, a turkey leg, anytheeng. Only the burp of a splurtsar can bring back the Deerector."

"We don't have any food," I said. "And we kind of killed the splurtsar."

"No!" she said over the phone. "Then I don't know what to do . . ."

There was a long pause.

"Lunch Lady," I said. "Are you still there? Director

Z's face is starting to turn blue."

"Okay," she said. "Wait. I have an idea: burpcessitation."

"Burpcessitation?" I asked.

"Burpcessitation," she confirmed. "You need to eat a little bit of the splurtsar. Well, maybe more than a little bit. You really need to bite off a few good chunks. Swallow it down fast, jump around, and then burp directly into the Deerector's mouth. Burp hard. Like you're doeeng mouth-to-mouth. Only you're pushing your burp into hees lungs. Hopefully the essence of splurtsar will combine with your digesteeve juices and create the appropriate antidote."

"This is crazy!" I yelled. "But his face is completely blue. I've gotta do it!"

"Then put the phone down and hurry!" yelled Lunch Lady. "Then let me know what happens."

I threw the phone down on the ground and ran over to the already-rotten corpse of the splurtsar.

"What do you have to do?" asked Gordon.

"No time," I yelled, grabbing the backside of the hairy, stinky little space creature, and taking a huge bite of his rump.

"Oh, that's just gross," said Ben. Despite being on the moon, and not in zero gravity, he vurped all over himself.

I choked back the rotten flesh and went in for

another bite, this one deeper and juicier. I could smell the dead splurtsar all over my mouth, in my nose, practically in my ears. Its blood stung a little. Its flesh tasted like a piece of chicken left out in the sun for a week.

"Mmmm, space bacon," chuckled Murrayhotep. "Nom, nom, nom!"

"We should give you black nectar more often," said Shane. "I like this new Murrayhotep."

"Zip it, kung fu weenie," said Murrayhotep.

I went for one last bite, just to be sure, this time hitting bone.

"Whatever you're gonna do, hurry!" screamed Nabila. "I can barely feel a pulse."

"I just need to jump around," I said, but because my mouth was filled with dead flesh, it came out, "Iush neeho shum-row."

I forced myself to swallow every last piece. My tongue searched around my mouth for any missing scraps. I gulped those down as well.

I jumped up and down on my way to Director Z. Lunch Lady was right—this was making me really gassy. In fact, now I was worried I would blow chunks directly into Director Z's mouth. I was starting to get stomach cramps, and the room was spinning.

My friends, who still had no idea what was going on, gathered around as I got on my knees, leaned down to Director Z's mouth, tried not to pass out, took a deep breath, and BUUUUUURRRRPPPPFFFFFFFFFffffffff!

I clamped my mouth down on Director Z's, burping the largest burp I had ever burped in my life directly into his lungs. His chest rose in front of me. I gave it all I had, pushing out every last bit of gas, and then for good measure, lifted my head, breathed in one more huge breath, and . . .

BRRRRRIIIIPPPPPPFFFFFFffff!

I clamped my mouth down once again. Once I was sure I didn't have any more gas to give, I stood up, took two steps back, and passed out into Gordon's arms.

The last thing I remembered hearing was Murray saying, "To tell the truth, even I'm impressed."

Meet the
New Boss

When I woke up, Director Z was over me. This time, he was the one slapping me in the face.

He had the silver cell phone tucked under the crook of his neck.

"Yes, he's perfectly fine, Ms. Veracruz," he said calmly. "Yes, it was a close call. I will be eternally grateful . . . again. We'll speak again once we're on our way back to Earth, which should be shortly."

"Are you okay?" I asked Director Z, the smell of splurtsar still on my breath. My mouth felt fuzzy and tasted like I had licked Gordon's armpit after a big football game.

Griselda, who had finally made it to the cave, stood

next to Grigore. She saw me licking my pasty lips.

"It's okay, dearie," she said. "That will pass soon. I didn't pack the right herbs to help clear it up quicker."

Director Z held the phone down to me. "Yes, I've never felt better. Ms. Veracruz would like to speak with you," he said.

I grabbed the cell phone.

"Oh, Chrees!" yelled Lunch Lady. "You've saved the day once again. Those of us stuck on Earth, listening to everything all unfold, well, we're all so happy and proud of you."

"What do you mean, 'we'?" I asked. "Do you mean the Nurses?"

"Well, the Nurses, yes, and they do say hello, even though they're mad at you," said Lunch Lady. "But someone else has taken a special interest in your trip to space. Principal Prouty's grandfather is a resident of the Retirement Home."

"Whoa," I exclaimed. "No way!"

"What?" asked Shane, but Lunch Lady started talking again.

"Do you really think we'd be able to keep the huge secret of the five of you doeeng what you do at the Retirement Home without the help of the principal? What about all the work I've had to do to cover up the fact that you're on the moon? I've needed quite a bit of help. Your parents are more likely to believe lies from the principal, and it's much easier for her to administer the memory-eraser serum."

"Mr. Bradley's totally in on it, too, isn't he?" I asked. "His breath smells like one of his parents must be a zombie."

"Actually, Mr. Bradley—"

BLLLLLRRRZZZZZP!

"Hey!" I said to Director Z, handing him his phone. "She just cut out."

Director Z stared suspiciously down the tunnel. The glowing globes began to flicker in the cave. We could hear footsteps tramping toward us from deeper in the moon.

CLOMP CLOMP CLOMP.

The werewolves on top of Murray began to growl. Murrayhotep giggled with glee.

"Go!" Director Z commanded the vampire bats. "Warn the others."

"Warn the others about what?" I asked.

"He's coming to get you!" said Murrayhotep.

A dark hooded figure appeared in the tunnel, leading a dozen guards with huge spears, and whips made of electricity. One held an ax that broke into two sharp edges, curving in opposite directions.

The werewolves slowly backed off Murrayhotep, growling, as the hooded figure leaned down to pick up the mummy.

"Ah, Zorflogg!" said Murray. "It's not really all that great to see you. In fact, I must admit, you scare me to death. Here's a funny fact, when I was older—"

"There, there," said Zorflogg. "I knew that you were afraid of me from the first time you came to visit me and talk about how you were going to deceive all your friends." Zorflogg brushed a bit of moondust off Murray's shoulders. "Now, tell me something true that I don't know."

The mummy looked deep into Zorflogg's hood. I tried to see in, but all I could see were two glowing eyes. It was just too dark.

"Well, let's see," said Murrayhotep, scratching his chin. "I tried to kill the Director and blame it on the splurtsar. Yes, I think I was so occupied with that task that I didn't even see the werewolves when they jumped me. I'm dreadfully sorry about that, but what can I say?"

The mummy held his hands up in a sort of "what are you gonna do" way, while the guards closed Shane, Ben, Nabila, Gordon, Director Z, and me into a small circle. The werewolves bolted, and a few of the guards broke off to follow them.

"Let them go," yelled Zorflogg, and he held up a single gloved hand.

The guards obeyed.

"Now, let me be honest as well," Zorflogg said

ominously, "despite the fact that I haven't ingested any black nectar."

He walked closer to Murrayhotep and put both of his hands on Murrayhotep's shoulders. Murrayhotep shrank under the cold stare that came out of the hood.

"Let me be very, very honest," Zorflogg continued. "You have disappointed me very, very much. I've given you everything. Immunity. All the lebensplasm you'd want to drink. Not only did you try to kill this Director, but you failed so miserably that he is, in fact, now immune to black nectar. I've lost a prized splurtsar. You've proven yourself untrustworthy."

Murrayhotep whimpered. "Please . . . I . . ."

Zorflogg continued, "Let's see, what other truths can I bring up . . . Ah, yes. Fail me again and I shall destroy you utterly. Now get back to the mines and GET TO WORK!"

"I'm grateful that you haven't destroyed me, Master," said Murrayhotep. He hung his head and left the cave.

"Who are you?" Nabila said, defiantly stepping up to him. "What do you want?"

"I want it all," said Zorflogg, "but allow me to start with a snack."

Zorflogg picked up Nabila by her legs and flipped her upside down. Nabila squirmed and shook, trying to break free.

"Help!" she screamed. "Ben! Shane! Director Z!!!"

Give Me the
Moon Juice!

We lunged forward to help Nabila, but two of the guards cracked their electric whips together, connecting them and forming an electric barrier.

"Aaaaaahhh!" Nabila's screams echoed through the cave.

We watched helplessly as Zorflogg slowly brought Nabila's feet toward his head. With a slimy hiss, a black tongue emerged from the shadows of the hood and licked the bottom of her shoes.

"WHAT. IS. HE. DOOOOING?" Nabila screeched, her face red from being hung upside down.

The tongue retreated into the hood with a SLURP, and a great MMMMMMM echoed through the caves, shaking moondust off the cave ceiling.

Without warning, he swung Nabila over the electric barrier directly at us.

"GRRRWAAAAH! OOF!"

We cushioned her fall and crashed down like a heap of scared bowling pins.

"Such a paltry treat," said Zorflogg, "but enjoyable nonetheless. I noticed that the deep grooves in her sporty sneakers collected a fair amount of lebensplasm from walking through this newly formed moon chasm. Sometimes I like to enjoy it unrefined. Frivolous, I know. I cannot wait to mine this newly found section."

"That would explain the moon muck," said Shane.

"You're mining lebensplasm?" Ben asked. "What for?"

"So he can drain the moon—the original monster and the source of all the Earth's lebensplasm," said Director Z.

"The moon's a monster?" I asked.

But Director Z continued, talking directly at the hooded figure.

"Then, once you've destroyed the moon, you'll take all the pendants to solidify your hold over the Earth and all its inhabitants. Isn't that true, Cordoba?"

"Don't make me tell you again, you powerless fool, Cordoba is dead. I am Zorflogg! And, yes, the world shall be MINE."

He grabbed Director Z by his neck and lifted his head up into the ceiling of the moon cave, crunching his head against moon rock.

"I don't believe it," said Director Z, spitting his words out through Zorflogg's grip. "You were a terrible Director—you couldn't even control your Retirement Home! How dare you think you could control the Earth? Especially in your corrupt state—drunk off the power of lebensplasm."

"You were a Director?" I asked. "A Director who drank monster juice?"

"Yes, he was the first and only half-human, half-monster Director," Director Z said, his face turning red as he tried to pull the massive gloved hands off his throat. "But he grew corrupt, trying and failing to use the monsters under his charge to take over the world. He grew his strength by ingesting monster juice—"

"Oh, now you're calling it monster juice?" laughed Zorflogg. "What a delightful little joke for the kids."

". . . too much monster juice for his human side to handle," Director Z continued. "For a human to drink monster juice more than once, though it would give him much strength, would most certainly be fatal. The overdose of juice literally melted both parts together—the rotten, dead human side with the evil, monstrous monster side—and now he must drink monster juice to survive. That is his real reason for draining the moon.

How foolish the other Directors and I were to banish him to space. We never thought he could unlock the secret of the moon."

"Silence, you fool!" yelled Zorflogg, and he flung Director Z down onto the ground. "It is true that at first, I merely needed the monster juice for me, to keep myself alive. But now I see that it is the key to a new monsterdom on Earth. I would kill you if it were not for the knowledge that you possess. No, I won't make the same mistake that brainless mummy almost made. Guards! Take him back to my throne room! Prepare the zapeel! We must work even harder now that my precious splurtsar has perished."

Two guards stepped forward to grab Director Z.

"Don't touch him!" yelled Gordon, and he jumped forward to protect Director Z. He was blocked with a great ZAPPPPP!

And he flew onto the ground.

"Gordon!" I yelled.

Shane got into a karate pose.

"We can't fight them!" I said, pushing Shane back. Then I added in a whisper, "Not now. Not yet."

As the guards dragged Z away, he gave me a little wink and a smile.

"What Chris says is true," said Zorflogg. "No one can fight my new breed. Not without facing certain death."

We helped Gordon to his feet and brushed the moondust off his shoulders.

"New breed?" mumbled Gordon. "What new breed?"

"Since the beginning of time, the world has always had Retirement Homes for monsters," said Zorflogg. "When enough people forget about the monsters that once frightened them, they lose their power. With the invention of movies and the Internet, everyone was convinced that monsters were just made up. Creations. They just couldn't exist. But we were real—and we were losing our powers. Some had become so weak that they were withering away into nothingness. Monsterdom would soon fall."

"If you're so concerned about monsterdom, then why are you trying to destroy it?" I asked.

"Because the monsters of old proved to me they are too weak. I tried to get the old monsters under my direction to rise up and control the Earth as was our birthright. But they failed me. And I'm glad they failed me. When your Director and the other Directors banished me to space, it was here, on the moon, that I realized monsterdom needed a fresh start, with a new breed, and a new set of rules."

"What makes you think you'll be able to take over the world?" asked Nabila.

"Thanks to the Tentacled Heads of Andromeda," said Zorflogg, "I have power beyond my wildest dreams."

"The tentacled heads of what now?" asked Gordon.

Zorflogg turned swiftly to Gordon, "Oh, you're familiar with them, most certainly. They've already dined on one of your friends."

Zorflogg clapped his hands, and the unmistakable sound of wet burps echoed down the tunnel. But they were different somehow. The smell of vurp filled the room.

"Oh man," said Ben. "If that's what I smelled like on the ship, I'm so sorry."

"Nope . . . nope," coughed Shane. "This is so much worse."

A dozen of them entered the cave, floating inside the moon just as they had in zero gravity. We tried to dodge them as they floated past, but their writhing tentacles reached out and with a POP POP POP left little red marks on our cheeks.

They surrounded Zorflogg, and he greeted them. "Oh, my dear, dear friends!" he said. Their tentacles gently stroked him, and he purred like a cat.

"When I saw them here, on the moon," he said, "I knew I had found the perfect creature. They were the only beings I had ever seen capable of absorbing lebensplasm and depositing it back. They regurgitated *pure* lebensplasm. I provoked them, feeding off the delicious cloud of lebensplasm they attacked me with, and soon they were tamed, and their DNA is now in every one of my creations. They began to call me 'Zorflogg' in their native tongue, and since they have shown me my new, true power, I knew I must take the new, true name they gave me."

"But what does the moon have to do with this?" asked Nabila.

"Once the moon falls, I'll have the Earth in my grasp, and my new breed will rule!" Zorflogg said.

"Wait," said Shane. "If the moon falls, won't it crash into the Earth and obliterate everyone there?"

"Young fool, I don't actually mean that it will fall." Zorflogg was perturbed. "I meant I would defeat it. You know . . . FALL. In that sense."

"Well, I for one think you should have been more specific," said Shane.

"SILENCE!" yelled Zorflogg.

"Yeah, silence, dude," Ben said, shuddering.

"I will give you one chance, and once chance only, to join me," said Zorflogg. "You all seem so fresh, so smart. You made it all the way up to the moon, and I'm sure that those worthless monsters didn't help you. It would be a pity to have to enslave you along with those old fossils. Join me! Join me in my laboratory and let me make you the first humans to carry the Andromedan gene. When the time comes to take over the Earth, you can convince your fellow humans to make the same choice."

I stepped up to Zorflogg defiantly. "Absolutely not!" I yelled.

My friends stepped behind me. "No way!" they said.

"Well, that is a deeply unfortunate choice on your part. For I won't stop until I change the fate of monsterdom forever."

"I'd like to see you try!" yelled Gordon.

"Instead of accepting my invitation, you and your irrelevant monster friends will see nothing but the deepest, darkest recesses of the moon for the rest of your days," Zorflogg announced. "You shall be my slaves, forced to work an eternity in my mines, which are staffed by all my failed creations, doomed to crush and purify moon rocks into monster juice."

Zorflogg clapped his hands, and guards came forward to grab my friends and drag them away.

"Where are they taking them?" I asked.

"To the mines, where their eternal work begins," he said. "And you, too, shall join them. But first there is something of mine you possess, and I shall take it from you."

His hand, cold even through the thick black gloves he wore, wrapped around my wrist, and he dragged me deeper into the moon.

Doomed!

"Chris, I would ask you to consider joining me," said Zorflogg, his voice echoing around his throne room. "I've heard much from Murray about you and the way you almost foiled his plan. Well done."

As Zorflogg headed to the massive throne, chiseled out of moon rock, I could see that he wasn't walking so much as floating. He folded the bottom half of his robes, spun around, and came to a rest on the seat. The throne began to glow the same green as the globes of light we had seen in the tunnel.

"The way I see it, you have two choices," said Zorflogg from the comfort of his chair. "Join me as a top-ranking lieutenant and assist me in taking over your pitiful world. I also know from Murray your love for space. I'm quite sorry to ruin your moon trip, but I could certainly, once all of the taking-over-the-world business is done, promise that my friends from Andromeda would take you on a tour of their home galaxy."

"What's my second choice?" I asked.

"Slavery and death."

"That sounds fine to me," I said, though it didn't sound fine at all. It actually sounded quite terrible.

Zorflogg sighed from his throne and floated over to me once again. His cold hand lay over the pendant that I wore under my shirt.

"Then again," hissed Zorflogg, his sour breath pouring all over my face, "perhaps you aren't as smart as I thought. You did, after all, bring this pendant directly to me."

He reached into my shirt through my collar, and I shivered.

With a quick snap, he pulled the pendant off and held it up in the light.

"Wait a minute . . . ," he growled, tilting it so that the light from the giant globe that hung in the center of the throne room shone through it.

"Is there a problem?" I asked.

"There most certainly is," yelled Zorflogg, "This is another *fake*! But how? It must be on the ship. There is absolutely no way you could have made it to the moon without its power driving the monsters along."

"You are correct," I said. "There is absolutely no way I could have gotten the monsters to do what I needed them to do without the power of the pendant. But once we were in the moon's orbit, I jettisoned the pendant into deep space. It nearly cost us our lives, because I certainly could have used the power during the landing. But now it's out there in space. Better get your little Andromedan doggies to go fetch! Now who's the fool?"

"How DARE you!" he yelled. "To the mines with you! Do my bidding, slave!"

With two powerful claps, he summoned two powerful guards, who dragged me out of the room.

We stood in a massive cave deep in the moon, crude tools in our hands. We awaited our "trainer," who would give us instruction on the kind of work we would be doing until the end of our days.

"But I saw you command the monsters *after* we got off the ship," whispered Shane. "So I know you still have the pendant."

"Well, you know that, and I know that, but thank goodness, Zorflogg doesn't know that," I replied.

"How'd you do it?" asked Gordon. "You know . . . convince him."

"I just insulted him," I said. "I knew that if I made him feel stupid, he would be too angry to see that I was actually tricking him."

"Good tactic," said Nabila. "So, where is it?"

"Somewhere safe," I said. "Somewhere I hope Zorflogg doesn't think to look. I've already told you all too much. It puts you in danger."

My friends looked at me, waiting for me to tell them where I had hidden it, but it was the one secret I had to keep deep inside myself.

The cave we were in was so large that there was barely any echo. Through the eerie silence, a troop of guards hauled in all the monsters who had been pulled off the ship.

The monsters were lined up behind us, ready for what we were told would be "training." Around us, in fields of boulders, strange creatures tapped away at the moon rocks with different odd-looking instruments. Occasionally, someone (or rather, something) would roll up with a wheelbarrow to cart off the moon rocks to a massive machine that crushed them. Everyone looked exhausted and miserable.

"Is that Murrayhotep?" asked Shane. He pointed behind a small mound of moon rock on the other side of the massive cave. Two small furry and fanged creatures were working at the moon rock, chipping away at it slowly. Another creature that looked like an anteater with wings waddled over to the fallen moon rock to snorf it up.

"I think so . . . ," I said.

Murrayhotep pulled out a small glass vial of green, sinister-looking fluid.

"Monster juice," I said. "It must be the daily ration that Zorflogg gives him for having betrayed us."

Murrayhotep drank the bottle down greedily, his red tongue flitting around inside the bottle to lick up every last bit.

"Ew," said Nabila.

Murrayhotep got up, wiped off some moondust, and straightened his bandages. He started to walk toward us, but then suddenly, with a smack of his lips, walked back and crouched behind the rocks once more.

"He's going to have another bottle!" Gordon said. "That greedy old fart."

"Maybe he needs a little extra after the splurtsar attack?" Shane wondered.

We watched as Murrayhotep practically inhaled the second bottle.

"No, I think he's just . . . ," I started.

"Addicted," Ben finished. "Now, quiet, he's walking right for us."

Murray walked toward us, but not in a completely straight line. He sort of zigged and zagged.

He almost stumbled when he stopped in front of us.

"I think he acts even older with the monster juice," Gordon said, snickering.

Murray straightened up right away, his eyes going from unfocused to focused in a snap.

"Keep your trap shut, you sssniveling little sssnot," he said.

With that, Murray pulled a huge whip out from under his bandages and held it high.

"He's still slurring his words," Nabila whispered to Ben.

"You too, Nabila!" snapped Murray. "This issssn't a game. You're a slave in a moon mine! I'm your bossssss now. And don't ssschtink I forgot about that time you unraveled my wrappingssss!"

He brought the whip up over his head, and I instinctively jumped in front of Nabila, waiting for the blow.

Twenty-Three

"I've been wanting to do this for a long time," growled Murrayhotep.

I crouched and cowered, waiting for the whip to come snapping down on me.

"Let's not be too hasty, Mister Mummy."

"Back off, Twenty-Three!"

"Huh?" I said, and turned around. A small green creature stood between Murray and me. The creature was toddler-size, and looked sort of like a lizard crossed with a tabby cat. Stripes of fur crisscrossed his scaly body.

"Zorflogg said to train these humans in the next three hours, and that's what I intend to do," the small green creature said. "I think that's what you should help me do, as well—if I were you, I'd want to do exactly what Zorflogg said. You're already on his bad side after the stunt you pulled with the splurtsar."

Murray looked at the small creature for a moment longer and then lowered his whip.

"You heard Zorflogg," Murray said. "Three hours! Better get to crackin'!"

Murray snapped the whip right at the small green creature's feet.

"Ha-ha-ha!" The small green creature laughed. "Get to crackin'. I get it, I get it . . ."

Murray headed off, and the small green creature stepped in front of us and raised his hands to get everyone's attention.

"Hello?" he said. "Hello, all! My name is Twenty-Three, and I'll be training you on the proper procedure for the extraction and refinement of lebensplasm from moon rock."

A few of the monsters moaned, "Hello, Twenty-Three."

"Now, most of the creatures I train have to start from scratch since they were only recently created by Master Zorflogg," Twenty-Three continued. "But I'm sure you guys bring a little more to the table. Everyone knows what a moon rock is, correct?"

There was a general rumble of "yes," "yeah," and

"um, I think so" from the crowd.

"Okay, great!" said Twenty-Three. "And I'm sure everyone knows what a pickax is, correct?"

Again came moans of "yes" from the crowd.

"Wonderful," said Twenty-Three. "Let's get started."

Twenty-Three gave us the entire rundown of the process behind collecting and processing moon rock: breaking it into the right-size pieces, collecting it for the crushing machine, having it crushed and then boiled into the proper concentration. He showed us how to use pickaxes, tongs for the sharper pieces of rock, and our masks, which were needed for the extrafine moondust.

"Okay, well, you were a really great group, and I really appreciate that you paid attention to everything I had to say today," said Twenty-Three at the end of his training. "Does anyone have any questions?"

"Yeah," Gordon whispered to me. "Why is he so happy?"

"I think he's the only guy more excited than Chris to be on the moon," Shane whispered back.

The crowd of monsters started shuffling away to different parts of the cave.

"You know how much I wanted to surround myself with amazing moon rock," I whispered. "But not like this . . ."

"Did you have a question, guys?" Twenty-Three asked, walking over to us. "If not, you should probably get to work. Zorflogg isn't a big fan of idle chatter. He runs a professional moon, that guy."

He flashed us a big, lizardy smile.

"Okay, I've got one," said Nabila. "Where does all the moon rock go once it's crushed? You know, for refining?"

"Oh, wonderful question, earthling," replied Twenty-Three. He rubbed his scaly hands together, so excited to answer the question. "The crushed moon rock is vacuumed into processing vats in the next cave over. Very high security over there—even I'm not allowed. And I don't blame them—I would totally sneak a drink of the high-powered stuff."

"Why is your name Twenty-Three?" I asked.

"That's sort of a long story," said Twenty-Three, looking around for Murrayhotep or any of Zorflogg's other guards. "Are you guys familiar with the sangala creatures Zorflogg created?"

"Yes," Nabila said. "We were plagued by them just before we took off for the moon. Disgusting things. Terrible things."

"Well, I am one," said Twenty-Three.

"What?" Nabila asked. "Oh, I'm so sorry. If I had known . . . I mean, you don't look like a sangala."

"That's okay," said Twenty-Three. "I don't like the final versions, either. You see, I was version twenty-three of the sangala, which is how I got my name."

"Version twenty-three?" asked Shane. "What do you mean?"

"It's hard work perfecting the DNA splicing and biology of creating new creatures," said Twenty-Three. "Some of Zorflogg's creations were relatively easy to make. Sussuroblats were a breeze. And the membranium already existed—Zorflogg just needed to modify them slightly. I've heard rumors that the scientists have even made the skin better since then. The sangala, however, was a tough creature to make. They had to look like cats or dogs as they absorbed monster juice, all the while hiding a reptilian gene that could explode forth at any moment. It took Zorflogg twenty-four tries to get the sangala right. I was the twenty-third try, and the first to result in a living creature."

"Oh right," said Shane. "Yeah, I can see how you could be a sangala now. The mix of cat and lizard. The sharp teeth. Except, you're so nice. And so smart."

"Exactly," said Twenty-Three. "Which is why I was rejected. Aside from the fact that the lizard part of me was already showing, Zorflogg couldn't send hundreds of friendly creatures out to collect monster juice—the worst damage I could do was talk the old monsters to death with intelligent-but-boring conversation. So he kept me on the moon, doomed for all eternity to work the mines, just like you guys. And just like all the other rejected creations."

"So why are you still so happy?" asked Gordon.

"I guess it's just in my nature," replied Twenty-Three. "I must have the happy gene in my DNA. Plus, I'm a trainer, not a laborer. And I get all sorts of tasty grubs to eat from Zorflogg. I mix them with cat treats. Yum!"

"Yeah, that sounds delicious," said Ben with a burp.

"But I guess I'm okay because I know that this is all going to end soon," said Twenty-Three.

"What do you mean?" I asked.

"Well, the mines won't be open much longer," said Twenty-Three. "The Andromedans have always been here, hiding on the dark side of the moon, attracted by its lebensplasm. It gives them energy, but they could never figure out how to drain the moon's lebensplasm directly. Now Zorflogg is working on figuring it out for them. And when that happens, then it's all over—SLURP!—and done . . . and then I hope to finally visit Earth."

"Yeah," said Gordon, "it will be great to see all the screaming and explosions and violence and destruction when Zorflogg's minions take over the world. Just peachy."

"Well," said Twenty-Three, slapping Gordon on the back of the leg, "I, for one, will be happy for the change. All right, guys, better get to work. It was great talking with you!"

"I guess he really does have the happy gene," I said. "Totally creepy."

"Well, at least we made a friend," said Shane. "Someone to help us out. Someone to show us the ropes and teach us things. Now we know what Zorflogg meant by 'when the moon falls' . . ."

"I, for one, hope that we won't be here long enough to need help," I said. "We've got to think of a way out of this situation."

Twenty-Three walked away and Murrayhotep rushed up to us, whip raised high.

"Get moving, you worms," Murrayhotep said. "Or this time, you will taste my whip!"

Moon-Mine Blues

Four hours later, it felt like we had been on the moon for a hundred years.

"Maybe Twenty-Three was right," Shane huffed. "We should be happy that we won't have to do this forever. Let's hope Zorflogg teaches the Andromedans to drink monster juice soon."

"And then what?" asked Nabila. "We'll be doomed to do something else terrible for all of eternity. Like crush poor old monsters into pulp. At least Ben is finally getting in shape. I've been trying everything I can to get him to build a little muscle mass."

"Aw, shucks," Ben said, blushing and crushing another rock proudly. "That makes this whole doomed-to-die-on-the-moon thing worth it."

"You know, it wouldn't be too bad to have a little Andromedan DNA," Gordon said, chipping away at the moon rock. "I mean, I was a sussuroblat for a while, and it wasn't too terrible. I certainly didn't have to mine moon rock all day long."

"No way," I said, bringing my pick down on the next rock with a SHCRACK. "We can't give up. Plus, I don't think the offer is on the table anymore. Zorflogg is too mad with me after I rubbed in the fake pendant."

Murrayhotep stood up from the outcropping of moon rock he was sitting on and yelled, "Less talking, more mining."

A knee-high creature pulling a wagon approached to collect our stones. His skin was gray and wrinkled like an elephant's, but he had the pink nose of a pig. Every time he snorfed, a little bit of black goo sprayed out.

"A failed splurtsar," I said, and patted him on the head. "Which number are you? Do you have the happy gene?"

The little guy just snorfed again and moved along.

Once we had filled the wagon with rocks, I looked up to see that Murrayhotep had left his post.

"He's off to drink another bottle!" I said, dropping behind the mound of moon boulders I was working on. "Guys, gather around, quick!"

My friends dropped their pickaxes and rushed over.

"I've been brewing up a crazy idea," I said. "But I think it's the only way to get out of here."

"What is it?" Shane asked.

"We drink the monster juice," I replied.

Everyone stared at me like I had an arm growing out of my head.

"We drink the *what* now?" asked Gordon.

"The monster juice," I said confidently. "We drink the monster juice."

"But how?" Nabila asked. "You heard Twenty-Three: The refined monster juice is in another heavily guarded cave."

Gordon shook his head. "Forget 'how,' let's talk about why. This doesn't sound like the best idea."

"Not to mention," said Ben, making a retching sound, "how am I going to keep it down?"

"This is crazy," said Nabila. "Director Z said that it could kill us."

Gordon nodded in agreement.

"I like crazy," said Shane. "Plus, Director Z only said that using it more than once could kill us. Which makes me think that using it once would be okay. Tell us more, Chris."

I looked up to make sure Murrayhotep wasn't on the way back from his juice break.

"This is what I'm thinking," I said. "We're young humans, and won't need to drink too much monster juice to feel an effect. We could share one of Murrayhotep's bottles."

"What do you think it will do to us?" Ben asked.

"I hope it transforms me into a werewolf," said Shane. "I think I'd make an awesome werewolf. Karatewerewolf!"

"I have no idea," I replied. "But I'm sure it will make us powerful. Powerful enough to fight through whatever comes our way."

"Will we be invincible?" asked Nabila.

"I don't know," I said. "I just know we'll be more powerful than we are now. Hopefully powerful enough to fight our way into the secure section that contains all the pure monster juice. Then we let all our monsters feast on the supply, destroy Zorflogg, and get the heck off the moon."

"What if it doesn't work?" asked Gordon. "What if it just makes us sick? What if it works differently for kids? What if we d—"

"Look, I'm not going to force anyone to do it who doesn't want to do it," I said. "I'd love to just have the monsters drink the monster juice, but they need too much, and we might not have enough time to hatch a plan like that. Does anyone else have a better idea?"

"I'm in," said Shane.

"Me too, I guess," said Ben, who retched again.

"I can't think of anything better," said Nabila.

"Okay," said Gordon. "What do we need to do?"

"We need to create a distraction," I said. "Something that will keep Murrayhotep so busy that he won't notice when we snag a bottle of monster juice from his wrappings."

"Ooooh," said Shane. "I think I've got a good one. We need to talk to the werewolves."

"You and the werewolves! How are they going to help?" I asked. "They can't howl anymore. They've got muzzles when they're in dog form."

"You keep talking and I'll put a muzzle on *you*!" said Murrayhotep, who was back on his outcropping of rocks, watching us.

"We'll have to figure this out later," I whispered. "You *know* he's gonna take another break."

"Let's hope he doesn't drink all of it," Ben said.

"Shut it!" yelled Murrayhotep. "Get to work!"

"I feel bad for Frederick," said Shane. "He has no idea, does he?"

"No idea whatsoever," I replied, perfectly cracking into a moon rock with my pick. "Hey, I'm getting pretty good at this."

"We couldn't risk letting Frederick know the plan," said Nabila. "He might not have gone along with—"

"Shhhh!" said Ben. "It's Murrayhotep!"

Murrayhotep walked up to Gordon, who was slamming a large rock down onto a smaller one.

"Don't do it like that, you dimwit!" growled Murrayhotep. "You've got to use your pick, or all the juice crystals will be ruined."

"Man, I can smell the monster juice on his breath all the way over here," Ben whispered to me.

"You most certainly can," said Murrayhotep, quickly turning toward Ben. "And all that delicious lebensplasm has given me sharp senses—including my sense of hearing. So keep your lips sealed, or I'll come over there and sew them shut."

Behind Murrayhotep, Pietro and Howie started to rub their ragged, overgrown sideburns swiftly.

Knowing that Murrayhotep was listening closely, I looked at my friends and squinted, hoping they knew I was saying "get ready!"

Frederick was busily crushing rock with his bare hands, sending showers of monster-juice crystals everywhere. (Murrayhotep would not be pleased.)

The werewolves crept up on him from behind, and . . .

ZAAAAPP!

"Gaaah!" screamed Frederick.

The werewolves began rubbing their muttonchops again. Howie took off his shirt, exposing his hairy back.

Pietro rubbed Howie's back furiously, and sparks jumped off the hair that stood up on the top of the werewolves' heads.

"Stop it, guys," said Frederick. "Please don't."

Murrayhotep turned his attention away from Ben and toward the giggling werewolves.

"Knock it off!" yelled Murrayhotep.

But it was too late.

"Here I come," yelled Pietro. "I'm comin' ta getcha!"

ZAAAAAAAAAAPPPPPPPP!

Frederick shot up so high that his head got stuck in a crevice in the ceiling of the moon cave.

Murrayhotep ran to grab the werewolves, but they transformed into muzzled wolves and ran around—and in between—his legs.

"Okay," I said. "Now's my chance. Get ready! We're going to have to guzzle it down quickly."

I ran up to Murrayhotep, who was half bent over, trying to stop the werewolves. I saw two bottles sticking out of the wrappings on either side of his butt. I snatched them both and ran back to my friends.

"Hurry!" I said.

I passed Shane one bottle and pulled the cork out of the other.

GULP!

"Ugh," I said while passing it to Ben. "I feel like spiders are crawling around in my stomach."

"You didn't have to tell me that," yelled Ben, and he GULPED. He retched almost immediately.

"Hold it in," yelled Gordon, and he GULPED.

I looked over to see if Shane and Nabila had finished their bottle.

That's when I heard Murrayhotep yell, "What do you think you're doing?"

Monster Juice Madness

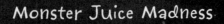

Now, as a kid, my instinct would have been to cower in front of Murrayhotep in fear, saying, "Sorry, sorry, sorry."

But I wasn't just a kid anymore.

Instead of opening my mouth to say sorry, I opened a mouth full of fangs and let out a "BRWAAAAARRRGH!"

Murrayhotep's eyes bugged out of his head. He backed off, tripping over a moon rock, and knocked himself out.

I panted, feeling the power of the monster juice coursing through my veins. I looked over at the others. Ben had turned a shade of green, but not because he was sick.

"I've got webbed hands," Ben said, staring at the new green flesh between his fingers. "Swamp creature." He reached up to feel his gills.

"Aw, fang it!" Shane said. "I mean, I really wanted werewolf, but vampire feels pretty good." He licked his teeth. "I vant to suck your blooood."

"Uggghhh," said Nabila. "Urrggh."

"Zombie?" asked Ben.

"She'll eventually learn how to talk," said Shane.

Nabila turned to him with a blank expression. She cocked her head and said, "Brains?"

"See?" said Shane.

"Uggghhh," said Gordon. He was crumpled up on the floor.

"Looks like Gordon got zombie, too," Ben said.

"Noooo," Gordon said. "It made me so sick. Ugh, my stomach."

I padded over to Gordon and pushed my muzzle into his side to try to get him to roll over.

"Chris," said Gordon, still clutching his stomach, "get this dog off me."

I was about to ask, "What dog?" when I realized he was talking about me.

I was a werewolf.

"AROOOOOOO!" I howled. It felt amazing.

The cave shook, and Frederick fell out of the ceiling.

"Thanks," he moaned.

"Awesome!" yelled Shane.

Murrayhotep was awoken from his stupor, and popped his head up in disbelief, staring at us again.

The other slaves and their guards took notice, and once the shaking stopped, they all stared at us in silence, wondering what was going to happen next.

Nabila took one look at Murrayhotep and bolted toward him, her arms outstretched, drooling, her glasses tilted awkwardly on her nose.

"Braaaaaaaiins," she yelled.

"Okay, forget what I said on the spaceship, now *that's* the fastest zombie I've ever seen," said Shane.

"Guuaaaaaaaarrds," yelled Murrayhotep, and he scrambled up to run.

I barked at Shane, whose job it was to relay the plan.

"Residents," he yelled, his vampire voice carrying through the cave. "We're going to take the secure section, that contains the pure monster juice—"

I barked at Shane again.

"I mean the pure lebensplasm," he continued. "Those who are not residents, help us and you will be accepted into our monstrous ranks. We will not hesitate to destroy you if you stand in our way."

All the slaves, our old friends and our new friends, threw their tools to the side and rushed to the doors that led to the secure monster-juice holding area. We rushed to join them as they pounded on the doors.

Before we could even get our footing, the huge iron doors blasted open. Guards in black hooded capes poured in on foot. Above . . .

"Andromedans!" Ben yelled.

Instinctively, I jumped up and, with my powerful werewolf jaws, grabbed the tentacles of one of the Andromedans. The sound of the crunch sent excitement through my furry body. I swallowed a bit of the disgusting blood and enjoyed the feeling. I flailed my head around to pull the Andromedan down onto the dirty moon-rock floor. It hit with a thud, sending a ripple through its disgustingly swollen skin. The zombies, still angered by the loss of their friend, approached it and began ripping into the bulbous head.

I took down another and another. My muzzle was wet with green Andromedan blood, and I licked my lips, panting with hunger and excitement.

Shane turned into a vampire bat and flew directly into the Andromedans' heads, breaking the huge, zit-like bulges on the top and spraying the monsters below with delicious juices. Not a lot, but enough to get them excited. Zombies swiped. Vampires snarled. One banshee screamed at just the right volume and pitch, and one of the Andromedans exploded, sending a waterfall of monster juice down.

"Waaaahoooo," screeched Bat Shane, tickling my sensitive werewolf ears.

Ben and Nabila were swiping away at the guards, who were charging in two by two. Ben was using his webbed hands to deflect electric charges with ease, and his scaly skin was protecting him from the massive axes, and occasional bites from Nabila, who was chomping in every direction.

I could see giant tanks of monster juice through the doors. We pushed ever closer, the monsters getting excited to see the bounty ahead.

"Make a push for it!" yelled Ben. "Come on, everyone. Once we get into that room, you'll be bathing in monster juice."

"Not quite so fast," yelled Zorflogg as he flew through the doors with dozens more Andromedans.

Shane landed next to me and POPPED back into his human form.

"Whew," he said. "Flying takes it out of me, I gotta say."

I barked in the direction of Zorflogg.

"Oh, I didn't see you come in, Mr. Zorflogg," said Shane.

Even Nabila knew that was a brain she was incapable of chewing on. We stood face-to-face with Zorflogg and his floating heads. Nobody knew who was going to make the first move.

The cave was once again silent. Then, from the corner, Gordon said, "Mommy, I want to go home. I ate too many corn dogs and I think I'm going to throw up."

I had forgotten about Gordon.

Zorflogg pointed to our sad, sick friend and commanded, "Destroy him!"

The Andromedans flew toward Gordon, and we followed as quickly as we could, Shane once again frantically biting and scratching their faces to slow them down.

But there were too many.

As we reached Gordon, I jumped up to grab tentacle after tentacle. Shane, Ben, and Nabila formed a protective circle around Gordon, pushing back any guard that approached, while helping me with the Andromedans.

Shane jumped up and sank his teeth into one of the Andromedans. A SCHLUCKING sound could be heard as he drained it dry.

"Stop!" Nabila yelled at Shane. "You can't drink monster juice a second time! You'll die!"

I called to Shane to stop, but all that came out was a loud howl.

Everyone turned to watch as Shane drained the Andromedan of a giant mouthful of monster juice.

His eyes grew wide and his head shook briefly before he turned to us and smiled.

"Man, that was refreshing!" he said.

"Huh," Ben said, struggling with a tentacle. "Maybe it didn't harm him because he's in monster mode. I'm still not going to risk a second sip."

We continued to push off the attack as best as we could, and it was all going very well, until the Andromedans started vurping.

"I'm starting to feel really light-headed," said Shane.

"They're starting to absorb our monster juice!" I yelled, suddenly in human form once again.

"Thank goodness I can talk again," said Nabila. "Wait, I can talk again! Did I eat any brains? Please tell me I didn't eat any brains!"

"Forget about your brains," I yelled. "Everyone, we have to push harder or we're done for!"

But the other monsters were weakened by the vurping and started falling over and flailing about, like roaches after a hit of Raid.

BURP BLIP BLURP.

The Andromedans kept burping their acidic vurps.

"Oh gross," said Gordon. "The burping is making me totally sick."

"Maybe *you* should try burping," said Ben. "That's always helped me."

Gordon continued to writhe in agony while trying to force a belch out of himself. The harder he pushed, the more his body convulsed. His stomach started pulsating madly. I was sure that an alien would pop out at any second. The shaking got worse as the throbbing mass moved from his stomach and started working its way up toward his mouth.

"Watch out!" Shane yelled as he covered his face. "Something's coming out, and I bet it's going to be grossmazing."

Gordon's eyes opened wide as his whole body lifted off the cave floor. His mouth flew open wider than any mouth should be able to. That's when it happened.

BLUUUUUUUUUUUUUUUUUUUUURPUH!

From somewhere deep inside Gordon came the most moon-shaking, neighbor-waking burp known to mankind . . . or moonkind. I was pretty sure that, despite the fact that it was 250,000 miles away, people could hear it on Earth. It was that epic.

And it stank worse than anything imaginable. Like rotten eggs on a summer day times a million.

A tunnel shook open behind us. And for a moment, the Andromedans pulled back. Gordon's burp made them too stunned to vurp anymore.

"Go, hurry," Shane commanded, covering his nose and moving monsters quickly through the newly formed crack and into the cave beyond.

We held our ground at the beginning, but were soon failing.

"We just have to retreat!" I yelled.

Ben and Nabila followed the monsters. Gordon

swayed in front of the Andromedans, relieved and stunned from his burp.

BLURP BURRRP BRAAAP.

"Gordon," I yelled, rushing up to him. "We have to go! We've got to get into the new cave as quickly as we can. The Andromedans have recovered!"

Shane and I each put a shoulder under Gordon's arms and rushed away from the Andromedans into the narrow passage to the next cave.

"Gah!" Shane yelled as an Andromedan tentacle snagged his leg.

"Shane!" I yelled. "SHANE!" I was able to grab his arm, but I had to drop Gordon to do it. He fell to the floor with an OOOOOOF.

I used both hands to pull Shane toward me, but my grip was slipping.

BLURP BURRRP BRAAAP.

A green cloud settled itself around my head. It smelled like a thousand babies had spit up dog barf all over my face.

"Gordon," I growled, the last of my werewolf strength leaving me. "Go get somebody to help. I can't hold on much longer. The vurps! I'm getting so weak. I'm not even a werewolf anymore!"

I looked back into the cave, and yelled, "HELP!"

Gordon slowly made his way to his feet, clawing at moon rock to rise and face the Andromedans.

"It's time to fight burps with burps," sputtered Gordon. "Let's do this."

He sucked in the air like a huge vacuum, rumbling and vibrating as he did it. The moon rock around us trembled as he cleared the air of all of the vurp. His eyes watered as he inhaled and inhaled, his face turning blue, a great PPPPPPRRRRUUUUBBBB sound resonating from his body.

The Andromedans began to retreat. They dropped Shane, and he landed directly on top of me. I tried to push him off.

"Wait, we might want to stay down," he said. "This is going to be awesome."

For a few seconds there was complete silence. From deep in the cave, a witch yelled, "What's going on?"

I looked up at Gordon. He shook in place, his eyes bugging. He slowly opened his mouth.

BRRRRRAAAAAAAAAPPPPPPGGGGLLLLL.

The green spew of the Andromedans was blown back into their faces.

GGGGGGGGLLLLLLAAAAARRRRRP.

Gordon kept going. The Andomedans screeched terribly as they flew backward into the cave.

PPPPPPPRRRRRRUUUUUPPPP.

Gordon stopped for a second, took in one last quick breath, and—

BURP!

—sent one last insanely loud thunderclap of a burp through the bodies of the Andromedans.

Every single Andromedan head exploded into a fiery, fleshy, chunky shower of green, green, and more green.

"Yeah!" I screamed.

But before I could high-five Gordon, the passageway crumbled around us.

Out of the Frying Pan . . .

Gordon lunged forward and scooped up Shane and me at the same time.

"Whoa," yelled Shane, bear-hugging me to keep from falling out of Gordon's arms.

Gordon turned around in a snap and ran like a crazy but strong chicken, dodging huge white boulders as they came tumbling down.

"Go, Gordon, go!" I yelled.

Gordon jumped out of the passageway just as the ceiling caved in.

Ben and Nabila, along with all the monsters, screamed and cheered as Gordon laid Shane and me on the floor.

Even the small failed splurtsar squeed with delight, a bit of black nectar spraying itself all over Gil's scaly butt.

Gordon took a bow and passed out.

"He's going to need quite a nap," said Twenty-Three.

"Twenty-Three!" Shane yelled, standing up. "Dude, you made it!"

"Yes," said Twenty-Three. "And you'll be happy to know that I'm not the only one."

Twenty-Three gestured over to a crowd of monsters, which parted to reveal . . .

"Director Z!" yelled Ben, and he waved with his still-webbed hand.

Director Z waved weakly, and then his head drooped onto his chest. He swayed like a zombie.

"He's still in shock from the last 'treatment' Zorflogg gave him," Twenty-Three said. "But he should be fine. I saw him in the High Security area and led him out when nobody was looking."

"Awesome!" said Shane. "But what'd they do to him?"

"Zorflogg supercharged his—"

Twenty-Three was cut off by screams.

A tall two-legged creature with goat's hooves and the beak of a hawk screeched terribly as it ran up to all of us. It flapped its tentacles with fear.

"Does anyone speak hawkish?" Twenty-Three

asked. "What's wrong, Glebdorf? Calm down and use your words."

"Sector 78!" screeched the bird/squid/goat/human. "Sector 78!"

"Sector 78?" asked Nabila.

"Oh no!" said Twenty-Three, smacking his lizard face with his claw/paw. "I should have known. We're in the supply room of Sector 78. I *knew* this looked familiar."

"Where are the supplies?" I asked. "And what's the big deal about Sector 78?"

A great roar echoed through the cave.

"Sector 78 is the last laboratory Zorflogg ran, but it was overrun by the creatures he created. Zorflog sealed it—and the old lebensplasm mine—off, but we dug so close to it with the new mines that when your friend burped, he reopened it!"

"What sort of creatures are we talking about here?" asked Ben.

"Well, that one, for instance!" said Twenty-Three, pointing at the front of the supply room.

A massive woolly creature lumbered into our cave. Its dirty coat was ragged and in some places bloodied.

"He looks really hungry," I said.

It opened its mouth and roared.

Two more of the massive creatures appeared.

"Wow, this cave felt pretty roomy until those guys got here," said Shane.

I knew we had to attack before they did, or when they charged, they'd scatter us all over the room and would have control.

"Zombies!" I yelled. "Grab Director Z and bring him over next to Gordon. Protect them both!

"Everyone else," I said, "chaaaaaaarge!"

"Gaaaaaaaaaaa!" the monsters from Gallow Manor cried.

The rejected monsters looked confused and scared, but with a quick "c'mon, guys" from Twenty-Three, they fell in line with us. In fact, the first in front of all of us was the small rejected splurtsar.

He ran up to the woolly creatures, and with a great achoo, snorfed a little bit of black nectar into the eyes of one of them. He then jumped up and chomped it with his piggly little mouth, holding on tight.

"ARRRRRGGGGH!"

The others charged. A giant zombie frog with the head of a battering ram jumped into a second woolly creature and knocked him over with a loud OOOOOOF!

The third was suddenly scared and tried to turn around to run.

But it was too late.

The monsters reached the three woolly creatures, and in a flash of fur and flesh, all that was left was a woolly pile of bones and a great circle of blood. Vampires picked meat out of their teeth. Werewolves fought over one of the great creatures' leg bones. Witches collected the wool to determine if it had any magical powers.

We stood in the doorway of the supply room, looking in on a massive, state-of-the-art laboratory built into the moon rock.

"Much of the equipment has been destroyed by the angry creatures that once roamed freely," said Twenty-Three. "Once it was sealed off, the creatures had to fend for themselves."

There was a screeching sound, and huge tentacled heads floated into the laboratory.

Twenty-Three pushed me away from the door.

"Don't let them see you," he hissed. "Or they'll take your brain out through your eye sockets."

Nabila twitched.

"I've seen it before," Twenty-Three continued. "And it's not pretty. Those massive floating heads are the same heads that Andromedans have, but Zorflogg altered them to collect brains instead of lebensplasm."

"How are we going to get past them?" I asked.

"I'm not sure," Twenty-Three replied. "Maybe they're full and won't notice us. Their heads must be filled with dozens of brains—human brains, brains of the new creations, brains of some of the monster and alien guards."

"Did you say brains?!?" Nabila yelled, and ran past us and into the next room. "Aw, YES! I've never been hungrier in my whole entire life."

"Looks like she's still got a little zombie in her, after all," said Shane.

"Nabila!" I yelled. "Stop!"

But there was no stopping Nabila.

There was a scream from the floating brain collectors as she entered the room.

A bloodcurdling scream.

A *hungry* scream.

...And into
the Membranium

Nabila rushed toward the floating heads and jumped like a possessed wildcat onto the closest tentacled brain collector, ripping into its squishy head with her teeth. She tore a pretty good-size hole for just using her mouth and then dipped her hand in, rummaging around for brains, while the head flew around the room trying to knock her off. The others were closing in to help, gnashing their disgusting teeth that were stained green from all the brains.

"C'mon, we gotta get her before she gets herself killed," I yelled.

"Yahooooo!" yelled Nabila, riding around the room on the brain collector like it was a rodeo bronco. While holding on, she shoved gray matter into her mouth.

I rushed into the room with Ben and Shane, followed by the vampires and Roy.

One of the brain collectors got close enough to get ahold of Nabila with its tentacles. She didn't seem to notice anything but the brains as it pulled itself closer to her and opened its toothy mouth with a hiss.

"Nabila," cried Ben, but she just didn't notice.

The vampires quickly turned into bats and flapped in front of the brain collector that had ahold of Nabila. Perturbed, it loosened its grip a little, and Grigore flitted above the head and turned back into a human, forcing it down to the ground. Roy lumbered over and crushed it.

They did the same with the remaining heads, with more monsters rushing in to help. Soon, knowing that Gordon and Director Z were safe, the other zombies were asked in to feast on the bounty of brains.

Nabila still held on to the first head, which flew higher and higher.

"Nabila, watch out!" I yelled through cupped hands. "It's going to crush you against the moon rock ceiling!"

The brain collector picked up speed, pushing up faster and faster.

CRASH!

Nabila's head hit the ceiling, and her grip started to loosen. The brain collector floated down and then up again—

CRASH!

—hitting the ceiling once again. This time, the impact knocked both of them out, and they came tumbling down toward the ground.

All the vampires were on the ground. Camilla reacted first, quickly turning into a vampire bat and flying up to slow Nabila's fall. As they collided, she transformed back into human form and tumbled toward the ground.

The last of the brain collectors hit the dusty floor first.

Camilla and Nabila landed second in a great pile of what appeared to be dead skin.

"Membranium!" Ben yelled as he rushed over to help.

Camilla, remembering the horrors of Paradise Island, clawed her way out of the pile of skin.

"Get them off me!" she shrieked, her black shoes slipping and squeaking as she made her way to the top of the huge pile.

"What about Nabila?" Ben yelled as Camilla rushed past him into the storage room.

Ben dove into the pile headfirst, with the agility that only a fish could have.

I screamed, "Ben!" and was about to jump into the pile myself when Twenty-Three grabbed my shoulder.

"Don't worry!" yelled Twenty-Three. "Those

membranium are harmless. You have to lead them to their victim and slip them over its head before they wake up enough to cover it. And they're not attached to a host, so they do nothing."

Ben exploded out of the pile of skin, dragging a moaning Nabila with him.

We helped her up, and she was able to sit on a busted old office chair with a huge chunk bitten out. Blood, crusted with moon rock, seeped over her eyes.

"Oh, my head," she said. "It aches so much."

The anteater monster I had seen collecting moondust in the mines came over to me and snorfed at my feet, shaking its hairy little rump back and forth.

"What is it?" I asked.

It pointed its trunk up at Nabila's bleeding head.

"Um," I said, "you want to snorf up her blood?"

It snorfed what I could only assume was "yes" and shook its hairy rump even faster.

"Okay . . . ," I said doubtfully, and picked up the little guy.

I felt its chest expand, and it snorfed up all the blood and moon rock, using its thin little tongue to work out the bigger chunks.

"Ack," Nabila said. "That tickles!"

When it finished, I put it back down again.

"You look great!" I said to Nabila.

"Uggghhhhh," Nabila said.

"Should we get you more brains?" asked Shane, rushing over to one of the zombies that was feasting away on a brain collector.

"Hey!" the zombie protested as Shane swiped a huge wad of gray matter out of its hand, brought it over to Nabila, and shoved it into her mouth.

"Bleeechh," she choked.

"I think that brain collector knocked the last of the zombie out of you," said Shane with a smile.

She barfed all over Ben.

"My, how the tables have turned," said Ben.

Everybody laughed and laughed . . .

. . . until the room began to shake. The beakers and flasks that were left on the shelves tumbled to the ground and shattered.

"Oh no," I said, "what's next?"

A great moan tore through our bodies, shaking our hearts. We held our hands up to our ears to keep them from bleeding.

"That's not any of Zorflogg's creations," said Twenty-Three. "That's the moon. The moon is screaming."

Moon Drain

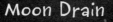

"Everyone grab a membranium!" I yelled over the rumbling and moaning. "Pull it over you!"

The monsters in the supply closet ran into the room as Shane and I passed out membranium to everyone we could as quickly as possible.

A huge boulder shook free from the ceiling and landed on Katherine the witch.

"Noooooo!" Griselda screamed. "My sister!"

All that was left of Katherine was one leg that poked out awkwardly from beneath the boulder. Griselda pulled at the leg as other, smaller stones tumbled from above, knocking her in the head and shoulders.

"Hurry, Griselda!" I yelled. "Or you'll be next!"

Shane grabbed an armful of membranium and passed them to Pietro, who had already put on his.

"Run these to Director Z and Gordon, fast!" Shane yelled over the rumbling.

Huge rocks continued to fall, bouncing off the monsters who had put on the membranium. Those that were too slow didn't stand a chance.

CRUNCH!

The small anteater monster was crushed under a rock.

"Noooooo!" yelled Nabila.

"Hurry, everyone, hurry!" I yelled.

And then, as quickly as it had begun, the moon stopped shaking.

Before we could even breathe sighs of relief, a great screech tore through our ears.

SQUEEEEEEEEEEECH.

"Is that the moon again?" I asked Twenty-Three.

"No, that's the intercom!" said Twenty-Three.

"SUCCESSS!" Zorflogg's voice boomed through speakers hidden all over the room. "The test was a success!" We could hear all his lackeys applauding through the intercom.

"What test?" Shane asked. "Did we pass?"

"I don't think he can hear you," said Twenty-Three.

"The Andromedans have learned how to drain the moon, my scared little children," said Zorflogg over the intercom. "I don't know where you are, and frankly hope the creations I've left scattered around my compound are chewing on your bones as I speak, but just in case, I wanted to make sure tell you about this fantastic news. For this is really all your doing."

His voice broke up for a moment, a shot of static echoing through the room.

"You see, you forced my hand. I wanted to take my time with the moon, to learn how to cultivate 'monster juice,' as you call it. But, in a burst of inspiration, I've moved the process forward. I'll just have to be a little wasteful and drain it all *now*! And why not? It will just make things easier for me on Earth. I've searched your ship, and there is nothing on it. But I will have all eternity and enough lebensplasm to find all the pendants soon. Now you are truly worthless to me. Servants, load up for takeoff! Andromedans, gather above the Apollo Quadrant. My ship will meet you there. Thank you, scared little children, for showing me the way! Wish me a bon voyage, and I wish you a good evening and the quick, painless death of which you are not even worthy."

SCCHHHPPLLUUUURCH!

The intercom cut off. There was silence in Sector 78.

"We've got to destroy that monster before he lets the Andromedans drain the moon!" I said, pacing around nervously. "But how? Wait . . . first things first. Twenty-

Three, how much time do we have?"

"I would think it would take at least twelve hours for Zorflogg to prepare his ship and get into position in the Apollo Quadrant," said Twenty-Three.

"Are you sure?" asked Shane.

"Yes," said Twenty-Three.

"What is the Apollo Quadrant?" I asked. "I've never heard of it."

"It's the area in the moon's orbit that lines up directly with the moon's mouth," replied Twenty-Three. "I think Zorflogg wants to be right above it just in case the moon spits up any raw lebensplasm as it coughs its last breath."

"Whoa, whoa, whoa, wait," said Shane. "So what are we actually talking about here? I just want to be clear."

"Yes, because clarity is your thing . . . ," snickered Nabila. "Ow, my head."

"The moon is a monster, and it has a mouth?" asked Shane excitedly.

"Yes," said Twenty-Three. "The moon is the First Monster, sending its lebensplasm-rich rays down onto the Earth. Monsters soak up the moon like humans soak up the sun."

"How did you not know this?" Shane asked me.

"Have you ever heard of science?" I asked. "I'm pretty sure Mr. Stewart never said anything about the moon being the First Monster."

"Are you sure?" asked Shane. "Because, as you know, I never pay any attention at school."

"Twenty-Three?" Nabila asked. "What did Zorflogg mean when he said that destroying the moon would 'make things easier for me on Earth'?"

"The monsters on Earth will wilt away quickly without the power of the moon. It looks like you've gotten him worried and now he's going to drain the moon completely. Well done!"

"But no moon means no monsters," said Ben. "Oh man."

The monsters started to screech and moan. The zombies began wandering around aimlessly, bumping into walls and weeping. Even Director Z lifted up his head for a moment and moaned.

"Don't give up!" I yelled, and the monsters jumped. "We can't let him destroy the moon!"

I stood up on a half-eaten examination table in front of all the monsters. They turned and looked up at me.

"We will not let the First Monster fail! Somehow, some way, we will prevail over this evil!"

Even Zorflogg's rejected creatures began to gather around me as my speech got louder and more impassioned.

"We're inside a huge source of monster power!" I yelled. "Perhaps the biggest source of monster juice in the known universe! We have twelve hours to figure out how to tap into that power, break out of these caves, and get into space! Let's—"

"Guys, guys!" yelled Gordon from the storage space. "Get in here . . . NOW!"

The monsters growled low growls, and I saw the hair rise up on the backs of the monsters who had hair.

"Oh, man, what's next?" I yelled, and jumped off the table.

We rushed back into the storage space, ready to face another threat.

Master Plan

We were ready to attack.

Screaming and growling, we ran into the room ready to strike fear into the heart of whatever disgusting creature had sent Gordon flying to us for help.

Director Z wandered in front of the door, a little drool oozing down his chin, as we charged through. He shrieked with terror.

Gordon's eyes bugged with fear as we rushed to the back of the room.

He held up his hands and waved us off.

"Guys!" he yelled as he stumbled backward. "SHHHHH! Shut up!"

The monsters around us frothed at the mouth and

shook like crazy, ready to tear into whatever happened to make the mistake of walking into the room.

I gave him a strange look.

"Just shut UUUUUP!" he insisted. "Please, Chris, just shut them up!"

"SILENCE," I commanded.

The monsters fell silent.

In the quiet, I could hear the echo of faraway voices.

"What's that?" asked Nabila.

"I think they're guards," said Pietro, his ears twitching slightly.

"Where is it coming from?" asked Ben.

"Look!" Shane said, pointing at a dark corner of the storage room. "A hole in the wall."

There was a human-size hole that must have shaken open when the moon was being tested. Through the hole, I could see the eerie yet familiar glow of the strange globes.

"It's the first tunnel we walked into!" I gasped. "The way back to the ship!"

"That's what I wanted to show you!" said Gordon. "Now keep it down! Or they'll hear us."

"Too late," said Pietro, his hand wrapped around his ear to collect sound better. "They've heard us and are coming to investigate."

"What!" Gordon yelled. "You idiots!"

"Now *you* shut up," I said. "Look—the rocks that fell

out of the wall to make the hole are still sitting in here. Everyone grab a rock and fill in the hole quick. We need to make it look like it was never here. Hurry!"

Monsters large and small rushed up to grab whatever size rock they could to fill in the hole.

"Hurry," I said.

"We need to get some of the bigger rocks in there," Shane said.

Frederick, who was good and charged up from the zapping that the werewolves had done to him, grabbed a big boulder and slammed it into place.

But it wasn't quite enough.

The voices in the tunnel got louder as Roy stomped up and grabbed the largest boulder. He lifted it over his head, ready to slam it home.

"Wait!" Ben whispered. "Gently!"

Roy gritted his teeth and slowly, achingly set the boulder into place with the faintest *sssscccccccrch*.

We all stayed very, very quiet. Even the wildest of the monsters knew that they should keep it down.

The concerned voices passed the newly filled hole, and Pietro shoved his ear up against the pile of rocks.

"They've moved on," he said.

"Are you okay?" Shane asked Gordon.

"Zorflogg woke me up with his crazy message," said Gordon. "I've just been sort of resting since then. Until I heard the guards and crawled over to see where it was coming from, only to see the globes."

"That means we have access to the ship," I yelled, excited.

"SHHH!" scolded Pietro. "They're still close."

"I never got to thank you," I whispered to Gordon. "You saved me."

"You saved me, too!" whispered Shane, and he gave Gordon a very slow high five.

"You saved *all* of us," said Nabila. "You were amazing."

"Yeah, man!" said Ben. "How do you feel? That sounded like the most relieving burp in the history of man. I'm totally jealous."

"I feel good," said Gordon. "Exhausted but good."

"I know what you mean," I said. "I'm beat. This is the first time we've stopped running since we landed on the moon."

I slumped down on a moon boulder.

"Me too!" said Shane and Nabila at the same time.

"I could really use a drink of blood . . . um, I mean, a nap," said Shane. He checked his teeth with his tongue one more time. "Nope . . . all gone."

"I feel pretty good," said Ben, flexing his webbed hands a little. "Swampy and fit."

"I could have napped for a few more years," said Gordon. "But something hit me in the head. A boulder, now that I think of it . . . like, as big as the one under your butt, Chris. But why wasn't my head crushed?"

"You're wearing a membranium," Shane said. "Pietro slipped it over your head while you were sleeping."

"We're all wearing them," I said.

"Ugh, that kinda freaks me out," said Gordon. He turned green and hugged himself.

"It's okay," I said. "Twenty-Three said they're not attached to a host. In fact, it's good! We have a little extra protection, and I'm guessing we're going to need it."

"How can we be sure?" asked Gordon. "I'm going to feel itchy. We better not have to wear them for too long. Maybe I can burp again and blow it off. I don't have time for all that fartin'."

"Be careful it doesn't get blown back in your face," said Nabila. "That was one incredibly powerful burp."

"Blown back . . . ," Gordon said, thinking.

"What is it?" Shane asked.

"I think I've got an idea!" yelled Gordon.

Nabila started to *shush* him, but Pietro said, "It's okay, they're gone."

"What is it?" I asked.

"Are there more membranium?" Gordon asked.

"There's a large tank deeper in the laboratory, right before you get to the old refining machine. There might be some more in there," said Twenty-Three. "Why?"

"We need to stuff the Andromedans inside the membranium!" Gordon yelled, pacing around and

328

slamming his fist into his hand. "Yes! Wrap them up tight. Then, when they start vurping . . ."

"Their vurp would expand the membranium," added Shane. "Even if they were in space."

"And then when they burped their thunderburp—" said Nabila.

"They'd blow themselves up," I finished.

"I mean, you saw what happened when I burped," said Gordon. "The epic sound waves destroyed them all. So, what if we could find enough membranium to toss on every last Andromedan?"

"There's no guarantee there are any in the tank," said Twenty-Three. "But you never know!"

"We've got to give it a try," I said.

As if to back up my statement, another sad, low moan came from the moon. The room shook slightly.

"I think he agrees," Gordon said.

"What makes you think the moon is a 'he'?" asked Nabila.

"Fine," said Gordon. "She agrees. Or it agrees."

"I think our best bet is 'it,'" said Shane.

"We just have to hope that there are enough membranium in there," Gordon said.

"And that we don't get eaten alive . . . ," added Shane.

"What do you mean 'we'?" asked Ben, pointing to his gills. "I think this is more of a 'me' thing. A swamp thing."

"You're still fully powered up?" I asked.

"As far as I can tell," Ben said.

He lifted up his shirt and slapped his strong, scaly abs.

WHORF!

With a splatter, a little green ooze spewed out of his mouth.

"Strange," he said. "That felt good . . ."

"Great," I said. "We've got a ship, even if it's half-busted. We've learned how to create monster juice from moon rock, and there's another refinery on the other side of the lab. We just need to grab the membranium, power up the monsters, and get on board."

"So what do we do about the half-busted ship?" said Nabila. "If we pull away from the cave, all the air will get sucked out of the huge tear."

"Frederick," I said, "do you know how to repair it?"

"Sorry, Boss," he said. "When I'm in the system, I can tell what's going on with the ship, but I can't do much more than turn things on and off."

"Can you seal off the cargo hold?" I asked.

"I can close the doors, yes," he said.

"But then how would we fit everyone on the ship?" asked Ben.

Director Z wandered back over to us again. His head was down, and he was snoring.

"I bet you he would know," I said. "Once we get the

330

monster juice flowing, we should give him a drink and see if it snaps him out of this. He knew about the ship before we did. Maybe he knows how to repair it."

"There's no need to wait," said Shane, pulling a small glass bottle out of his pocket. "Nabila and I didn't drink all of ours!"

He pulled out the bottle and handed it to me.

"Is it enough?" I asked, staring at it.

"There's only one way to find out," said Gordon, who stopped Director Z as he wandered past in his endless circle. Gordon tilted Director Z's head back, and the Director snored loudly.

SNNNNNNNNNAAAARRRRRCHHHH!

Gordon propped his mouth open for me . . .

SNNNNNNNNAAAAA—

. . . and pinched his nose. I let the oozy monster juice drip into his mouth.

GULP.

Director Z snapped to attention, eyes blazing red, and pulled himself swiftly out of Gordon's grasp.

"I will destroy ALL you!" Director Z yelled.

He grabbed me by the neck, and fangs sprang out of his bloody mouth.

I saw stars as he tightened his grip.

Moon Madness

"Director Z!" yelled Shane. "Let him go!"

"Director Z!" Gordon yelled. "Director Z! Listen!"

Gordon jumped up and grabbed Director Z's hands, but they didn't even budge.

I could feel myself passing out, and saw the monsters rushing toward Director Z as the light faded from my eyes.

His grip released and I hit the floor, and Director Z yelled, "WAIT!"

I looked up to see Director Z shaking as he struggled to control his monstrous powers.

But the monsters closed in. They would not listen to him.

The vampires hissed at Director Z, disgusted by his violent outburst. The werewolves growled a low growl. Even the smaller creatures rushed forward. A small zombie squirrel chattered its teeth. Roy picked up Director Z even easier than he had picked up the rock before, and held him above his head. My mind was still woozy from lack of oxygen, my body was beyond exhausted, but before Roy could slam Director Z against the rocks . . .

"WAIT!" I yelled.

This time the monsters listened.

"Put him down," I said to Roy.

Roy threw him onto the floor.

"OOF."

"You forgot to say 'gently,'" said Shane.

We ran over to Director Z and helped him up, hoping he was himself again.

"Are you okay?" I asked him.

"I think so," he said, licking his new vampire teeth. "Are you okay?"

"I think so," I said.

"You gave me monster juice?" he asked. "That must be the reason for my sudden anger. My apologies. It was the first time in hours that I had any thought in my head, and the thought was an overwhelming one: 'kill.' I have to say, I have a newfound respect for the residents now that I've felt the powerful emotions they experience."

A few of the monsters around us nodded, agreeing with him.

"How did you know that I hadn't drunk monster juice before?" Director Z asked me. "You do realize what would have happened if I had."

"We didn't really think it through," I said. "We just did it. We really need your help."

I updated Director Z on everything that had happened since Zorflogg took him away. A few of the monsters added details here and there.

"So, you see," I finished, "we need to figure out how to repair the ship, power up the monsters, and lead them to battle with the membranium in hand. And then there's the question of how to defeat Zorflogg. I haven't even begun to figure that out. My brain hurts. I'm totally tired. Totally burned out. I'm so glad you're back."

"As am I," replied Director Z. "However, I can help you in very limited ways. As you saw from before, the monsters won't take orders from me anymore. They would have killed me if you hadn't stopped them. I have no pendant. And I'm *very* proud that you've held on to yours. Well done. Not even I had thought of hiding it there."

"That reminds me," said Shane. "I've been meaning to ask where—"

Before he could ask where, Director Z continued, "It is you who must lead them into battle, Chris."

"But you still know so much," I said, trying hard not to whine. "You have to teach me what you know. And what about the ship?"

"I will guide you as I can," Director Z replied. "And as for the ship, I'll explain to Frederick the way he can focus his power to melt the crack back together. Once the residents have drunk the moon's fresh, rich monster juice, we can get on board, make the repair as quickly as possible, and head into orbit. And I think that your idea of using the membranium is a good one, Gordon. I think it will work. But you are correct—we still must figure out how to defeat Zorflogg in his well-shielded ship. He is a relentless creature. He will stop at nothing now that he's set his mind to destroying the moon."

"Tell me more about Zorflogg," I said. "You knew him? Why does he hate the old monsters so much?"

"He doesn't believe in the Code of Monsterdom, for one," replied Director Z.

"What's the Code of Monsterdom?" asked Nabila.

"It lays out all of the rules that monsters must obey in a world of humans," said Director Z. "I won't get into details—in fact, I mustn't, or I'd have to kill you—but the part of the Code that Zorflogg finds so terrible is the rule that says monsters are only allowed to scare humans, not harm them. They are required to maintain a balance with the human race."

"I take it he'd rather just eat us?" asked Shane.

"It's more complicated than that," replied Director Z. "The Code was laid down to protect humans, but Zorflogg believes that the monster race should rule the Earth. He aims, with the help of his new breed, to take over the world. Any old monsters that don't fall into place shall be crushed along with the human race. He believes that by not rising up with him, the old monsters proved they, too, must be destroyed."

"So we'll destroy him first!" yelled Gordon.

"Yeah," yelled Twenty-Three, his lizard fist in the air.

"It remains to be seen if that is possible," said Director Z. "However, I think that Zorflogg has made one mistake that might help us."

"What's that?" I asked.

"He's turned his back on the moon," said Director Z. "Zorflogg is right to think that the moon—the First Monster—holds the key to all power in monsterdom. But what Zorflogg has forgotten because he is so drunk on power is that the moon is itself an incredibly powerful monster that can give power to other monsters."

"So we're not the only ones who are given power by the moon?" asked Howie.

"Yes and no," said Director Z. "Werewolves have always had a special relationship with the moon—a closer bond. Have you ever noticed how, of all the monsters in the retirement home, it was they who had the most power when you first arrived, Chris?"

"Yes," I said. "Pietro was always winning all the bingo games."

"I knew there vas a reason!" yelled Grigore, and he shook his fist at Pietro.

All our monsters began to protest, and Director Z held up his hand to silence them.

But everyone kept yelling at Pietro.

Director Z gave me a look.

"Oh right," I said.

I held up my hand to silence them.

They obeyed.

"Yes, the werewolves were more powerful," continued Director Z. "Because they spent more time with the moon. They ran in moonlight, no matter how tired they were. They had conversations with the moon. But all monsters are influenced by the moon's power. And the moon can choose which monsters to give the most power to."

"Wait," said Shane. "The moon talks back?"

"I always thought I was just hearing voices," said Howie.

"Knowing you," Gordon said, "you might just be hearing voices."

"So how can we use the moon to our benefit?" I asked.

"That is another great mystery," said Director Z.

"The moon usually keeps to itself. But you've already been helped along—more than once—and I'm sure the moon is very much interested in aiding in our success. If we win, the moon rises again. I'm sure we'll be rewarded greatly."

"And if we don't win," said Nabila, "not only are we dead, but the entire world as we know it is gone. POOF!"

"Oh man," I said, clutching my stomach. "It's sickening."

"I agree," said Shane. "Thinking of the end of the world will definitely give you indigestion. Or garlic. Garlic and I don't get along."

"You're tellin' me," said Vlad.

"No, that's not it," I whispered to Shane. "I have to . . ."

"Have to . . . ," Shane said.

"Number two," I whispered.

"What's the big deal?" Shane asked. "I think there was a bathroom in the laboratory."

"Because . . . ," I whispered even more quietly.

"What?" Shane asked, leaning in.

"I ate the pendant," I whispered. "That's how I hid it. And I don't want the monsters to know, because what if it freaks them out that I pooped all over their pendant?"

"I see," said Shane. "Can I help?"

"No," I said. "I'm pretty sure I need to do this alone.

But I really appreciate that you asked, despite the fact that it's totally weird. I'm just not looking forward to eating it again."

"Did you know some nomads eat their own poop?" Shane asked. "To battle dysentery."

"No way!" I yelled. "How do you know these crazy facts?"

"Go on, then, nomad," said Shane. "Do your thing."

I slowly limped away, trying not to go in my pants.

"The rest of you get a little sleep," said Director Z. "It'll be the last bit of rest that you'll get before—"

"The monster space battle to end all monster space battles?" Gordon asked.

"I wouldn't say it exactly that way," said Director Z. "But yes."

"Yeah, guys," I yelled over my shoulder, "you heard Director Z. Take a nap. I've got some important business to take care of."

Director Z gave me a thumbs-up as I headed for the bathroom.

Take the Plunge

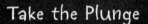

It took me so long to do my duty, clean off the pendant, and—after several failed attempts—force it down again that by the time I got back to everyone else, I had no time for napping. I just had to push forward. My body ached from lack of sleep and the thought of what was floating around inside me.

"How was it?" Shane asked, stretching after his catnap.

"Not so bad," I said. "But it made me realize how hungry I was. The only thing I've had since we left Earth was the pendant—twice—and little bits and pieces of Andromedans."

"Don't forget the monster juice," said Shane. "That

stuff has to be packed with essential vitamins and minerals."

Pietro had his hairy ear pressed up against the wall.

"I hear lots of growling and yelling," he said, listening hard. "Something about Sector 66."

"Sector 66 is where everyone loads into Zorflogg's ship," Twenty-Three said. "Ah, how long I've dreamed of that day."

"No time for dreaming, Twenty-Three," I said. "We have a lot to take care of, and it makes me nervous that Zorflogg's ship is already being loaded."

"First stop: creepy moon laboratory!" yelled Shane.

Twenty-Three guided me, Ben, Nabila, Shane, and Gordon into the laboratory along with half of the monsters. Director Z and the other half of the monsters stood watch near the filled-in hole in the wall, just in case someone (or something) broke through.

We passed by the rotting carcasses of the brain-eating Andromedan mutations.

"Would you care for any leftovers?" Shane asked Nabila.

"Please don't joke," she said, vurping a few brains into her mouth. "Ugh, they taste even worse on the way up."

"At least you're full," I said.

As we went deeper into the laboratory, whole chunks of ceiling and wall had crumbled all over the floor.

The lights that weren't completely shattered flickered ominously. We walked past cages that smelled even worse than the brain-eating Andromedan carcasses.

"I wonder what was in there," said Ben.

"Whatever it was, I hope it's gone for good," said Nabila.

I looked nervously into each dark corner as we approached. The hair on the back of Howie's neck raised as he turned into dog form, knocking a tray off an experiment table. Wendy the banshee screeched.

"Well, if anyone's down here, they'll know where to find us," I said.

"Sorry," said Wendy.

We all paused.

Listening . . .

Waiting . . .

All we could hear were the huffs and puffs of the older monsters.

The small rejected splurtsar nervously nudged Gordon's pant leg.

"Wha!" he yelled, surprised. "Back off, bacon! Haven't you ever heard of personal space?"

The little splurtsar SQUUUEEED around the corner.

"Sounds like he's okay," said Twenty-Three, and he kept walking. "We're good!"

We turned the last corner, and saw a towering glass

tank, crusted with dark green, slimy algae.

"How are you going to see in there?" Nabila asked Ben. She held his webbed hand tightly.

"I'm not sure," Ben said. He craned his neck to look all the way up to the opening of the tank at the top, near the ceiling of the massive cave. "I don't even know how to get into it."

We walked up to the tank. The closer we got, the more it smelled like sewage.

Ben took a deep breath. "Oh man," he said. "That smells great!"

"My brother!" yelled Gil, walking over to Ben. "I knew that you were one of my kind. I could see it in you. The way your body couldn't control the spew that came out of it. You barf like a swamp creature!"

"Swamp creatures barf?" asked Ben. "I thought you guys all had swamp gas."

"Yes," he said, "I was gifted with the beauteous swamp gas. Some of the strongest of my kind. But there is also swamp muck . . ."

"Diarrhea," said Shane. "Right?"

"The swamp chunks . . . ," said Gil.

"Barf, right?" asked Shane.

"And the swamp nuggets . . . ," said Gil.

"Boogers?" asked Gordon.

"No," said Gil. "I'm referring to those beautiful sticky chunks that get stuck between my webbed toes."

"Oh, toe jam!" I said.

"I like to call it 'fin jam,'" said Gil. "Our kind is so used to the wet world, lots of fungi and other things grow all around us. And liquid or gas always spews from deep in our bodies. I knew the way you spewed, you were one of us!"

He gave Ben such a huge hug that a juicy little fart escaped from both of them.

"Whoa," said Ben. "That felt weird."

A growl from deep inside the tank broke the awkward silence.

"Be careful," I said. "We have no idea what's in there. Or do we, Twenty-Three?"

"No, not for sure," said Twenty-Three. "But I think the only underwater creatures that were ever created by Zorflogg were the membranium. Maybe different types of those? Any membranium without power, like the ones we need, would be deep in the bottom of the tank. Be wary of any membranium that you see floating near the surface."

"Got it," said Ben. "I'm ready."

Gil grabbed Ben by the finned hand and squeezed tight.

"I will explore this disgusting tank with you!" he exclaimed. "I will not fail you, my brother!"

"Are you sure?" asked Ben. "I think that I'd be better off alone. I can handle whatever's down there."

Something slimy and black scraped against the glass in a flash. A deep roar rattled our teeth.

"Where's the Kraken when you need him?" asked Shane.

"On second thought," said Ben, "it might be good to have some company."

"Great!" yelled Gil, and jumped onto the glass wall of the tank using his hands as suction cups.

"Wait!" Ben said. "We can do that? Awesome!"

Ben quickly took his clothes off and jumped up on the glass with Gil. His scales covered up any sensitive areas, but Nabila still blushed.

SCHLUP SCHLUP SCHLUP.

Ben and Gil slowly made their way up to the top of the tank and jumped in with a SPLASH.

Then it was deathly silent.

We stood and watched, waiting for something to happen.

"I feel like it's been twenty minutes," said Gordon.

"One minute and twenty-three seconds," said Twenty-Three.

CRUNCH CRUNCH CRUNCH.

"What's that?" asked Shane.

Nabila and I rushed up to the tank.

CRUNCH CRUNCH CRUNCH.

"Are they being eaten alive?" asked Nabila.

"Sorry, it's just me," said Jill the zombie.

She nervously nibbled her nails.

CRUNCH CRUN—

"Stop it!" I yelled. "You're hitting bone!"

Nabila turned to the tank.

"I wish I could see what's going on in there," she said.

"I wish I could hear what's going on in there," I said.

"I hear you!" said Ben.

There was a cheer behind me, and ahead of me through the muck, I could barely make out Ben.

"How are you able to speak?" I yelled.

"Fartspeak," he fartsaid, a few bubbles rising from his scaly swamp-creature butt. "Found membranium!"

He pointed at Gil, who we could barely make out collecting dozens and dozens of membranium at the bottom of the tank.

Suddenly, there was a flash. Then a second. Then a third. It was so intense, it hurt my eyes, even through the algae.

"An electric eel," I yelled, pointing behind Ben. "It's huge!"

The eel flashed once more and knocked Gil over with its gnarled tail.

"I forgot about the eels," said Twenty-Three.

"Did you say 'eels'?" I asked. "As in 'more than one'?"

"Well, on the bright side, at least they'll be able to see what's going on in there," said Shane.

"If that's the bright side of what's going on in there," said Nabila, "I'm a little worried about what the dark side is."

Ben pushed off the glass and swam over to Gil, picking him up quickly. Nabila pressed her face against the glass to get a better look, but another eel came out of nowhere and zapped the algae, cooking it against the glass.

"I can't see what's happening," she yelled.

"We're okay," fartyelled Ben.

But it looked like a thunderstorm was trapped in the tank. The eels zapped constantly. The water began to bubble at the top of the tank.

"Hurry, Gil!" Ben fartscreamed.

There was another huge flash, and then . . .

"Arrrrgh!" Ben fartscreamed so loudly it rattled the glass and our ears.

"Ben!" screamed Nabila.

A huge net, filled with membranium, flew out of the top of the tank—a huge, wet ball. It hit the ceiling and flew down to the floor, bouncing once, twice, and coming to a stop against the far wall.

Gil exploded out of the tank and grabbed onto the ceiling.

"Waaaaagh!" he yelled.

An eel splashed up and out of the tank after him, headed right for his frazzled old swamp-creature butt, mouth open wide, razor-sharp black teeth exposed.

FLLLLLUUUUUUUURRRRRRRPT!

Gil farted directly into the gaping mouth of the eel. Dazed, it crashed into the ceiling, and then flopped back into the tank.

"Oh man, that's epic!" yelled Shane. "Yeah, Gil!"

Gil fell from the ceiling onto the lip of the tank, quickly SCHLUP SCLUPPING down the side.

"Where's Ben?" screamed Nabila, rushing over to Gil. "Where is he? Is he safe?"

"I tried so hard," said Gil. "But he's not a swamp creature anymore."

"What does that mean?" Nabila yelled. "Go back in there and get him!"

"I was too late," Gil said, and he put a webbed hand over his face and began to weep.

Barfball

Nabila began to cry. Shane walked over and hugged her. Some of the monsters started to sniffle and wail.

I stomped over to Gil, holding back tears. I needed answers.

"Too late?" I asked, grabbing him by the shoulders. "What does that mean?"

"I failed him," he said. "He'll never be a swamp creature again. I took away his gift."

"How?" I asked. "He had a membranium on."

"His fartspeaking filled it up slightly," said Gil, green ooze coming out of his nose. "One zap from the eel was all it took to weaken the skin. A second drained him of—"

BAAAARRRRRRRF.

"What was that?" asked Nabila. "That is the exact sound Ben makes when he's sick!"

She rushed up to the tank one more time and screamed, "BENNNN!"

"Ugh, I'm choking," a weak voice came from somewhere.

"Look," Gordon yelled, pointing at the net of membranium. Barf oozed out of the sides.

WHAAARRRRRF.

More chunks spilled out of the tightly wound ball of membranium. It splashed out of the sides like a geyser.

"Get. Me. Out," Ben said.

Camilla quickly turned into a vampire bat and used her extremely sharp teeth to cut into the netting. All at once, the netting broke, sending barf-soaked membranium spilling out onto the moon-rock floor. With it came . . .

"Ben!" yelled Nabila. We all ran over to him, slipping on the membranium.

"I'm okay," he said. "Just sick."

"And naked," I said, covering his butt with a barf-stained membranium.

"So everything is normal again," said Shane. "None of us are monsters."

"Like I said," Gil said, walking over with Ben's clothes, still sniffling, "Ben has lost his powers. I'm so sorry, my brother. When the last eel zapped the swamp creature out of you, I threw you into the middle of the membranium and tied up the net. I figured you'd be safe in there."

"It was a bit rough coming out of the tank," said Ben. "How many times did I bounce? It felt like seven hundred."

I shielded him while he got dressed.

"No wonder you were sick, *habibi*," said Nabila, gently stroking his wet hair. She pulled chunks of goo out of his ears.

"He's sick because I let those terrible creatures drain his powers," wailed Gil.

"No, he's sick because he's Ben," I said, lifting him up and patting him on the back.

"You saved me, Gil," Ben said. "Thank you. I couldn't have stayed a swamp creature forever, anyway. That wouldn't have worked out so well at school."

"What happened with the membranium?" I asked Ben. "Gil said your bit of fartspeaking weakened it."

"It might have been because it was stretched," Ben said. "But I think it was actually because of the eel's electric shock."

"Yeah, it must be weakened by electricity," Gordon said. "Look at what Gil was able to do—fart that gnarly fart right through it!"

"I don't think we'll be dealing with any electricity

in space," I said. "But I don't think we can trust the membranium we have on to protect us. And how can we be sure that the membranium won't just pop when the Andromedans thunderburp?"

Before anyone could answer, Director Z came rushing into the room.

"Chris," he said, panting. "Pietro's telling us that he can't hear anything but the rumble of an engine."

All of Zorflogg's rejected creations began to chatter nervously.

"The engines start warming up about thirty minutes before takeoff," Twenty-Three said.

"But we don't even know how we're going to deal with Zorflogg's ship when we get up there!" I said, already feeling defeated. "And we've still got to refine enough monster juice to power everyone up."

"With all those eels blasting electricity around the tank, I got an idea," said Ben. "I mean, an idea about how to deal with Zorflogg's ship."

"What is it?" I asked.

"Remember those globes plugged into the moon?" Ben asked.

"You mean, the glowy ones?" asked Shane.

"Yes," said Ben. "Those. They're tapped into the power of the moon somehow. What if we did the same thing and ran a cable from the moon to our ship?"

"That would have to be a really long cable," I said,

turning to Twenty-Three. "Is there something like that on the moon?"

"There might be some extra cable in the old refinery," replied Twenty-Three. "It's just up ahead, in the next set of caves."

"Well, let's get going," I said. "We've got an insane amount of work to do to mine monster juice in preparation for takeoff. Director Z, please come with me back to the supply room. I'll grab the rest of the monsters and guide them back to the refinery. You get on the ship and get it ready. I know for sure that it needs some repairs."

"I'll do what I can," he said.

"Everyone else, get to mining," I said. "Twenty-Three, do you think you can turn on the refiner?"

"I'll try my best," he replied. "Some of the other creatures that worked in the other mine got a peek at the old refiner before it was off-limits. They might have some insight."

"Great!" I said.

Director Z and I jogged back through the laboratory to the supply room.

"Chris, wait just one minute," said Director Z.

"What is it?" I asked as we stopped in front of the terribly smelly cages.

"I just wanted to say that you're doing great," said Director Z. "Really, I mean it. You remind me of myself . . . in my younger days."

"Thanks, Director Z," I replied. "That means a lot."

"Just remember one thing," he said.

"What's that?" I asked.

"Sometimes, to be a Director of monsters, you need to be monstrous," he said, flashing his vampire teeth. "Don't hesitate to show them who's boss."

I paused for a second, thinking about his advice . . .

. . . and then we ran for our lives.

Things Just
Got Crazy

Thirty minutes later, everyone who could hold a pickax was still slamming one into rock. The room was hazy with moondust. Monsters grunted and gasped. Zorflogg's former slaves ran around, desperately trying to feed the crusher. Twenty-Three was on the other end, watching what was coming out.

"Earthlings," said Twenty-Three. "This isn't good."

"What do you mean?" I asked, throwing down my pickax.

I almost tripped over a cat-size slug pulling along a wheelbarrow as I approached Twenty-Three. The refining machine sputtered and shook, tickling my toes inside my shoes when I approached. My teeth felt jittery.

GRRRRRIIIIIINNNNNNNNDDDD!

"It's only one small flask worth of lebensplasm," said Twenty-Three. "There was probably a reason Zorflogg abandoned this machine. The combination crusher-refiner never quite worked."

"That's nowhere near enough!" I yelled. "The monsters are already weakened from all of the mining."

"The good news," said Twenty-Three, "is that we were able to find more than enough cable to connect the moon to your ship." He pointed to a huge pile of coiled-up metal cable behind the refiner. "I kind of figured we would, since everything around here is powered by the moon's energy."

"In other good news," said Shane, "you're soon going to be able to visit Earth, Twenty-Three!"

"If. We. Survive," Nabila said. "Why do you guys always forget?"

"I think it's because Shane has the happy gene, just like Twenty-Three," I said. "C'mon, I need everyone to get serious."

Suddenly, my feet felt like they were going to fly out from under me, the ground shook so hard. My teeth went from jittery to jackhammery.

"Zorflogg's ship must be taking off," said Twenty-Three, holding on to the machine.

"Well, I'm not so happy anymore," said Shane. "I'm ready to get serious."

The shaking slowed and stopped. The refiner stopped with it, choking on the last bits of moon rock.

RRRUUUUUNNNNNCCHHHSPPPPLLLLRRRFT!

"Well, we don't need that piece of junk anymore anyway," Gordon said, kicking its metal legs. "OW!"

"But we need your foot!" I yelled. "Everyone, focus! We've got to get into the ship as soon as possible. Gordon, Shane, Roy, and Grigore, grab the cable and run it to the ship. Twenty-Three, hold on to that bottle tight. It's not much, but we'll ration it out to the weaker monsters. Everybody, go, GO, GOOO—"

PPPPPPPSSSHHHHHHHHHHTTTTT!

A huge geyser erupted in the middle of the cave, spewing gooey, creamy, green slime everywhere.

"Pure, unrefined lebensplasm!" Twenty-Three screamed.

The monsters stood, frozen in place, as the geyser stopped, and the last of the monster juice splashed down onto the ground with a SPPPPPPLLLLLUUUURT!

"The moon . . . ," said Shane.

". . . is helping us," I finished.

A small pond had formed in the middle of the cave.

Before I could tell the monsters what to do, they all ran up to the edge and jumped in.

"Wahoooo!" yelled Pietro, and he dove in headfirst.

"Don't drink it all!" yelled Jill.

All the monsters laughed and howled with glee.

"First come, first served," yelled Frederick, and he belly flopped in, splashing the goop all around.

A bit splattered on Nabila's arm.

SIZZZLLLE.

"It burns!" she yelled. "Get it off!"

"I guess Director Z was right," said Ben, rushing over to her. "We can't ever touch this stuff again."

Before Ben could get there, Twenty-Three crawled up Nabila's leg lapped up the monster juice on her arm. His eyes turned red immediately, and he hissed. He opened up the small flask of monster juice he was carrying, pulled out the cork, and GULP GULP GULP!

He screeched and dug his lizardy claws into Nabila.

"Twenty-Three, that hurts," she yelled.

"Feels. GOOD. To. MEEEE," he moaned.

"GET HIM OFF ME," she yelled.

Gordon rushed up and pulled Twenty-Three off Nabila. He flung him onto the ground, but before he hit, wings burst out of his back, and he took off for the pond.

He dove into the muck with the rest of the monsters, who were completely submerged. Random hands popped out of the surface. An occasional bubble popped, sending a roar echoing through the huge cave.

"Something tells me this isn't going to be good," said Gordon, backing away from the pond.

The monster juice bubbled and frothed, and slowly lowered, revealing heads with angry red eyes.

SLLLLUUUUUURRRP.

"Guys, get out of here!" I yelled to my friends. "I'm not sure I'll be able to control them."

SLLLLLUUUUUUURRRROOOOOOOOAAARRR!

The monsters emptied the pond and began frantically licking the sticky monster juice off one another.

"I barely recognize them," Shane said. "Look at Grigore."

Grigore's fingers were long and bony, with terrifyingly sharp fingernails at the tips. He opened up his mouth with a great, satisfied roar. Every single tooth was a fang. He flexed his powerful arms, and the popping of his joints echoed throughout the cave.

The monsters stumbled up out of the sticky hole in the ground, their arms outstretched.

"Go!" I yelled to my friends. "Get to the ship! Tell Director Z to get ready. Grab the cable and run it through the tear."

ROOOOOOAAAAAR!

The cable began to unspool as my friends ran. The crazed monsters followed.

"STOP!" I commanded so loudly that the cave shook, small rocks shaking out of the ceiling and raining down on us.

The monsters all turned slowly to me, their bodies heaving as they huffed and puffed. They were strong.

They were insane with monster power. They were the most terrifying monsters I'd ever seen.

Jaws snapped. Frederick was so powered up, he sent a shower of sparks into the air.

All at once, they rushed at me.

"How dare you disobey your Director?" I yelled, holding up my hands. "Or have you forgotten that I hold the pendant of power?"

Some stopped, whimpering as they realized what they had almost done. Just as many kept rushing toward me, the zombies stumbling forward in the lead, their arms pinwheeling like crazy.

Remembering what Director Z had told me, I let the zombies come at me . . .

. . . and ripped off John's arm.

The other monsters stopped, stunned.

I held his arm high and said, "You will listen to me, or you will be punished!" John's finger pointed at them.

"I am your Director, and you *will* do what I say. I am not your enemy. I am your friend. My friends are your friends. The Andromedans are the enemy. You will listen to me. You will listen to my friends. You will listen to Director Z. And we will crush the Andromedans!"

A great roar went up in the cave.

"To the ship!" I yelled, pointing with John's arm. "Let's show the Andromedans the real terror that awaits on the dark side of the moon!"

Takeoff!

By the time we reached the tunnel with the glowing globes, the moon rock was shaking violently around us.

The moon was in trouble.

As soon as the last of us crawled up into the ship, Director Z turned Frederick back around so he was facing the huge metallic tear in the cargo hold.

"Remember what I taught you!" he commanded. "Seal it up!"

Frederick looked at me doubtfully.

"You heard me down there," I said. "You are to obey my friends and Director Z."

Frederick reached out his long, strong arms and grabbed either side of the tear.

"ARRRRRGHHHHHHH!"

He pumped his energy into the metal, heating it so he could bend it back into place.

As the tear closed, we could see the passageway the moon had opened up earlier crumble away with a great crash. The vacuum of space rushed in, sucking all the air through the crack.

Frederick was being pulled into the crack. The werewolves rushed up and bit into his pants to pull him back.

"Hurry!" I yelled. "Seal it up, Frederick."

"WAAAARRRRGH!"

He pulled the crack tight and, with a great electric shock, melted the two sides into place.

ZAAAAAAAP!

"Get to the engine room," Director Z said to him.

Frederick looked at me once again.

"Do it!" I said.

The ship shook violently.

"The Andromedans must already be attacking the moon," said Nabila. "We've got to hurry."

"I'm sure some of them will be drawn to the ship when we take off," I said. "And we'll battle them in space, above the moon. Everyone gear up!" I tossed John his arm. "Those who don't need to breathe will still need jetpacks. Don't forget to grab a membranium!"

Everyone rushed to the supply closets.

"I must stay on the ship," Director Z said. "If the monsters don't obey me in the heat of battle, it could be devastating. You saw what happened with Frederick, but I think he understands now. Plus, I can pilot the ship and figure out with Frederick how to work with whatever energy the moon provides us through the cable. If we can focus it up to the front of the ship, we might be able to send a concentrated blast forward."

"Let me know when we're close enough to the Andromedans," I said. "Then I'll have Frederick blow us out of the cargo hold."

"I'll make sure the door is pointed right at the Andromedans," said Director Z.

He rushed up to the bridge. The ship began to hum and whirr. Frederick must have sat down in the electric chair.

I rushed over to my friends, who were almost completely suited up in the leathery space suits that we found on board. Ben locked his glass helmet into place with a PPPPSSSSSSSSHT.

"These are actually pretty comfortable," Nabila said. "But I hope that crazy old scientist knew what he was doing. Something tells me he didn't have any time to test this stuff out. And I'm sure he had no idea about the Andromedans."

"Let's hope the membranium do what they're supposed to do," said Gordon. "The ones on us and the ones we'll be putting on them."

"I'm thinking if we get them on the Andromedans right before they thunderburp, they should hold," I said. Then I turned to the crowd of monsters. "Did you hear that? Wait until the last minute to slip the membranium over the Andromedans."

They all growled in agreement, from the smallest of Zorflogg's creations to the tallest banshee.

The ship lurched forward suddenly and rose above the moon.

"Helmets on, everyone!" I yelled. "Here we go!"

With the reduced g-forces and lack of atmosphere, it wasn't long before we were up in the moon's orbit, floating around the air lock.

The monsters chattered nervously. I turned to my friends.

"Guys," I said, "be careful out there. Let the monsters do most of the work. Try to stay away from the battle. Just move them around where they're needed. They're so much stronger than us."

Twenty-Three flapped over to Nabila, drooling slightly.

"Get that freak away from me," she screeched.

"We've all got to work together," I said. "That goes for both of you."

"Tasty," said Twenty-Three.

"Gross," said Nabila. "Kill Andromedans! Kill any

Andromedans that are far from me."

"Yes, Tasty," said Twenty-Three. "For you I will do."

"We're all set, Chris!" yelled Director Z over the intercom. "I've got them in my sights."

"Is everyone ready?" I asked through my helmet radio. I tucked a few membranium under the belt of my space suit.

"ROOOOOOAAAR!" said the monsters. My head ached from the noise.

"All monsters, please mute your helmets," I commanded.

"Ready," said Nabila.

"Let's do this," said Shane.

"I wish I were still a swamp creature," said Ben.

"I hope this isn't how I die," said Gordon. "I always pictured myself dying on the field."

"This is a new kind of sport," said Shane. "Andromedan wrapping."

"Frederick," I yelled, "open the air lock doors in five . . . four . . . three . . . two . . . one . . ."

PSSSHOOOOOOT!

We were sucked out of the air lock by the vacuum of space, and flew directly toward hundreds of hungry Andromedans.

Battle for
the Moon

"Whoooooaaaa," I yelled, flying uncontrolledly through space.

"Don't forget your jetpack," said Shane. I looked over to see him come out of a spin with the perfect thrust.

But I was too dizzy to figure out how to do the same thing. Just before I spewed all over the inside of my helmet, I slammed into something squishy and came to a stop.

BLURB PLUP BLUUURP!

"Guys, I'm surrounded by three Andromedans!" I yelled.

Their vurp splattered all over my glass helmet as a

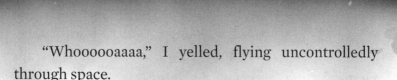

great green cloud formed around me. I tried to thrust away, but a tentacle wrapped itself around my leg, and I dragged it with me.

"Guys!" I screamed, but all I could hear from my friends were the same crazed screams I was giving off.

They were as terrified as I was.

I looked around to see more Andromedans than there were monsters, but the monsters were putting up a fight. Vampires with jetpacks flew around crazily, puncturing Andromedan heads with their sharp teeth and claws. Werewolves in space suits used their insane strength to pop the Andromedans' bulbous growths, sending green steam everywhere.

The vurping of my Andromedan was slowing down, and I could hear a deeper rumbling.

"No!" I yelled, knowing that the Andromedan was about to thunderburp. Suddenly remembering the membranium, I crawled up to the head of the Andromedan using its tentacle and whipped a membranium out of my belt. It opened its mouth wide, and I slammed the membranium down over its head. Just as the membranium sealed tight . . .

CRACK! POP!

The Andromedan thunderburped, blowing its own head apart and popping the membranium all over me in a spray of green goop.

"Gaaaah," I yelled as I cartwheeled backward.

I couldn't even tell what direction I was headed in. I was moving fast and getting faster by the second. If I didn't stop soon, I really would spew all over my helmet. As I spun, the moon came in and out of my view. I saw even more Andromedans on the moon—thousands—their heads pulsating as they drained it.

They got closer each time I saw them.

I was about to land in the center of them.

"Heeeeeeelp," I screeched.

In a flash, Shane grabbed me, and my spinning stopped.

"I gotcha, homey," he said.

"I'm so dizzy," I said. "My head aches. I think I popped an eardrum."

"Yeah, a nasty side effect of having to put the membranium on at the last minute," he said. "By the way, what happened to 'staying away from the battle'?"

"It wasn't my choice," I said.

I got my bearings and pushed off Shane. We rocketed away from the moon and back toward the battle. Above, monsters clashed with Andromedans, but except for the occasional thunderburp, it was completely silent. There was one large thunderburp, and another Andromedan popped, sending a monster flying toward the moon.

"Here," Shane said, handing me his membranium. "I'm going to get him."

He rocketed down, and I rocketed back up.

Most monsters had already run out of membranium and were now fighting with the tools they had left—fangs, claws, and jaws. I watched as Twenty-Three destroyed Andromedan after Andromedan, somehow able to push himself from one to the next with ease.

Two vampire bats flitted uncontrolledly past me. They must have lost their jetpacks when they transformed. I grabbed them and flung them back at a pair of Andromedans who were vurping all over a stunned Howie.

I saw Shane fling the monster he had caught back into the battle and rocket over to Gordon, Ben, and Nabila, who were in a tight circle. They were trying to collect the random body parts of monsters that had been thunderburped apart. Arms, legs, and heads floated everywhere.

I rocketed over to them.

"This doesn't look good," I said. "The monsters are getting destroyed, and—"

BEEP BEEP BEEP.

"What's that?" I asked.

A red light on Gordon's wrist was flashing, and we could hear an alarm inside our helmets.

"I don't know, but I'm having a hard time breathing," he said.

"Your oxygen is low," Director Z said over the intercom. "You need to get back on the ship as soon as you can. You only have a few minutes."

BEEP BEEP BEEP.

"Mine is low, too," said Nabila.

"We've got to get back to the ship!" I yelled.

"Correct you are," yelled a voice inside our helmets.

"Director Z?" I asked.

"No, it is I, Zorflogg, coming through on all frequencies," he said. "I've taken the liberty of listening in on your feeble attempt to destroy my beloved Andromedans, and I just can't take your whimpering anymore. You've already harmed too many of the most perfect creatures in the universe. You *do* have to get back to your ship. But that's going to be a little difficult if I blast it into atoms, isn't it?"

"Look!" Shane yelled, and he pointed to the moon's horizon.

A huge ship, with a jagged black spire on its nose, rocketed toward us. Behind it was a huge cloud of Andromedans—more than I had seen on the surface of the moon.

"Zorflogg," said Director Z, "leave these innocent children alone."

"Innocent children?" sneered Zorflogg. "There is nothing innocent about them, especially that sneaky yellow-haired one. I don't know how, but he got the pendant back. There's no other way to explain this madness. You never could have gotten these insane creatures into orbit without a pendant. But even a Director can suffocate. And so he shall."

Now all our suits were beeping. I looked behind me to see our ship in the distance. We were between it and Zorflogg's ship when the spire on the front of his ship glowed an ominous red, and—

ZAP!

A laser beam blasted our ship, blowing a chunk of metal off the back. Its tail pointed down toward the moon, and it began to fall.

"Noooooo!" I screamed. "Director Z!"

There was no reply.

Boom!

"What do we do?" asked Shane.

I knew I couldn't answer, or Zorflogg would hear. I turned off my radio and motioned to Shane to do the same. I pushed my glass helmet against his, hoping the sound would travel between the two.

"Our only hope is with Director Z and Frederick," I screamed. "We've got to keep the ship from falling into the moon's gravity and crash-landing. Hopefully they can give us that blast we're looking for."

It was no use, he couldn't hear me. I repeated myself, this time slowly and simpler, hoping that Shane could read my lips.

"How?" I thought he mouthed back.

"We get below the ship and thrust our jetpacks as hard as we can," I said, miming along. "We give Director Z as much time as we can."

Shane gave a thumbs-up.

I turned on my radio again.

"Everyone who can hear me," I yelled. "Follow me and bring the others with you. Do as I do!"

We thrust down to the ship. The monsters followed.

BEEP BEEP BEEP.

"I wish these suits would shut up," Gordon gasped.

"If they did, I think that means you'd be completely out of oxygen," I replied. "Everyone, try not to breathe heavy."

"Yeah, right," said Ben.

"Are you okay?" I radioed Director Z. "I don't care that Zorflogg can hear—just let me know you're alive."

Still nothing.

The Andromedans followed, vurping all the way.

First my friends and I arrived. We got under the tail of the ship and pushed on it as we thrust our jetpacks.

"Are we doing anything?" Gordon asked.

"Hard to tell," I said.

The monsters joined us, and the extra thrust helped. But soon the Andromedans arrived, and half the monsters had to fight them away from us. Soon, vurp filled the space around us, and I was worried that we'd soon be thunderburped into oblivion.

"Keep it up!" I yelled.

"Keep what up?" asked Zorflogg. "You really think you can keep the ship from falling? You fools! Stop this insolence."

The vurping suddenly stopped, but not because a thunderburp was about to happen. It was because Zorflogg's ship was only one hundred feet above us. The Andromedans scattered.

"Good news!" yelled Shane. "It's working!"

"Bad news!" I yelled. "We're about to get blasted. Everyone back off."

The monsters scattered. In the panic, everyone was bumping against one another to get out of the way. The nose of Zorflogg's ship glowed red and—

ZAP!

—blasted right between Gordon and me. Gordon went tumbling down toward the moon. Shane rocketed off to catch him. Monsters exploded from the heat. Howie's fur caught fire inside his suit.

"I've been hit," said Nabila. "I think my arm is burned. It hurts. My suit is okay."

"I'm coming," said Ben.

Through the radio, I could hear monsters moaning. Between the Andromedans and the last blast, our powered-up monsters had been nearly drained of their energy.

Suddenly, my suit stopped BEEPING. I could barely breathe.

"I don't think we're going to make it," I said to Shane.

"I disagree," he said, and pointed at the cable connecting the ship to the moon. It glowed a brilliant white-green.

"YES!" I screeched.

"Yes, what?" Zorflogg asked. "Answer me."

Up above, I could see the nose of our ship glow the same white-green.

It crackled like Frederick crackled when he had too much energy.

I was nearly breathless, but was able to say, "How's this for an answer?"

BLLLLLRRRRZZZZZZZT.

A great jagged ray of moon plasma erupted out of our ship and blasted Zorflogg's!

"Arrrggh, noooooooooooo!" Zorflogg's voice came through static. "I can't believe I didn't crush you when I had the chance."

His ship fell past our ship and plummeted to the moon below.

"Eat moondust," Shane said, shaking his fist.

"This ship is designed to survive any crash, you little fool," said Zorflogg. "And in the meantime, my Andromedans will feast upon your measly bones."

"So we *are* doomed," said Ben, rocketing back with Nabila.

The Andromedans raced back, surrounding us with their vurps.

"I tried so hard," I said, wheezing.

"You did a good job, Boss," said Griselda. "I'm so proud of you, young man."

The monsters formed a tight protective circle around us, but it was no use.

"You guys are the best friends a space captain like me could ask for," I said, delirious.

"You're not half bad, yourself," said Shane.

"Is it okay if I cry a little?" asked Gordon.

"Please just shut up and die," said Zorflogg. "I . . . oh no! Aaaaaaaaah!"

"Look!" yelled Gordon, and he pointed down at the surface of the moon.

The Andromedans stopped vurping for a moment.

A huge grinning mouth had appeared on the moon's craggy surface, and as Zorflogg's ship got closer, it opened wide, and a massive tongue curled out of it.

Zorflogg's ship crash-landed on the tongue and bounced deeper into the mouth.

"Nooooooooo—" Zorflogg's scream was cut off, and over the intercom, we could hear CRUNCH MUNCH MUNCH.

The mouth drooled slightly as the moon enjoyed its snack.

Thousands of Andromedans, enraged, vurped once

more, ready to destroy us, but suddenly—

BRRRRAAAAAAAAPPPPPPPP!

The moon burped the loudest burp in the universe. It blasted right past us and all the monsters, instantly shattering the heads of the thousands of Andromedans. A white-green haze floated down to the moon. North of the mouth, a nose exploded from the ground, and two nostrils the size of Rhode Island breathed in deeply.

SNNNNIIIIIIIIFFFFFF.

A great laugh shook our space suits.

But I was too weak to laugh.

"Need," I said. "Ship. Need. Air."

My fingers slipped off my jetpack controls. But I felt someone—maybe it was Shane, maybe it was one of the monsters—guide me back to the cargo hold of the ship.

We floated for another moment in silence, and then there was a hiss of oxygen as the room filled with air.

But it was too late.

I blacked out . . .

. . . only to be awoken by Grigore.

"Don't give up, Boss," he said, and slapped me across the face.

"HWWWAAAAAH!"

I breathed for what felt like the first time in my life. White light exploded in my head. I looked around to see everyone else gasping as well. Nabila moaned in pain as Griselda tended to her burn. Gordon threw up so hard that he began doing cartwheels in the room. Some monsters had been reduced to parts. Twenty-Three appeared limp and lifeless. Camilla floated past me in freeze-dried vampire bat form—doomed to be stuck in that shape for all eternity like some sort of bat jerky.

"I hope it was worth it," I said.

"Oh, it was worth it," Director Z said, floating over to me. "You've saved the moon, monsterdom, and the entire human race."

"I know," I said. "But I've lost so many friends."

"Your friends are fine," said Director Z. "They just need a little R & R. They'll be on the right track in no time."

"No, I mean all my monster friends," I said. "Look at them. They're more beat-up than I've ever seen them. The ones that are left, anyway."

I floated over to Howie, whose fur was burned off completely. He shivered in the cold cargo hold, his body twitching violently.

"Oh, Howie," I said, trying to comfort him.

"Hooooooooowl," Howie howled weakly.

Below us, at the point where the cable from the moon was connected to our ship, the metal glowed a brilliant white-green.

The same plasma that had shot out of the nose of the ship now connected with every single one of the monsters. Their eyes became bright, and they puffed out their chests. The chunks of leftover monsters pieced themselves together to re-form monsters that we thought were lost.

"Wow," said Shane. "The power of the moon."

With a brilliant flash, the light was gone.

And many of my monster friends were back and better than before.

"YIPPPEEEE!" everyone cheered.

Monsters hugged monsters. Kids hugged monsters. Kids hugged kids. Some kids kissed other kids.

"Ew, stop it, Ben!" said Nabila.

"Sorry, I couldn't help it," Ben said.

"Hey, Boss!" Grigore said, floating over.

"Grigore, you look amazing!" I said, and awkwardly hugged him. "Black hair! Not one wrinkle!"

"Yeah, and not jacked up on monster juice, either," said Shane. "That was pretty freaky!"

Grigore ended the hug and handed me a bloodstone on a gold chain. "You almost lost your pendant," he said.

"This isn't mine," I said.

"If this isn't yours, then vhere is yours?" Grigore asked, confused.

"We Directors always have something up our sleeves," I answered. "Don't we, Director Z?"

I placed the pendant over his head.

"You're BACK," yelled Shane, and high-fived Director Z.

"Thanks to Chris," said Director Z, "we're all back."

Headed Home

We landed our ship back on the moon and quickly made repairs. We searched for the ship that Murrayhotep had taken to the moon. Once we found it, Director Z put the coordinates for our town into the system.

"There," he said. "Now you'll be able to sit back, relax, and enjoy the ride."

"Are you sure one of us shouldn't come back with you on the Victorian scientist's ship?" I asked.

"Well, now that I have this back," he said, touching the bloodstone necklace hidden under his suit, "I shouldn't have too much of a problem. Plus, that old ship is so rickety and unreliable that it's only suitable for monsters."

"I wish we could stick around a little longer," Gordon said. "I was really looking forward to playing football on the moon."

"Well, I suppose we could stay," said Director Z. "But not too much longer. It's getting hard to keep track of all the lies we're telling your parents, and there could be more Andromedans on the way. The new ones wouldn't know how to drain the moon, but they would probably be quite upset that their friends are no longer here. I wouldn't want to be here to witness their anger."

So we played football on the moon, with Shane and me leading a team of vampires and zombies, and Gordon, Nabila, and Ben leading a team of werewolves and banshees. My team won 24–14. Gordon blamed his space suit, but I think he just didn't have a good grasp of how to use the gravity and lack of air to his advantage.

"I can't believe I have to tell everyone back home that I lost a football game to you!" said Gordon. "Are you *sure* I can't mention we were playing on the moon?"

"It would probably be best if we kept that secret," I said.

We stood in front of Murrayhotep's ship, the monsters in front of us proudly waving good-bye.

"Thank you!" Grigore yelled, and he flashed his sharp fangs with joy.

"Get home safe!" yelled Jill.

"Howl if you need us," said Howie.

"It's so good to see them so strong," said Shane as we stepped on board.

"I know," I said. "Now they really don't need us anymore."

"I wonder, if they don't need us, are they going to eat us now?" asked Ben. "I always worry about that."

"We know," said Nabila. "But there's the Code of Monsterdom."

"Oh right," Ben said. "But these guys haven't had anything good to eat since—"

"Stop it!" we yelled.

After takeoff, I floated next to the window with Shane, sad to see the moon getting smaller.

"You still have your telescope," Shane said.

"I guess," I said. "But after having been on the surface, even underneath it—literally, inside it—it won't ever be the same."

"I'm sure we'll make it back one day," said Shane. "It's safe now that Zorflogg's gone."

"And good riddance," I said. "That guy was terrible."

"And his breath was insanely bad!" said Gordon.

"The only person in the universe with worse breath than Mr. Bradley," said Ben.

We all laughed.

"It was all the monster juice," Nabila said, laughing harder.

We laughed until we snorted, and then Shane and

I looked out our window, this time at the blue ball that was getting larger.

"Hey," Shane broke the silence. "I wonder what ever happened to Murrayhotep."

Want more Monster Juice?

Here's a little taste from the

Tomb of Brain Ooze!

Prologue

The mummy entered the dank chamber and lit the torches one by one. The flickering light reflected off of the liquid that filled the jars, vats, and open Tupperware around the room.

"I'm baaaaaaaaaack!" growled the mummy, and something within each of the containers trembled. Ooze gushed out and splashed onto the sandy ground.

"I'm back, and I don't have any time

for chitchat," said the mummy. He clapped his hands twice, and a fine white dust flew from his bandages. "We've got to get down to business straight away."

Two figures appeared in the doorway that had been chiseled through a rock wall. They crouched down low to get through the doorway without harming their bird heads. Their beaks clicked as they bowed low to the mummy.

"Yes, yes, do come in," he said. "Make it snappy— we've got a lot of prep work to do."

The bird-heads went back through the doorway, and returned quickly with another mummy. This one was motionless as they carried it into the room. They bowed again and dropped it at the feet of the first mummy, who was alive and very impatient.

"All right, all right," he said, snapping his fingers. "Enough ceremony. Stop bowing and give me the Blade of a Thousand and One Souls already!"

The bird-heads clicked their beaks in anger, but obeyed. One reached behind its back and unsheathed a long, curved blade that started narrow near the hilt and widened toward the point. Before the bird-head could bow and present it to the mummy, the mummy snatched it away.

"SQUAWK!" yelled the bird-head.

"Get outta here!" yelled the mummy in reply.

They held up their hands in protest, clicked their

beaks, and hissed, but backed out.

Once they were gone, the mummy turned his attention back to the containers.

"Now . . . ," he said, swinging the sword carelessly with one hand while searching around the chamber. "Where are you, Tutankhamen? Tonight your body shall burn to feed your brain."

He strolled around, peering into jugs, lifting up the larger Tupperware containers and peering underneath, making sure not to spill the precious juices on his head.

Finally, he came to a laundry basket lined with a trash bag.

"Aha!"

He plunged his hand into the ooze and pulled out a pulsating brain.

"Tutankhamen!" he screeched. "I. Can't. WAIT. To eat you!" He held the brain up high. "So young. So fresh. With the exception of our new visitors', your brains will be the richest. Your brains will take me *soooo* many places—deep into so many minds!"

The brain squirted a purplish-black goo directly into the eyes of the mummy.

"WARGH!" he yelled, dropping the brain— SPLUNK—and the sword—CLANK.

He used the bandages on his hands to clean his eyes. Once he opened them again, he gasped and pointed at the brain.

"Nooooo!" he yelled. "Look what you've done to yourself."

The brain was starting to disintegrate into the sand. The mummy picked it up, blew off all the sand that he could, and then plopped it back into the trash-bag-lined laundry basket with a PLOOOP.

"How dare you disobey your master on a night such as this?!" he yelled, picking up the sword. "Tonight of all nights! YOUR night. The night that has been thousands of years in the making. The night we will drive what's left of your spirit from your body and back into your MIND!"

The angry mummy raised the sword high and brought it down onto the lifeless mummy in the sand. FWACK. The head rolled into a corner. FWACK, FWACK! No more arms. FWACK, FWACK!

"How does that feel, Tut?" screeched the mummy.

"Noooooooo!" yelled the dusty old head on the ground. "What you're doing is wrong, and the spirits shall make you pay."

"Zip it, Tut," said the mummy. "I didn't actually need you to answer. It was a rhetorical question!"

FWACK, FWACK, FWACK!!!

The mummy went on and on, until Tutankhamen's body was just a pile of parts. He gathered up all of the parts and placed them in the center of the room. Then he grabbed Tutankhamen's head and held it so that his eyes pointed at the pile.

"Take a good look!" said the mummy. "It will surely be your last."

With his other hand, the mummy grabbed one of the torches from the wall and threw it on the pile.

SCHWWOOOOOF!

Tutankhamen's body parts caught on fire almost immediately.

"Noooooooo," screeched the head. The laundry basket began to bubble and froth in anger.

"AMAN-RA!" boomed the mummy, holding Tutankhamen's head high.

An eerie purple glow filled the room. The flames danced around Tutankhamen's parts like orange and purple snakes. The body crackled and snapped, and the pieces started folding into one another and sent sparks to the very top of the chamber. Then the sparks blew back down, hitting the liquid in the vats and containers with little hisses. Before the fire got too low, the mummy threw Tutankhamen's head on the very top.

"Sizzle, sizzle!" the mummy yelled.

"You. Will. PAY!" said Tutankhamen's head on top of the flaming pile, his mouth opening wide with a CRACKLE.

The mummy pulled out a vial from somewhere in his wrappings, popped out the stopper, took a mouthful, and blew the liquid over the burning pile.

"ANUBIS-DUN!" the mummy yelled.

There was a low moan, and then, POP-POP, both of Tutankhamen's eyes exploded juicily.

The fire died down quickly, and with a POOF, a large cloud of purple and red sparks swirled, gathered, and tumbled into the laundry basket.

The mummy peered into the basket and, with a grin, said, "Yes. YESSS. Glow with your newfound powers. GLOW. And grow. I'll be back to eat every last bit of you, you false king. You and all those who came before you. And after."

A large scarab beetle scampered into the room and stopped at the feet of the mummy. The mummy raised his sword high once again and chopped off the scarab's head. He leaned down, picked up the body, and tipped its oozing green fluid into his mouth.

SLLLLLUUUUUUUURP!

He dropped the shell and sword and flexed his muscles.

"I am the only ruler now!" he yelled. "Now . . . who's next?"

ABOUT THE AUTHOR . . .

M. D. Payne is a mad scientist who creates monsters by stitching together words instead of dead body parts. After nearly a decade in multimedia production for public radio, he entered children's publishing as a copywriter and marketer. Monster Juice is his debut series. He lives in the tiny village of New York City with his wife and baby girl, and hopes to add a hairy, four-legged monster to his family soon.